THE SUNKEN CHASE

Also by Cap Daniels

THE
SUNKEN CHASE

CHASE FULTON NOVEL #18

CAP DANIELS

ANCHOR WATCH
PUBLISHING
** USA **

The Sunken Chase
Chase Fulton Novel #18
Cap Daniels

Published by:

ANCHOR WATCH
PUBLISHING
** USA **

13-Digit ISBN: 978-1-951021-34-4
Library of Congress Control Number: 2022909529
Copyright ©2022 Cap Daniels – All Rights Reserved

Cover Design: German Creative

Printed in the United States of America

The Sunken Chase

CAP DANIELS

Chapter 1
My Robot and I . . .

Although I have many character flaws, running from a threat is not one of them. No one who knows me would ever say, "Chase Fulton is a coward," but running is exactly what I was doing on that morning in May of 2007. I was running from a pair of pursuers bent on destroying me. They were relentless and unlike any adversaries I'd faced in my time as a covert operative.

For the first time, my team, including my handler, Clark Johnson, was powerless to intercept and dispatch my pursuers. Their bullets would have no effect on my foes. In many ways, this fight was mine and mine alone. Believing I could outrun those who were determined to drive me into the ground and force me from the battlefields where my country needed me most was a ridiculous lie I could never let myself believe.

No, running from my foe is not how I would ultimately overpower them, but at that moment, on that scalding-hot sand on which I ran, I was doing everything in my power to leave my pursuers exhausted and incapable of battle when they inevitably caught me. The fight was unavoidable, and the strength I was forced to muster came from deep within my soul. I would defeat them, if in no other way, through sheer determination and force of will. That was not the first time I'd run because of the pair who were determined to drag me into the miserable pits from which they crawled, but it could've become the day I crushed them and finally returned to my life without their shadows falling over me and their will being stronger than my own.

When I finally crossed the line in the sand drawn by those who often expected more of me than I believed I was capable of giving, I pounded to a stop in the hardpacked sand at the water's edge, my breath coming hard and my heart pounding its rhythmic thud of life. I spun on the heel of the most recent iteration of my mechanical right foot that I still affectionately called "my robot" to face the critical eye of the most demanding force in my world: former Green Beret, my handler and tormentor, Clark Johnson.

"Not bad, College Boy. You broke eleven thirty this time. It's your best yet at eleven twenty-six for two miles, but anything short of sub-eleven isn't good enough."

As my chest heaved and I fought to catch my breath, I said, "Let's see you break eleven thirty, old man."

He grinned and tossed a bottle of Gatorade at me. "That's the beauty of being your handler and not your partner anymore. I don't have to break eleven minutes. In fact, I don't have to run at all if I don't want to."

"Maybe. But if you stop running, you'll weigh three hundred pounds in six months."

Instead of firing back with some witty retort, Clark bowed his head and dug at the sand with the toe of his boot. "You know, I miss it."

My heart finally returned to a normal rhythm. "I'm sure you do. I miss having you in the field with us."

"That's how this business is, though. A shooter either takes a bullet before he turns forty, or he's suddenly too old to make the starting lineup."

I finished the Gatorade and inspected the empty bottle. "Disco's over forty, and he's still banging it out."

"Yeah, but what you forget is that he hasn't been dragging his knuckles and kicking down doors since he was eighteen. He spent twenty years in the cockpit of an A-Ten. His body hasn't been through the same grinder as ours."

"You've got a point, there," I admitted.

He took a seat beside me on the sand. "Is it the foot or your head that's stopping you from breaking eleven minutes in the two-mile?"

I shrugged. "Maybe both. I'm definitely running from both, and they're putting up quite a fight."

He examined the metal rod protruding from the stump just below my knee. "I bet Mongo could build you a swim fin for that thing."

"There's a collection of electronics and a whole bunch of stuff that wouldn't enjoy a saltwater bath as much as the rest of me."

He said, "Yeah, I know, but I was talking about a fin to attach to the stump. You know . . . just a fin on a rod that would attach to that one. You could take the foot off and screw on the rod with the fin."

I joined Clark in studying my robot. "I'd give that a try."

He hopped to his feet and dusted off his shorts. "Come on. Let's get you back to the house and cleaned up. We've got a lunch date."

"A lunch date? With whom?"

He screwed up his face. "*Whom*? What kind of word is that? That must be some of that fancy talk you're paying a hundred grand to learn."

"I'm not learning fancy talk, you hillbilly. I'm building a soft spot to land."

He grabbed his chest with both hands and staggered backward. "That's insensitive and hurtful. I'm pretty sure I'm offended."

"I'm pretty sure you're not smart enough to be offended. Who are we meeting for lunch?"

He broke into a sprint and yelled over his shoulder. "If you beat me to the plane, I'll tell you."

My robot and I passed Clark in two hundred yards, but I didn't slow down. When he finally made it back to the airplane, I looked down at him from the portside pontoon. "Where've you been? You just got beat by a guy with one foot. I guess that means you're pushing us off the beach."

He leaned against the pontoon and caught his breath. "You cheated. You've got a bionic foot. Take that thing off, and let's see who wins."

I chuckled. "When you get finished passing out and blaming other people, pull the anchor. You can tell me about lunch *if* you still have the strength to climb aboard."

We commandeered our amphibious de Havilland DHC-6 Twin Otter during an operation over two years before, and thanks to highly placed government officials we pulled from the jaws of death, she became legally and rightfully ours. Her twin 680 horse-power Pratt and Whitney PT6A turboprop engines gave her the muscle to slightly outperform and out-haul our Cessna Caravan. It wasn't an airplane I would've bought since her performance was only slightly better than the Caravan, but since we picked it up for a steal, so to speak, she was a fun horse to have in the stable.

With the turbines whistling their beautiful song, I pulled the propeller controls across the detent, taking advantage of one of my favorite features of the Twin Otter: reverse. With Clark still winded but securely aboard, I backed the airplane off the sand and onto the placid water off the point of beach delineating Long Key from Bush Key just east of Dry Tortugas National Park. I completed the pre-takeoff checklist and turned the Otter's nose into what little wind was blowing sixty-five miles west of the southernmost point in the American mainland. The Otter leapt into the air as if she were homesick for the sky and carried us to a thousand feet over the imaginary boundary between the Atlantic Ocean and the Gulf of Mexico.

With the airplane configured for cruise flight, I turned to Clark. "You lost the race, so tell me about our lunch date."

He looked over the rim of his sunglasses. "We've been over this. I didn't lose. You cheated. But since I'm the better man, I'll tell you about lunch anyway. We're meeting a guy named Phil McCall at Alabama Jacks."

"Who's Phil McCall?"

He pushed his glasses up the bridge of his nose. "I don't really know."

"I'm not going to a lunch meeting smelling like a goat who's been running on the beach all morning."

Clark continued looking out the window as the endless blue water played out beneath us. "I'm sure they have a hose at Alabama Jacks. I'll be glad to squirt you down."

"I've got a better idea."

Thirty seconds later, the GPS and autopilot were programmed to take us directly to the Ocean Reef Club private airport run by our old friend Hank, who just happened to be a former spook but never spoke of his days in the clandestine service.

We touched down and taxied to the ramp, but when we shut down, it wasn't Hank who came through the mirrored doors of the terminal.

Clark and I climbed down from the Otter, and the ponytailed twenty-something co-ed raised her hand against the bright midday sun. In an undeniably Eastern European accent, she said, "Hello.

Welcome to Ocean Reef Club. I am Masha. I can get for you fuel, yes?"

I exchanged glances with Clark and turned back to Masha. "Does Hank's wife know you work here?"

The chiseled features of the Eastern Bloc beauty radiated amusement. "This is funny. Yes, she knows. I am *lány unoka*."

I stuck out a hand. "I'm Chase, and this is Clark, but I'm afraid you've stumped us with *lány unoka*."

"Is nice to meeting both of you. I am sorry for I cannot remember English word for *girl child of man who has Hank for father*."

"Granddaughter."

"Yes. Thank you! *Lány unoka* is Hungarian for *granddaughter*, but nobody knows Hungarian when not inside Hungary."

I said, "I have a little Russian and some Romanian, but I just learned my first Hungarian word."

"You are friends for grandfather, yes?"

"Yes, we've known Hank for years, and I'm glad to see he's getting some time away from the airport. Hank's son must've married a Hungarian woman."

"Yes, this is true. My mother is from Székesfehérvár. This is fifty kilometers from Budapest, and my father is diplomat. This is correct word, yes? *Diplomat*?"

Clark and I shared a knowing glance. "Yes, that's the right word." Tugging on my sweat-soaked T-shirt, I said, "If you don't mind, I'd like to get a shower."

Masha motioned toward the door. "Yes, of course. Inside is shower, and I will get for you fuel, yes?"

"Yes. Top us off with Jet-A, if you don't mind."

She asked, "You do not need with Prist for freezing, yes?"

"No, we don't go high enough or far enough north for Prist. We like the warm southern skies."

Clark followed me into the terminal. "What was that all about? Why would you ask her if Hank's wife knew she worked here?"

I couldn't suppress the chuckle. "Because Hank has a deep-seated weakness for Eastern European women, and Mrs. Hank would kill him if she found out he'd hired one who wasn't a descendant."

"Oh, that *is* funny. Now, get your shower. You're stinking up my airplane."

"*Your* airplane? What makes you think it's yours?"

He plopped down into an overstuffed chair and picked up a worn copy of *Flying Magazine*. "Because you've already got the Caravan. What do you need with another amphib?"

"With friends like you, who needs tax collectors?"

He touched a finger to the tip of his nose. "Exactly. Wait, no . . . That's not nice."

Masha had the Otter topped off, and she even cleaned the windshield that had become the final resting place for several hundred thousand bugs and one that may have been big enough to qualify as a bird.

I paid the fuel bill and left Masha a nice tip for the extra work. "Tell your grandfather we said hello and that we're glad he finally has some help around here.'"

"I will tell to him this, but I will be here only short time. I came to United States for university."

"Really?" I asked. "Which school?"

"I am to study oceanography for master's degree of professional science at Rosenstiel School of Marine and Atmospheric Science. Is college of University of Miami. I have already marine biology degree from Eötvös Loránd University in Hungary."

Clark waved a hand at the airplane. "I'm going to preflight the Otter while you two smart people talk about summa cum laude and stuff."

The seven-mile flight from the Ocean Reef Club to Alabama Jacks took ten minutes longer than expected. I flew a low pass over the restaurant that was perched precariously on the edge of Card Sound Road and studied the narrow canals running along both sides of the road. "Nope. I'm not trying that."

Clark leaned forward and surveyed the scene in front of us. "Come on, College Boy. I thought you were a real pilot, but I'm starting to lose faith."

I reached over, took his left hand, and placed it on the yoke. "Since it's *your* airplane, *you* have the controls."

He replaced his left hand with his right and moved his left to the throttle. "Since you put it that way, let Daddy show you how it's done."

We flew a traffic pattern over Alabama Jacks and turned final over the toll bridge. As Clark pulled the throttle back and we settled toward the narrow canal, I sent up a prayer that my handler was smart enough to abandon the approach that *his* airplane could never survive.

My prayer was answered as the powerlines crossing the canal passed beneath our pontoons.

Clark pushed the throttle forward and pitched the nose up. "It's your fault. You've been hogging the airplane, and I haven't had time to get proficient with her yet. But you just wait. Next time we're down here, I'll show you how to put ten gallons in a five-gallon bucket."

"They would've carried our remains out of here in a five-gallon bucket if you'd continued that approach."

We climbed away and circled over open water to the north.

Clark touched down on Little Card Sound and kept enough power to step-taxi to the bridge. "Help me watch for boats coming out of the canal."

I leaned forward and peered down the long, narrow stretch of water. "I'm not sure it's wide enough for us to taxi in there."

"We'll know in a minute," he said.

After dodging a few crab traps and something that looked like a carousel horse sticking out of the water, we nosed into the mangroves outside the legendary roadside eatery, and I stepped ashore and tied us to a tree.

Clark hopped ashore from the starboard pontoon, and I took him by the arm. "Let's have it. Who is this Phil McCall guy, and what does he want?"

He pulled his arm from my grasp. "I already told you. I don't know who he is, and that's probably not even his real name."

"If you don't know who he is, why did you agree to a meeting with him?"

"How else were we going to find out who the guy is if we didn't at least break bread with him? Now, hobble your one-footed butt up that bank, and try not to get hit by a truck. We've got some business to conduct."

Chapter 2
What's in a Name?

Picking out our lunch date wasn't as challenging as I'd expected. Sitting sideways at a table in the back was a man pretending to read the *New York Times* with a cup of coffee and two bottles of beer on the table in front of him.

"Let me guess. That's Phil McCall."

Clark said, "You're getting good at this. Pretty soon, you won't need me at all."

"I'll always need you. Who else am I going to harass?"

"You've always got Hunter."

I leaned close. "I'm a little bit afraid of Hunter. He might kill me in my sleep if I give him too much of a hard time. I'm not afraid of people I can outrun."

He gave me a shove toward McCall's table. The man lowered the paper and stared up at me across a pair of half-glasses. He gave a solitary shake of his head. "Sit down, Mr. Fulton. We've got a lot to discuss."

I rescinded my offered-and-ignored hand and slid into the seat across from the man. "My friend tells me you're pretending to be somebody named Phil McCall."

He slowly folded the paper, meticulously creasing every fold, and laid it on the table, perfectly aligned with the row of condiments. "What makes you think that's not my real name?"

"Just a hunch." I slid one finger behind the pepper shaker and pushed it a quarter of an inch from its resting place.

He never took his eyes from mine, but his hand, as if driven by a force even he couldn't name, slid the shaker back in line. I waited, expecting another mysterious question to fall from his lips, but he just watched me.

A moment later, he nudged a beer to each of us and raised his coffee cup to his lips.

I moved the bottle back toward the man. "No, thanks. We're flying."

He touched his coffee mug to the edge of the beer and pushed it back toward me. "It's just one beer. Surely you can still fly after one beer. Besides, who's going to know?"

Four years of undergraduate psychology and almost three years of post-grad work instantly became worth every penny. I lifted the beer and poured the equivalent of one sip into his coffee.

He stared down at the cup and then back at me. "Why would you do that?"

"It's just one sip. Surely you can still drink your coffee with one sip of beer in it. Besides, who's going to know?"

To my surprise, he raised the cup to his lips and took a long swallow.

Clark, in uncharacteristic style, sat in silence, watching and listening as the exchange between McCall and me played out.

"So, tell me, Phil—if I may call you Phil—why did you want to meet with us this morning?"

He turned his attention to Clark for a moment and then back to me. "I'm not interested in meeting with him. It's you I want to talk with."

"So, talk. But no more games. Tell me what you want and why you think I can get it for you."

He tilted his head and ran a finger along the sharp crease in the *Times*. "What makes you think I want something from you, Chase?"

"When I said no more games, that's exactly what I meant."

He raised a finger toward a passing waitress. "Excuse me, ma'am. Something was spilled into my coffee. Would you mind bringing me another?"

"Sure, hon. I'll be right back." She snagged the contaminated cup and replaced it with a fresh, steaming version seconds later.

He took a tentative sip and replaced the mug back to its previous, precise spot on the table. "Fair enough. I'll get to the point, but it won't be quick. First, I want to tell you a story about a little boy I once knew."

I checked my watch. "My time is valuable, Mr. McCall."

"Everyone's time is valuable," he said without looking up. "And it would appear we've reverted from Phil to Mr. McCall. That's interesting."

I leaned back against the well-worn seat. "No, that's not interesting. That's impatience."

He steepled his fingers and stared between them. "It was nineteen seventy-six, and Gerald Ford was the president. In February of that year, a massive earthquake rocked the Central American country of Guatemala. You were too young to remember it, but you were there, Chase."

He paused and lifted his cup while I pondered his introductory teaser. I wasn't ready to bite the well-baited hook, but he had my attention.

Involuntarily, I leaned forward but instantly regretted doing so. The upturned corner of his lip said he registered my interest.

The sin was committed, and I couldn't undo it. The one thing I could do was try to have it masquerade as something other than curiosity. "Like you said, Mr. McCall, everyone's time is valuable. Let's not waste any more of each other's precious time dancing around whatever point you're trying to make."

He pulled off his glasses, studied the lenses, and laid them on the table. "Have you ever heard of the Agency for International Development?"

"Sure, I have. It's an independent government agency who hands out most of the foreign aid the U.S. sends around the world every year."

He lowered his chin. "Play that back in your head, Chase, and let it roll around in there."

"I thought we weren't playing games any longer."

"It's far from a game, Chase. It's the way things are. There's nothing independent about the Agency for International Development. In fact, as I'm sure you've already learned, there are very few entities funded by American tax dollars that the federal government doesn't have its long, slimy tentacles woven through."

He paused for another sip while I considered his assertion. With the cup back on its mark, he continued. "In March of seventy-six, I was being paid by the United States Government with those tax dollars we mentioned. After the earthquake in February, the whole country of Guatemala looked like a trash heap in the jungle. President Ford sent a guy named Daniel Parker down there to make a speech. The last thing people want to hear when everything they own is piled under a billion tons of rubble is a speech, but that's what politicians do."

"I'm getting bored, Mr. McCall."

"Stay with me. We're getting to the good part."

The waitress made another pass, and I motioned toward McCall's coffee cup. "Can I get one of those, please?"

"Sure you can, sugar. How about you?"

Clark looked up. "No coffee for me, but I'd love a glass of water."

"No problem, baby. Do any of you want anything to eat?"

McCall answered for all of us. "Not yet, but maybe later."

"Okay, hon. I'll be right back with those drinks."

McCall said, "So, back to Guatemala. This Daniel Parker fellow, he was the head of the Agency for International Development, and he had an entourage of somewhere around a hundred people who followed him down there when Ford ordered him to go make that speech. I was part of that entourage, but I didn't work for the USAID. I worked for a three-letter government agency, and I went to work for them after spending three years snooping around the jungles of Vietnam making nasty little deals with nasty little people and doing nasty little deeds." He leaned back and turned his attention to the approaching waitress.

She set a cup of coffee in front of me and a glass of ice water in front of Clark. "Is there anything else you need right now?"

My handler said, "No, ma'am. Just a little privacy if you don't mind."

"Sure thing, sugar." And she vanished.

I tapped the table with my knuckles. "So, you were a spook."

He nodded. "Yeah, I was a spook, but I was on a humanitarian mission in March of seventy-six."

"A humanitarian mission?" I asked. "Why was the CIA conducting humanitarian missions in Guatemala?"

He closed one eye and stared at me with the other. "That's where you come in, Chase."

"What do I have to do with this story?"

"Keep your shirt on, boy. It'll all make sense before that long-legged waitress wanders back over here to flirt with your handler."

"What do you mean, handler?" I asked.

"Don't play dumb with me, kid. We're way beyond that. Do you want to hear what I have to say or not?"

"Let's have it."

He cleared his throat. "First, I have nothing to gain by lying to you. You can believe what I'm about to tell you, or you can hop back in that airplane of yours and never think about me again. What you do with this information is up to you. Is that clear?"

"What's clear to me is that you're still stalling."

He nodded. "When I flew to Guatemala in March of seventy-six, I wasn't there to support the Agency for International Development. I was there to find, recover, and repatriate James Fulton and his family."

The sound of that name hanging in the air between McCall and me sent a chill running down my spine. "My father?"

He swallowed another mouthful of coffee. "Yes . . . Your father, your pregnant mother, and you."

My mind imploded. *My pregnant mother in nineteen seventy-six? That can't be true.*

"My mother wasn't pregnant in nineteen seventy-six. I was born in January of seventy-four, and my sister wasn't born until seventy-eight."

He pressed his lips into a thin horizontal line. When his eyes met mine again, he spoke in a measured monotone. "Your mother was pregnant with your brother when the three of you went to Guatemala in the fall of seventy-five. They were planning to come back to the States for her to have the baby in April of seventy-six, but there was no way for them to know about the earthquake."

My mouth went dry, and I clenched my fists. "Are you saying my mother miscarried my brother?"

He sighed. "No, Chase. That's not what I'm saying. I'm telling you she had the baby a few days after the earthquake, but the conditions in that country in the weeks and months following the earthquake were deplorable. It looked like a warzone down there. There's no other way to describe it."

"So, what happened to the baby?"

He swallowed hard. "Your parents believed the baby was killed in an aftershock that brought down the communal house where they were living. The earth opened up and swallowed six or seven people. Some people who were there reported at least twice that many people falling into the sinkholes. The whole scene was utter chaos."

"My baby brother died in Guatemala?"

He slowly nodded. "That's what everyone believed, until . . ."

I pounded on the table and roared, "Until what?"

McCall reached into his shirt pocket and produced a photograph. He slid it across the table, and I stared into the image at my fingertips.

He tapped a finger on the picture. "Look at that man on the end."

The man could've been my twin except for his unkempt hair and beard and even number of feet.

"Is that my brother?"

"That photo was taken six months ago in San Miguel, El Salvador. We know the identities of every man in the picture except the one I believe is your brother. They're a band of forajidos . . . outlaws."

I grabbed the picture and pulled it close to my face. "I know what a forajido is. How and from whom did you get this picture?"

He reached for the photograph. "You can't have the picture."

The next sound from the table was the hammer of Clark's 1911 pistol being cocked, but McCall didn't flinch.

Clark said, "Not only are we keeping the picture, but you're going to tell us everything you know about it, who took it, who the other men are, and most importantly, why and how you have it."

Chapter 3

Unafraid

Phil McCall glanced down at Clark's pistol only inches away from his right side. "Look, boys. I've been around the world, shot, stabbed, left for dead, loved, hated, forgotten, and everything in between. If you think you're going to scare me by sticking a gun in my ribs, I need to prepare you for the most disappointing moment of your day. I've been dead since sometime in the early eighties. What you see are the remnants of a man who's been gutted and a mortal shell that refuses to lie down. I'm not afraid of dying. In fact, I look forward to it. The life I've lived has taught me two things in six decades. Real bad guys don't make threats. They just take what they want and dump the bodies. And good guys don't kill washed-up old spooks in roadside restaurants in the Florida Keys."

Clark didn't move his pistol, but he leaned toward the man. "Maybe you should've stayed in school a little longer because there are no such things as good guys or bad guys. There's only shades of gray of people in between. Now, you can keep playing the martyr if that's what rocks your boat, or you can get up and walk out of here with us. You may have been around the world, but you've never had a man like me pointing a gun at you. You see, my shade of gray is a whole lot closer to black than my friend's on the other side of the table. You're right about him. He won't kill you in this restaurant, but even *he* doesn't know if I will. When all of this plays out, it doesn't matter what you or Chase believes, because here's what I know. When the sun goes down tonight, I'll be sitting in my favorite chair, smoking a Cuban, and drinking Scotch half my age."

McCall ignored Clark and lifted the newspaper from the table. He carefully unfolded it and slid his half-glasses back onto his face.

When he'd positioned the *Times* between himself and me, I drew my knife and dissected the paper from top to bottom, precisely along its crease, leaving the man holding a piece in each hand. "My friend is right. I won't kill you in this restaurant, but you chose to turn this conversation into a confrontation, and I'm very good at destroying a man's will to continue the fight. You don't want or need the hell I'll pour down on you if you don't get up, walk out, and tell me everything you know."

As if his paper were still whole, he refolded it and let it fall to the table, misaligned with everything. "Okay, let's go."

I laid a twenty on the table and tilted my head toward the door. "You first."

We crossed Card Sound Road and descended the mangrove-covered bank toward the Twin Otter. I cast off the line holding the airplane to the bank and climbed inside. Clark stayed with our guest in the cabin while I taxied down the narrow canal and onto Little Card Sound. The twin turbines pulled us from the water and sent us soaring through the humid, early afternoon air.

For the first time, McCall cracked ever so slightly. "Where are you taking me?"

"Now, that's an interesting way to phrase that question," I said.

Although I couldn't see his face from my perch in the cockpit, I believed we'd proven to be more than the man claiming to be Phil McCall expected.

I said, "Most people who are unafraid would've asked, 'Where are we going?' instead of, 'Where are you taking me?'"

I cast a look across my shoulder to see McCall staring out the right side of the airplane.

Clark said, "I think our new friend is afraid of those alligators down there in the Everglades."

I cracked a smile behind the microphone of my headset. "In that case, I know just the spot."

We splashed down forty miles southwest of Key Largo in a shallow cut called Conchie Basin and cautiously taxied to a tiny speck of an island called Cormorant Key.

It took five minutes to stumble and weave our way through the rocky, tree-covered terrain of the island before reaching the perfectly clear interior. I took a knee, and Clark *encouraged* our new friend to sit. Resisting Clark Johnson's physical encouragement to do anything is futile, so McCall found himself sitting on the sand and looking up at the more dangerous of the Fulton brothers.

I said, "I wanted this to be friendly, but you wanted it to get rough. I guess even guys like you get what they want sometimes. Now, it's my turn to get what I want."

He continued staring up at me with one eye closed against the beating sun, and I motioned to the northwest. "The Everglades are five miles that way. There's even a campground and the Coastal Prairie Trailhead over there. All you have to do is swim the five miles, and you can disappear into oblivion. In fact, here's a bonus. The water is shallow enough to walk most of the way, but I seem to remember reading somewhere that the waters along the coastal Everglades are the only place on Earth where alligators and crocodiles live together, so good luck with that."

McCall's gaze fell to the white sand around him. "I guess they were right about you guys."

"Who was right about us?" I demanded.

"Some old friends," he mumbled.

"If those old friends told you we always mean what we say, then they were right, but now, you have firsthand knowledge of just how serious we are. My guess is that nobody, not even your priest, knows where you are. That gives us a piece of the upper hand. Your fear of gators gives us the rest. So, talk or swim."

His surrender, like most surrenders, came as a sigh. "What do you want to know?"

"Let's start with my family," I said. "Was that deployment to Guatemala in March of seventy-six the first time you met my parents?"

"It was the first time meeting your mother, but not your father. I knew him from Vietnam and some training after the war."

I considered his answer and analyzed it for signs of deception. "Did you see them again after you got us out of the country?"

"Our paths crossed a few times, but we never officially worked together. They were good people—strong, devoted, faithful people. And I see a lot of them in you."

There it is . . . The first sign of manipulation.

"Don't try getting under my skin with a trip down memory lane. I've been down that road, and it's a dead end. I don't know you. I don't have any way of checking out your story. And I have every reason to doubt you. I've caught enough bullets and blades to bleed out all the gullibility inside of me, so stick to the truth and stay off the emotions."

He shrugged. "Believe what you want, but anybody who knew Archie Fulton would agree that you're the same man he was, inside and out."

"Maybe so," I said. "But none of that matters now. He's gone, and I'm still here. That's what matters right now. If—and that's a huge if—my brother exists, I *will* find him, and I *will* give him a chance to walk away from the life he's living with those Central American banditos."

McCall chuckled. "How are you going to find him?"

I leaned down and stared into his skull. "If Archie Fulton were still alive, don't you believe he'd climb every tree and kick over every rock in the jungle to find his son?"

He chewed his bottom lip. "All right. I get it. Here's what I know. That picture was taken in November or December of last year."

"How do you know?"

He picked up a handful of sand and let it pour through his fingers. "Because I took the picture right before I killed Hector Domínguez, the guy standing next to your brother in the picture."

"What's his name?" I whispered.

McCall furrowed his brow. "I told you his name. It was Hector Domínguez."

"No. My brother. What's his name?"

He stared down at the sand again. "I don't know, but if I did, I swear I'd tell you. The Agency assigned him the designation of the Lizard."

"We'll revisit that later, but for now, what were you doing in El Salvador?"

"That's classified."

I pressed my booted robot against his shoulder and gave him a shove, sending him onto his back. "Let's go, Clark. This guy can swim or starve to death on this rock. I don't care which."

McCall scampered to his knees. "You didn't let me finish. What I was doing in El Salvador is classified and has no connection to your brother, but I was there with an old friend of yours, Diablo de Agua."

This guy is good.

I took a knee beside him. "You're doing it again. Playing my family card didn't work, so now you're trying to distract me with the Water Devil. Why is it so important for you to get inside my head?"

"I'm not trying to get in your head. I'm telling you what I saw. That's it."

I bore holes through his flesh with my stare. "Your verbal misdirection might play out just fine on some rookie shooter who's enamored by your résumé, but that ain't me, partner. I've seen and done too much to fall for your schoolyard psychology. It's as simple as this. I ask questions, and you give immediate answers. Classified, unclassified, I don't care. You answer my questions. If you balk one time, the next thing you'll see is the tail of our airplane climbing away. Got it?"

"It's not that simple, kid . . ."

I put a finger between his eyes. "It's exactly that simple. Question one. Why were you in El Salvador?"

To my surprise, he pushed my finger away. "They've got some real problems down there. There's a coup d'état afoot." He shot a look at my prosthetic. "Pardon the pun."

Clark choked back the laughter, and I wanted to stick my a-foot right up both of their a-asses.

"A coup d'état? That's nothing new in Central America," I said.

McCall shook his head. "No, it's not, but this one is particularly troubling. It is—or was—well funded and extremely well organized."

"Was?"

"Yeah, was. The good guys won, for now."

"Are you saying my brother was one of the bad guys?"

"No, I'm not saying that at all. I'm saying the men in that picture were mercenaries . . . extremely high-paid mercenaries. Four of them are now dead."

"And my brother?"

McCall spat between his knees. "Here's the skinny. I don't know for sure if the guy in the picture *is* your brother, but he sure looks a lot like you, and his age is right. He's definitely not Guatemalan, but he has the language, the mannerisms, and the bravado. He just doesn't have the look."

"You said the coup was well funded. Who's the financier?"

McCall's bottom lip endured more chewing. "Now you're asking big-boy questions, so I guess it's time for some big-boy answers." He glanced toward Clark and then back at me. "He knows how the world works, and you're about to get a primer in geopolitical reality. We financed it. The good ol' Red, White, and Blue."

The pinball machine my skull had become instantly locked up, full tilt. No matter how hard I struggled to put the shiny silver ball back in play, it wasn't happening.

Stalling more than probing, I asked, "How do you know?"

The nervous tick of lip-chewing ceased as McCall's confidence returned. "Because that's how it works. How do you think that little band of patriots who thumbed their nose at the King of England turned thirteen colonies into the world's only remaining superpower in a little over two hundred years?"

I was still flashing tilt, but McCall showed no signs of noticing, and he continued his dissertation. "We've been funding hostile takeovers since those guys signed the Declaration of Independence a couple hundred years ago. It's never going to stop."

I shook off my disbelief. "So, help me understand. We're paying for the coup, but you and Diablo went down there to kill off the mercenaries fighting for the overthrow. I'm afraid I'm not smart enough to understand that."

McCall stared up into the beating sun and wiped his brow. "Do you think we could take this into the shade?"

I placed a boot on his thigh. "Have we reached an understanding?"

"Yeah. I'll tell you what you want to know. You don't have to feed me to the gators. By the way, were you being serious about crocodiles in the glades?"

"That's what I've heard, but I've never seen one. We can wade around and see if we can find one if you'd like."

He groaned and popped his way to his feet. "Nah, I think I'll take a pass on that."

"I thought you might. Come on. We'll do a little better than shade. I know where there's a hardworking air conditioner and some soft chairs."

Chapter 4
Demons Old and New

We climbed back into the Twin Otter and blasted off to the northeast. Minutes later, Clark kissed the runway back at the Ocean Reef Club and taxied to the terminal.

McCall glanced out the window and shot a look back at me. "What's my car doing here?"

"I told you we aren't amateurs. Clark lifted the keys while you were giving your speech about not being afraid when somebody shoves a pistol in your ribs. Our man in Alabama Jacks brought it out here."

He shook his head and put on a look that could almost qualify as respect.

Stone W. Hunter waited on the tarmac as we climbed down from the airplane.

McCall glanced at my partner and let out a chuckle. "I should've known. You were the guy with coffee and a pack of cigarettes in Alabama Jacks, but you didn't smell like smoke, and your fingers weren't nicotine-stained."

Hunter gave him a wink and tossed the cigarettes to our new friend.

He squeezed the pack and looked down into the tiny camera lens it contained. "I guess the Cold War gadgets are still in style."

Hunter tucked the pack back into his pocket. "Classics never go out of style."

We pushed our way through the mirrored glass door of the FBO and caught Masha's eye as we continued down the hallway to the pilot's lounge.

I said, "We're going to need the lounge for an hour or so. Is that okay?"

She smiled. "Yes, this is okay, but please do not break anything."

I feigned offense. "Do I look like I break things?"

She lowered her chin. "You do not, but the others look to me like breakers of things."

"You've got a good eye, Masha. I promise I'll keep the breakers of things under control."

The door to the pilot's lounge let out a cry of resistance when I turned the lock, but the bolt finally surrendered, and our briefing room was secure.

"I don't think introductions are necessary," I began. "We all know each other, and the three of us are smart enough to know you won't give us your real name. With the formalities out of the way, it's time for you to spill your guts, McCall."

He closed his eyes and took in a long breath. "Okay, here it is. I'm an old, washed-up spook. People like me make great scapegoats. We're still sane enough to pull off simple missions, but just crazy enough to play a plausible lunatic. If I catch a bullet or a blade, it's no big loss. There's a thousand more just like me lined up to cash the government's checks and stick their noses into places they don't belong. That's why I was in El Salvador."

Hunter pulled four bottles of water from the cooler and tossed them around the room.

McCall caught a bottle, nodded his thanks, and emptied it. He continued. "When I was in Guatemala in seventy-six, on the mission to get your family out of there, the place was a hell on Earth. I've seen my share of dumpster fires, but that place looked like something the ground swallowed up and then spat back out. In times and places like that, a man has to make some decisions that will haunt him for the rest of his life." He fell silent and stared down into the pits of his memory.

I leaned forward. "What did you do, McCall?"

The long breath came again. "It's not *what* I did. It's what I didn't do. This way of life . . ." He paused and met each of our gazes. "This life of ours . . . It's no way for a man to live. It robs us of any humanity we ever had inside of us. It tears out our souls and shoves demons into the cavities left behind. We beat those demons back with pills and Jim Beam, but some of them like the painkillers even more than we do. They thrive on them, and little pieces of our sanity, until there's nothing left."

"Quit stalling," I ordered.

"I ain't stalling, Chase. I'm confessing."

"I'm not your priest. You can take your guilty conscience to God, but I don't need to hear it."

"Fair enough. When I shoved your family onto that airplane, your folks knew your baby brother hadn't survived. But . . ."

"But what?"

He let out the guttural moan of a dying animal. "But I wasn't so sure."

I sprang to my feet, but Clark grabbed my belt and forced me back into the chair. "Sit down, and stay down."

I jerked away from Clark and stuck a finger toward McCall's face. "Are you telling me you knew my brother was alive and you left him behind?"

McCall shook his head. "No, that's not what I'm saying. What I'm telling you is that I wasn't certain he was dead, but I had to make a decision that—"

I pushed from my chair again, but again, Clark yanked me back down.

It was my handler's turn to take control of the room. "Listen to me, McCall. We don't care about your angst or whatever demon you're running from. You're not going to find absolution here. That's between you and God. If all of this is some pitiful effort to clean up your guilty conscience, you're wasting your time."

McCall cut in. "You may not care now, but the day will come when there's not enough vodka in the Rodina to make you forget the unthinkable things you did when you thought you were the good guys."

"No more philosophy," I said. "Just give us the facts."

He leaned back in the overstuffed chair. "The facts are these . . . I was sent to get you and your parents out of Guatemala in seventy-six. I did that. The fear that's haunted me for thirty years is the fact that I probably made your brother an orphan. When I saw the man who I believed to be him, my suspicion was confirmed. That's why we're all here today. First of all, I wanted you to know so I could clean my slate before they throw me in the ground. Second, if a man has a brother, I think he should know."

I replayed his words through my head half a dozen times before saying, "How did you know?"

"How did I know what?"

"How did you know the man in that picture looked like me? You haven't seen me since I was a toddler in seventy-six. There was no way for you to know what I looked like as an adult."

McCall pulled his cell phone from his pocket and tossed it to me. "I thought you might ask that question. Take a look at my recent call list."

I caught the phone and thumbed through the call log. Third from the top was the name that ended my search. I shook my head and passed the phone off to Clark.

It took him only seconds to see the name Dominic Fontana, and he eyed McCall. "How do you know my father?"

McCall held out his hand, and Clark laid the phone in his palm. "Your father and I drew a lot of fire together when we were young and bulletproof. Men like us tend to keep in touch with our brothers-in-arms. I ran into Dominic with a woman who could've been his granddaughter on some island I can't pronounce a while back. We caught up, and the subject of kids came up. The little Cuban goddess perked up, but Dom was quick to shut that down."

Clark shook his head. "That's what I need . . . a baby brother from a sixty-eight-year-old pappy."

McCall said, "I don't think there's any danger of that."

I cut in. "We're losing focus. Let's get back on task. How did you know the man looked like me as an adult?"

"I was getting there. When I asked Dom about his son, he was gushing with pride. He even showed me some pictures. When I saw a picture of the two of you on a sailboat, my heart sank, and it felt like I'd been hit by a truck."

Clark leaned forward. "And I suppose my dad can corroborate all of this?"

"He can corroborate the chance meeting and the part about showing me the pictures, but I didn't mention what was going on in my head about Chase and his brother."

"*Possible* brother," I said.

"Take another look at that picture and tell me it's not more than a mere possibility."

As I studied the picture, everything else in my world faded out of focus. There was no question the man in the picture resembled me. He was tall, lean, and beneath his shaggy beard, I could imagine the same chin that appeared on every male relative who shared the Fulton name.

Clark stuck a thumb to the picture and slid it across the table toward himself. I watched his eyes glance from the picture to me and back again. He tossed the photograph into the air like a frisbee, and it floated to the table, still spinning. After eying McCall for a long moment, he turned back to me. "Pack your bags, College Boy. It looks like we're going to Guatemala."

Chapter 5
Those Who Can Count

On the northbound flight back to Bonaventure Plantation in Saint Marys, Georgia, the Twin Otter became a chamber of horrors for me.

Is it really possible for me to have a living brother? Could he know I exist? Would he care? Is it feasible for us to find him? And if we do find him, am I his enemy? Is he mine?

Clark pulled the microphone of his Bose headset to his lips. "I know you're the psychologist, but let me guess. You're trying to decide if it's possible that you have a brother . . . other than me, of course."

I stared out the window across the endless blue expanse of the North Atlantic. "Am I that easy to read?"

"Not usually, but I've been thinking about the questions I'd have if the hand was on the other foot."

"Hand on the other foot? What's that supposed to mean?"

He shook his head as if I were the weak link. "You know, College Boy, there are only three kinds of people on Earth. Those who can count, and those who cannot. And I'm definitely one of those."

I laughed for the first time in hours. "Sometimes I wonder if you and I speak the same language, but you guessed correctly. I'm wondering exactly that. What do you think?"

He adjusted his sunglasses and tapped his temple. "I've been running the whole thing through my supercomputer, and I've decided there's only three possibilities. One, the guy in the picture isn't your brother at all, and it's all a huge coincidence. Two, he *is* your brother, and we're going to have one heck of a time finding him."

He paused, leaving me wondering which of the three kinds of people I was. "Please tell me there's *really* a third option."

"I'm getting there. The supercomputer's churning, and the third possibility is the one I *really* don't want to think about."

Clark suddenly had my attention, and he continued. "I need to talk to my dad about that McCall character. If he is who and what he claims, I've still got one concern. I know one thing about retired spooks who didn't save enough money to retire . . . They make their living any way they can when their age starts with a six or higher."

I ignored the speck of water that was the Atlantic and dived headlong into the ocean that was Clark Johnson's bottomless mind. "Are you suggesting it's an elaborate setup?"

"I'm not suggesting it. I'm just saying it's possible."

"Great. Now my brain has something else to worry about. How long do you think it'll take Skipper to find him?"

Clark grimaced. "Let's run through our balance sheet. You list our assets, and I'll tick off the liabilities."

"Well, we've got a picture."

He looked over his sunglasses. "Get ready. I'm about to use a big word. Tell me about the *providence* of that picture."

"Okay, I get it. We can't trust McCall . . . yet. And I think you meant *provenance*."

"You knew what I meant, and I made my point," he said. "And I think that qualifies as a liability."

"Here's a definite asset. Diablo de Agua saw him, too."

He reached into the console between us and pulled out the satellite phone. "Here you go. Give Diablo a call."

I took the phone from his hand and dropped it back into the console. "Again, point taken. We may not have Diablo on speed dial, but Ginger can find him."

Clark held up a finger. "I'll give you that one."

I let my mind pore over the teacup of information we had. "I guess our balance sheet isn't very well balanced, huh?"

"It's a little heavy on the liability side."

With Clark at the helm, I drifted back into my world of hope, fear, and thousands of questions.

* * *

We touched down at what had been the St. Marys Municipal Airport until the city turned off the runway lights and sold the whole thing to us. Having our own private airport only minutes from my home was an expensive endeavor but worth every penny.

We refueled the Twin Otter and committed her back to the hangar she claimed as her own. Hangar number one housed the workhorses of our aeronautical fleet: the Cessna Citation, amphibious Caravan, Bell 212 Helicopter, Skylane, and the jewel of the crown, our 1944 North American P-51D Mustang.

The five-minute ride to Bonaventure in the ragged Volkswagen Microbus gave my mind another opportunity to worry, fret, and fear the coming days and weeks of my life.

"Penny! Are you home?" I called as we came through the kitchen door.

No answer came, so I bounded up the stairs to the ops center while Clark pillaged the refrigerator.

Skipper, our intelligence analyst, answered on the third ring from her home office in Silver Spring, Maryland. "Hey, Chase. What's up?"

"Hypothetical for you . . . If I told you I needed you to find a person in Guatemala or El Salvador from only a single photograph, how long would it take?"

"That depends. Is this person the only one in the picture, and is there anything in the background that might give something away?"

"I just scanned and emailed it. You should have it in your inbox."

"Checking now."

I waited in silent anxiety for her to see the picture. When her reaction came, I was not disappointed.

"Oh my God, Chase! Is that you? When was this taken? Who are those other people?"

"You sound like Penny when you rattle off questions like that. First, that isn't me, but he's the guy I want to find. Clark and I met a retired spook at lunch. He knew my parents and Dominic. He claims to have taken the picture, and he believes the man on the end is my brother."

"Are you kidding? How is that possible? I thought you were—"

I cut her off. "He claims he was sent to Guatemala in nineteen seventy-six to rescue my parents and me from the fallout of a bunch of earthquakes. He says my brother was a baby and that my parents believed he was killed in one of the quakes."

"What's the guy's name?"

"Phillip McCall. I'd put him in his mid to late sixties."

The sound of fingertips on keys echoed through the line until Skipper sighed. "There are sixteen former or current Agency case officers with the name Phillip McCall. Four of them fall into that age range."

"How about areas of operation?"

"Nine are, or were, Eastern Europe, and three in Central and South America."

"Can you get any pictures?"

"Seriously, Chase? You want pictures of current and former CIA case officers? Get real."

"Fine. How about this? McCall claimed to be close friends with Clark's dad, Dominic."

Fingers once again danced across keys. "Yeah, I can work with that. Stand by."

Two minutes, or perhaps two weeks later, she said, "The room is clean, right?"

"It is."

"Good. Look up."

I checked the screen to see a black-and-white picture of my lunch date. "That's him."

"I thought so. Here's the skinny. His name is Phillip Benjamin McCall, born June tenth, nineteen forty-five. That makes him sixty-two. He's a Naval Academy grad, SEAL in Vietnam in sixty-eight and sixty-nine. Purple Heart, Air Medal, Silver Star, Bronze Star. He was medicalled out of the Navy in seventy and went to work for the Agency in December of the same year."

"Okay, so he checks out."

"Not so fast," she said. "He checks out until nineteen ninety-seven, when he was killed in the line of duty on an official mission in Panama."

"What?"

"Yeah, it says here that he was believed dead, but his body was never recovered."

"That's interesting. I think it's time for a chat with Dominic."

The tones and light above the door warned me of Clark's arrival in the ops center. I looked up to see him with a sandwich dangling from his mouth and a bag of potato chips tucked beneath his arm.

"Get in here, Hungry Hippo. We need to call your dad."

He pulled up a chair and devoured the sandwich. "I thought we might make that call this afternoon. What have we learned about McCall?"

I brought him up to speed, and he said, "Hmm . . . a SEAL. I didn't see that coming."

"The killed-in-action thing is what caught me by surprise," I said.

Clark crammed his mouth full of chips and mumbled, "That's no big deal. I've been killed in action half a dozen times. Sometimes it's for the convenience of the Agency, but mostly it's for plausible deniability. You know . . . He wasn't *our* man. He must've been rogue."

"Whatever you say. Let's get your dad on the phone."

Dominic wasn't as quick to answer as Skipper. It took six calls to four different numbers.

"Can't you guys leave a retiree alone?"

Clark said, "What's wrong with a man calling his dad just to check in?"

"Nothing's wrong with that. But we both know this isn't a social call."

"Hey, Dominic. It's Chase. We had an interesting conversation with a guy who claims to be a friend of yours. Does the name Phil McCall ring any bells?"

Dominic groaned. "Hold on. Let me go inside." A minute later, he said, "Yeah, I know McCall. How did you cross paths with him?"

"He called us," I said.

I spent the next five minutes briefing Dominic on the situation, but he showed no signs of surprise. Instead, he asked, "When are you leaving for Guatemala?"

Skipper became the voice of reason. "We've got a lot more homework to do before we're ready to be wheels-up. Come get me so we can get started."

I stood from my chair. "We're on our way, but before we go, Dominic, is there anything else we should know?"

Dom's voice boomed through the speaker. "Yeah, there's just one more thing. McCall is a man of conscience. Men like him aren't good at the games we play. It gets under their skin, and they seek out every possibility to cleanse their soul of the atrocities they've been a part of. Keep that in mind when dealing with him. He's a good guy, but Catholic school implanted a guilty bone in him. Don't let him get you hurt in an effort to clear his conscience."

I said, "Thanks, Dom. We'll keep that in mind. And Skipper, we'll be there as fast as the Citation will fly. I'll call you fifteen minutes out."

"I'll be ready," she said. "In the meantime, is there anything specific you need me to do?"

"Find Diablo de Agua."

Skipper huffed. "I'm afraid that's outside even my ability, but I know just the person to make it happen. I'll see you soon."

We cut the lines and headed through the door.

I'd mastered the complex skill of climbing stairs with my robot foot, but descending them was another issue entirely. With no feeling in the foot, it's challenging for my brain to know when I've made contact with the stair tread on the way down. As I hobbled from the bottom step, Hunter came through the kitchen door.

He said, "There you are. We've got a huge problem at the barn. Come with me."

Chapter 6
Rough Shod

Clark and I followed Hunter down the back gallery stairs and across the yard at a sprint. As we approached the horse barn, the sound of cursing and bellowing filled the air.

"What's going on, Hunter?"

He either didn't hear me, or he chose to ignore me. We ran through the open barn doors into a scene beyond description. Hanging upside down from a line thrown across the rafters was a man of perhaps thirty, wearing dirty boots, well-worn jeans, and a black T-shirt. He squirmed and jerked against the restraints looped around his ankles.

Penny, my docile Southern belle of a wife, pulled a horseshoe from the coal-fired forge with a pair of steel tongs. The shoe glowed from the heat, and smoke poured from its surface.

I yelled, "What's going on here?"

Penny stomped toward the hanging man with the smoking steel shoe held in outstretched arms. "Stay out of this, Chase. It's not your fight!"

Overwhelmed by the chaos of the moment, I tried to piece together what was happening right before my eyes. Penny continued toward the doomed man, and I stepped between the two of them.

The expression on her face and scorned tone sent chills down my spine. "I mean it, Chase. Stay out of my way."

I dodged the scalding-hot weapon, and to my disbelief, she pressed the shoe to the left hip pocket of the man's jeans. White smoke billowed from the denim, and the smell of burning flesh wafted from the wound. She lifted a booted foot and gave the man a spin. When he swung to face her, she pressed the still blazing-hot horseshoe against his chest. The cotton T-shirt melted to his flesh, and he bellowed in agony as he pawed at his burns.

Penny dropped the tongs, and the shoe tumbled across the dirt floor of the barn. She then stepped around the hanging man and lifted a two-by-four from against a stall door. "The branding was for grabbing my ass, and this is for hitting Pecan!"

She wound up like Babe Ruth and swung for the man's head. Hunter's reaction was only slightly faster than mine. Stopping the swinging board wasn't an option, so Hunter threw a shoulder into the man's gut, swinging him out of the arc of Penny's board.

I yelled, "Enough! What's this about?"

Penny dropped the board and exhaled hard. "He decided to get a little handsy with me, and I let him off with a warning, but then he hit Pecan in the face with this board to get her to calm down. Just look what he did to her eye, Chase."

I had a long-standing and well-founded hatred for horses, but Pecan was the only horse on the planet I didn't loathe. She was a fourteen-year-old quarter horse who wouldn't hurt a fly. A line of dried blood lay just beneath her left eye, and I suddenly thought Penny had let the man off the hook too easily.

I took a knee beside his inverted head. "Who are you?"

He groaned. "I'm the farrier."

"Did you hit my wife's horse?"

He shuddered in pain and fear. "She wouldn't calm down and give me her hoof, so I had to get her attention."

"And how about putting your hands on my wife? Was that an attempt to get *her* attention?"

He roared. "She's crazy, man. I never touched her."

I looked up at the woman I loved who wouldn't tell a lie for a billion dollars, and I tossed the board back to her. "He just called you a liar, baby. Hunter and I are going outside to see if his truck will float. I think you can handle the rest."

The man yelled, "No! Don't leave me in here with her. She'll kill me!"

"Maybe you should've thought about that before you put your hands on her."

It was Clark's turn to become the mediator. He reached for the board in Penny's hand. "How about you give me the two-by-four, and I'll take care of the guy who used to be your farrier while you help Chase and Hunter with his truck?"

She reluctantly surrendered the board and followed me through the door. I'll never know what Clark did or said to the guy, but the last time I saw the farrier, he was running as fast as his legs would carry him in the opposite direction of the North River, where I'd threatened to send his truck.

Penny laid her head against my chest. "Thanks for coming, Chase. I would've probably killed that guy if Hunter hadn't found you."

I wrapped my arms around her. "You can't be killing people in our barn because they grabbed your butt and hurt a horse. But I think you made your point. Are you all right?"

"Yeah, I'm fine. It just pissed me off."

"I know. Maybe it's time to get rid of the horses."

She pulled away. "What? No! We'll get a new farrier, but we're not getting rid of the horses, no matter how much you hate them."

An hour later, the veterinarian treated Pecan's wound and said, "I'll put the word out about that guy. It won't take long for him to be unemployed. In the meantime, here's the name of a *good* farrier who doesn't behave the way he did." He handed us a card and pulled off his gloves. "Pecan's going to be just fine. She's a good old horse."

I stuffed a pair of hundred-dollar bills into his hand. "Thanks for coming out so quickly."

He pocketed the money. "No problem. It's always a pleasure. Call anytime."

It took half an hour to explain to Penny the surprise of my potential brother and Phil McCall.

When I'd answered her questions and given her all the info I had, Penny said, "I'll get a shower and come with you to get Skipper."

Through the years, men have justifiably complained about the exorbitant amount of time it takes for women to get ready to go anywhere, but those men weren't married to Penny Fulton. Ten minutes after entering the house, she was headed down the stairs with her wet hair in a ponytail protruding through the back of an Atlanta Braves hat. Penny was perfect right out of the box, without an ounce of makeup or any need for a designer wardrobe, and there would never be anything on Earth sexier than her ponytail from beneath a ball cap.

I followed my wife up the stairs of the Citation. "You do that on purpose, don't you?"

She giggled and reached for her ponytail. "You bet I do. Because that's exactly how the only man who's allowed to grab my butt likes it."

"You've got that right, Mrs. Fulton. Do you want to drive or relax?"

"I've had a big day. I think I'll sit back here in the comfy seats like somebody important while you boys fly me around."

"I think you've earned it," I said.

The flight from Bonaventure Field to Montgomery County Airpark near Gaithersburg, Maryland, took just over an hour, and Skipper was waiting by the terminal when we taxied up. Minutes later, she was aboard, and we were airborne and southbound.

By the time we landed back in St. Marys, Hunter had assembled the team in the ops center, and we had a mission to brief.

Skipper made short work of setting up the room and bringing the monitors to life. "Okay, gang. This one is a doozy."

She told the story of McCall and my brother in explicit detail, and she ended the briefing by showing a picture of the man who likely shared my DNA.

Mongo was the first to speak. "Well, if he ain't your brother, he ought to be. I've never seen two people look more alike without being twins."

Singer, our Southern Baptist sniper, spoke softly. "What do we know about the other men in the picture?"

"We believe they're all dead," I said. "McCall claims to have killed them with the help of another operative named Diablo de Agua."

Disco, our chief pilot, asked, "The Water Devil?"

I nodded. "Your Spanish is getting better. His real name is David, but he's known in the business as the Water Devil. I've never met anyone like him. The best way I can think of to describe him is a ninja who can outfight Mongo. The only problem is that he's not exactly connected to the rest of the world, so it'll take a few days to find him."

Skipper pulled off her glasses. "That's where you're wrong. I know somebody who can find him before the sun goes down."

"Get her on it," I said.

Seconds later, the analyst who taught Skipper the fine art of running operations came into focus on the master screen. "Hey, gang! How's everybody doing?"

Skipper hit the key, activating the bevy of microphones through the ops center. "Hey, Ginger. We're doing great. I hope we haven't pulled you off anything important."

Ginger pulled a pencil from the bundle of hair piled atop her head and shook it out. Her long red hair cascaded across her shoulders and changed her look from librarian to debutante in seconds. "Oh, no. I'm never too busy for my favorite protégé."

I took the reins. "We have a little seek-and-find mission for you if you're up for it."

"Always," she said. "Who are we finding?"

"Your favorite little Water Devil."

"Oh! In that case, that makes this a labor of love. I'll find him for you in a couple of hours. Do you want a face-to-face or just a conversation?

"Both."

"Consider it done. Is there anything else?"

Skipper said, "Nope. That does it. Let us know when you find him."

Ginger leaned toward the camera. "Hey, Mongo." She gave our giant a wink. "Oh, the big-brained, beautiful babies we could make." She held her thumb and pinkie to her face like a phone and mouthed, "Call me."

Mongo blushed and couldn't manage to get any meaningful words to fall out of his mouth.

Skipper saved the big guy. "Bye, Ginger."

Chapter 7
My Spirit

I loved every room of Bonaventure, but there was something special about the kitchen. That's where my team tended to gather while not in the ops center. That afternoon was no exception.

Clark, in his typical style, was back in the refrigerator. "Why don't you ever have anything to eat around here?"

I sighed. "You never seem to have any problems finding something to eat, but I've never seen you carry in a bag of groceries."

He eased the door closed and shoved several slices of salami into his face. "You know I'm not a shopper. Get off my case."

Before we could continue the banter, Skipper's voice filled the room. "Get back up here, guys. Ginger's on the line."

I scanned the ceiling. "When did we get an intercom?"

Mongo's chair almost sighed with relief when the big man stood. "I think it's been here all along, but you've just never used it."

We ascended the stairs and piled back into our seats just as Ginger's face filled the screen. "Guess who I found."

"You're a genius," I said. "Patch him through."

The analyst stroked a few keys, and the sound of birds squawking filled the room. She said, "Of course there's no video, and the audio is a little shaky, but here he is."

The quiet, confident tone of Diablo de Agua crackled through the speakers. "Hello again, my friend. I hear your team has grown since I last saw you."

"It has," I said, "but we'll make introductions later. Right now, we need to know about a mission you worked with an American named Phil McCall."

The line went silent for several seconds. Even the birds seemed to sense the weight of the coming conversation.

Finally, Diablo said, "The man in the picture . . . he has your spirit."

I screwed up my face. "My spirit?"

"Yes, your spirit. Just as shade from the bamboo doesn't feel the same as shade from the mahogany tree."

"You'll have to forgive me," I said, "but I don't understand."

The sounds of the birds returned in the distance. "Remember in Panama when I told you that you move and speak like your father?"

"I'll never forget that."

"It is the same with your brother. He moves and thinks like you. He is a dangerous man and very unpredictable."

I let the comparison wash over me for a moment. "You called him my brother . . ."

Before I could continue, he said, "Yes, there is no doubt of this."

Again, I found myself awash in a feeling I couldn't define. The thought of a brother—especially one who likely was my enemy twelve hundred miles away—left me tumbling inside my head. Until that moment, the proposition was merely a possibility, but hearing Diablo's confidence felt like daggers through my soul.

Singer, the man who'd become my moral compass, laid a hand across my forearm and gave a gentle squeeze. "Ask your questions,

Chase. Try to be objective for now, and we'll deal with the emotion afterwards."

I swallowed the lump in my throat and stared at the ceiling. "Can you find him again?"

Diablo asked, "Is this a question for me?"

"It is."

I expected a confident answer in the affirmative, but instead, I got, "With your help, I can. But it will not be easy . . . nor safe."

Instead of choking on his warning, I said, "What do you need from us?"

Without hesitation, Diablo asked, "Is Ginger inside on this?"

I said, "She's not been fully briefed yet, but if you'd like to use her as a contact, Skipper will make sure she's up to speed."

"Then I don't need anything directly from you other than your arrival date."

I turned to Clark. "Am I going alone?"

Clark's wasn't the only answer that rose from the table.

Everyone said, "No!"

The team gathered around the table was my family by choice, and every man was more of a true brother to me than anybody with my DNA.

"When and where?" I asked.

Diablo said, "I will be in the town of Puerto Grande on Bahía de Chismuyo in three days."

Skipper's fingers flew across the keys, and without looking up, she said, "That's sixty miles south-southwest of Tegucigalpa, Honduras."

I scanned the faces at the table, and Clark held up three fingers.

"We'll be there," I said. "How will we find you?"

Diablo chuckled. "I will find you, amigo."

With that, he was gone like the apparition he is, leaving my team sitting in silent wonder.

Skipper broke the silence. "So, I guess that means this is an official mission now."

Clark pulled his phone from a pocket of his cargo pants, pressed a key, and stuck it to his ear. When a voice answered, he said, "Team Twenty-One is down for at least six weeks." The muffled voice in the earpiece apparently put up an argument, and Clark rebutted with, "Because I said so." With that, he returned the phone to his pocket.

I caught his eye. "Do you think we can get this done in six weeks?"

Clark shrugged. "How should I know? I made up that number to keep my phone from ringing. Even if we need six years, I'll keep putting them off. I can't think of anything more important than this mission. Can you?"

I took in a long breath and considered his question. After a few seconds of drowning in the thought, I spun back to face my brothers and rapped on the table. "Here's the deal, guys. I'm going, but I don't expect all of you to follow me. Just like every other mission we accept, you always have the option to sit this one out."

Singer held up a hand. "This is ridiculous, Chase. You're wasting not only your breath, but also precious time. We're going . . . all of us. But before we do, we've got to put your head on straight. Maybe you and I should take a walk out to the gazebo."

I swallowed hard and felt my heart pounding. "No, let's do it right here, right now."

Singer eased himself back into his seat and rolled back from the table. He rounded Clark and pushed his chair away from mine. Having repositioned himself into Clark's spot, Singer began. "Chase, you know more about the academics of psychology than anybody in this room, but I've got a few years of actual practice under fire. There are three things I want you to consider before we lock and load."

Having spent hundreds of hours of my life under Singer's tutelage, I could feel the harsh reality of the lesson coming. "Okay, I'm listening."

He leaned back in his chair, and every eye in the room focused on nothing but our sniper's face. "First, it's imperative that you consciously put a set of priorities in place." He motioned toward the door. "Penny is just down those stairs, and she loves you more than even she can understand. Coming home to her has to be foremost in your mind during every second of this mission. Is that clear?"

I nodded, and he continued.

"Second, the man we're hunting may genetically be your brother, but his life experience has been vastly different than yours. You've heard the age-old argument about nature versus nurture. It's undeniable that this guy looks like you. If you and he share the same parents, that's the epitome of nature's hand in this, but what you must keep in mind is that he's spent nearly thirty years in an environment that's completely foreign to you, just as your environment is foreign to him."

Singer paused, apparently to give his statement time to sink in before continuing. "Even if we assume he is your biological brother, he likely has no clue that you exist. He was raised by God only knows who, and because of those three decades of nurturing, he's likely to have a set of values entirely opposed to yours and all of ours. Will you be able to separate the emotional attachment to a brother you never knew you had from the reality of the man inside the shell that looks a lot like you?"

His question was powerful, but my answer was weak. "Honestly, I don't know. Sitting here, it's easy to say yes, but predicting how I'll feel when I stand face-to-face with him . . ." I paused, realizing there was a critical piece of information I didn't have. Kicking a heel into the carpet, I spun to face Skipper at her console. "What's his name?"

She furrowed her brow. "What's whose name?"

"My brother."

Her eyes widened as if she'd seen a ghost. "I, uh . . . Give me a minute." She typed and clicked furiously for several minutes. "All I can find is 'the Lizard.'"

Singer's hand landed on my shoulder, and I spun back to the table. He said, "His name doesn't matter right now. Even if we knew his name, we have no way to be certain it's valid. I'm afraid we're getting off track."

The yearning to know his name scorched its way through my chest and into my very core, and I was certain Singer, despite his insistence, could see it.

Our sniper's confident, quiet tone cut through my ears. "What you're feeling right now is exactly why we're having this conversation. When was the last time you cared about the name of a man we were chasing?"

"This is different," I demanded. "We're not chasing my brother. He's not done anything wrong. When we pursue a target, we do so to eliminate an evil from Earth. As far as we know, he hasn't done anything wrong. That makes this mission entirely different."

Clark grimaced, and Hunter groaned.

"What?" I demanded.

Both Clark and Hunter stared at Singer, and the sniper pulled the only picture we had from a folder in front of him.

He slid the picture toward me and leaned in. "What's different about the other men in this picture?"

I stared down at the shot and studied the faces. "Those four aren't my brothers."

Singer reached for a marker from the cup in the center of the table and drew a red X over the face of the four men who didn't share my familial connection. Barely above a whisper, he said, "Those men are dead because of their involvement in a coup to overthrow a duly elected government."

He tapped his finger above the only remaining man in the picture. "It's time for you to accept the likelihood that this man is exactly the opposite of you."

For the first time, the sickening realization hit me like a hammer. Everyone else at the table knew my brother was, most likely, a dark, dangerous man, but that was a likelihood my mind wasn't capable of swallowing at that moment.

"That's the third thing, isn't it?"

Singer nodded. "Yes, it is, and it's the most important of the three. That man, regardless of his name, will not see us as a party of humanitarians trying to reunite a family. He'll see us as American mercenaries, just like the mercenaries who killed his four comrades."

Chapter 8

Go . . . Don't Go

I spent the remainder of the evening alone in one of my favorite places, the gazebo housing the eighteenth-century cannon overlooking the North River. I found myself trying to rationalize emotion. Such a task is impossible, and of all people, I should've known that. However, despite my years of psychological education, I believed that rule didn't apply to me.

Singer was right, but believing I could approach the mission of finding my brother with the same mindset I'd carried into battle, time after time, was ludicrous. If we were successful in finding him, what would I say to him the first moment I stood staring into his eyes as if gazing into a mirror?

Hello, I'm Chase, your big brother.

The sound of footfalls behind me pulled me from my stupor, and I looked up to watch my anchor step into the gazebo. She held two tumblers of beautiful, honey-colored whiskey over ice. "I thought you might enjoy having a drink with your wife."

I accepted the glass, and she nestled onto the arm of my Adirondack chair. We touched the rims of our glasses, and I said, "Here's to the calm before the storm."

The cool, smokey whiskey warmed my throat and left me feeling human again.

Penny slid from the arm of the chair and onto my lap. She whispered, "I don't know what it feels like to be where you are right now, but I want you to know this will always be home for you."

I met her gaze. "Bonaventure?"

She kissed me softly. "No. Bonaventure is a place. Home is a feeling, and I love being that for you." She laid her head against my shoulder and stared out over the black water. Her breath against my skin felt like life itself, and suddenly, a brother a thousand miles away who didn't know I existed seemed to dissolve into the darkening sky.

Penny sighed. "Is it dangerous?"

"Is what dangerous?"

"Chasing a guy who *might be* your brother through the jungle."

"Clark seems to think it is, but I don't know. It's not like I'm there to capture or kill him. I just want to look into his eyes and tell him he has a brother."

"What if he has no concept of family? Have you thought about that?"

I swallowed another sip and placed my glass on the wooden deck of the gazebo. "Everyone has a concept of family. It may not be the nuclear family, but a sense of belonging to a close group, even if they're not blood relatives, is something our brains naturally develop. He'll understand the bond of brotherhood, even if he wasn't raised in a traditional family."

She ran her fingers through my hair and smiled. "You're thinking like a psychologist instead of a brother."

"I guess I am, but there's a pretty good reason for that. It's been a long time since I've been anybody's biological brother, and when I complete the doctoral program next month, I'll be a bona fide psychologist."

She kissed me again and pushed against the arms of my chair. "I know I'm crushing you, so I'll get up."

I wrapped my arms around her waist. "Don't you dare. I love you right where you are."

She relaxed. "How long will it take to find him?"

"I don't know, but we have an insider down there. He's a strange little guy named David, but everybody calls him Diablo de Agua."

She frowned. "Water Devil?"

"Exactly. I've only worked with him once, but he's basically a Central American ninja, if you can imagine such a thing. He's silent and absolutely lethal in the jungle, but if you put him in the water, he has no equal."

"Not even Hunter?"

"Hunter is the best combatant I've ever seen in the water, but the thing about Diablo is, you'll never see him or hear him. Hunter tends to make a little noise when he throws punches in the water."

Penny shivered. "I don't know how I feel about that, but I'm glad he's on our side."

"Me too," I said. "Hopefully, there won't be any need for that side of Diablo's skill set. His value on this mission lies in his intimate knowledge of the area and the fact that he's actually seen my brother."

"You keep referring to him as your brother as if you already know for a fact."

I lifted my tumbler and considered her point. "I guess you're right. Maybe I just *want* him to be."

She touched the tip of my nose with her index finger. "Just don't let that desire lead you into doing something careless. Remember, I'm your family and your home. Don't throw that away and get killed by chasing a maybe."

There was nothing I could say that would ease her fear, so I simply held her and watched the river flow slowly by, just as it had done for thousands of years.

* * *

Ten hours later, the sun rose over Cumberland Island, but I wasn't in the gazebo to watch coastal Georgia take its first breath of morning light. I was in the armory wrestling with my ever-changing packing list. Our operation would not only take us into the jungles of Central America, but also the streets and towns that were, in many ways, far more dangerous than the canopied rain forest.

"Sidearms and SBRs?" Hunter asked.

"Sidearms for sure," I said, "but I don't know about the short-barreled rifles. I'm leaning toward packing as light as we can. We're not going to have a resupply point, so we'll have to hump everything we pack everywhere we go."

Hunter grimaced. "I hadn't thought of that. This is starting to sound like a beans and bullets trip."

"That's part of the beauty of operating in the jungle. There's always plenty to eat and usually a good supply of fresh water."

"In that case, forget the beans and pack more bullets."

Clark bounded down the stairs into the armory. "Not so fast, kids. I just got off the phone with the Board, and we may be on hold."

"On hold?" I demanded. "I thought you told them we weren't available for the next six weeks."

"Take it easy, College Boy. I did tell them that, but I didn't expect what they had to say next."

I slid a rifle back into its rack. "I don't care what they have to say. As far as I'm concerned, there's nothing more important than finding my brother."

Clark said, "I thought I told you to take it easy. You cut me off before I could finish. The Board isn't trying to stop our self-assigned mission. They're trying to help us."

"Now you have my attention. But how is delaying our mission helping us?"

Clark took a seat on the bottom step. "Remember the boat that was anchored in the Sound when we came home from the narco-sub mission?"

I said, "The one like Captain Stinnett's ship? Sure, I remember, but what does that have to do with this mission?"

He flipped open his knife and picked at his teeth as if the blade were made of dental floss. After capturing and collecting the offending piece of whatever had gotten stuck between his teeth, he said, "It's ours now."

"What's ours now?"

"The boat. It's ours," he said as nonchalantly as if someone had dropped off an apple pie.

"What are you talking about?"

He pocketed his knife. "They gave it to a team in Virginia, and they did the sea trials with the Northrop Grumman designers and engineers, but they turned it down. Said they were squad-level operators and didn't like the idea of expanding their team to manage an asset that size."

I closed the locking bar across the rifle rack. "Are you serious? They turned down a ship?"

Clark shrugged. "That's what they said, but I don't understand it, either. Here's the kicker, though. If we don't take it right now, they'll move on to the next team, and I don't want that to happen."

"What do we know about the boat?" I asked.

He continued his shrug. "It floats, and it's painted haze gray. That's all I can tell you."

Suddenly, it was Hunter's turn to jump into the puddle with us. "What about a crew?"

Clark said, "Look, I told you all I know about the thing, so stop asking me questions. We get the boat if we want it, or they'll find someone who does. In my opinion, this changes our mission capability dramatically. We're done with inland ops if we take the boat, but we'll get every coastal assignment that comes down the chain."

I said, "I'm sure you're right, but we need to get back to Hunter's question. We're not a boat crew. I'm the only one of us with a captain's license, but I don't have the tonnage for a ship that size. That means we either have to send me to sea to get the time I need to up my license, or we have to take on a captain we don't know."

Clark's crooked grin said he knew more than he was admitting.

"Spit it out."

"You're forgetting about our new man."

"Our new man?" I asked.

"Yep. My brother Tony has all the license we need, and he'll graduate from The Ranch any day now."

The anxiety burned in my chest. "The timing is terrible. We absolutely have to get to Central America."

Clark sighed. "I knew it would come to this, and I've been practicing my argument for ten minutes. I understand how important it is for you to find this man who's probably your brother. It's important to all of us because we love you, and we know you'd fist-fight a chainsaw to help us if the roles were reversed, but if you can step aside from the emotion for a minute and look at the logic of the situation, I think you'll see that postponing this mission a few weeks likely won't change its outcome. We're going to find this man. I have no doubt. But it's not a time-critical mission. If we take the time to at least give the ship a look, it could change the future of our mission profiles for the rest of our lives."

I groaned. "I understand what you're saying, and you're right, but that doesn't make it any easier for me to swallow."

Clark stared between his boots. "I'm not going to insist. The decision is up to you, but I'm asking you to make it with your head and not your heart."

"How do we call off Diablo?" I asked.

"Ginger can take care of that. Are you sure you're okay with the decision?"

I nodded slowly, but I couldn't get the words to come.

Clark slapped his leg and hopped to his feet. "Okay, then. I'll tell Ginger and check on Tony. The boat will be here in forty-eight hours."

Chapter 9
Kidnapping Anyone?

I found Penny in her office opposite the library and stuck my head through the door. "Got a minute?"

She looked up from her monitor and smiled. "I've always got a minute for you. Besides, I'm going blind staring at this empty page."

I stepped through the door and took a seat across from my favorite screenwriter. "Writer's block?"

"I'm not sure if I believe in writer's block. I can write, so I'm not blocked. I just can't write what I want to put on the page."

"I have faith in you. It'll come."

She threw up her hands. "We'll see, but thanks for the confidence. What's going on?"

I curled the five toes I had left inside of my left boot. "It's a tough one. Hunter and I started the load-out for the mission to Guatemala to find my brother, but Clark interrupted."

"Interrupted?"

"It's a long story, but the short version is, we're postponing the mission so we can start training on a new piece of equipment."

She frowned. "What kind of equipment?"

"It's a new boat, but not just any boat. It's a ship."

She shuddered. "A ship? What do any of you know about ships?"

"Not much . . . yet. But we're going to learn. The people we work for offered the ship to a team sort of like ours in Virginia, but they turned it down."

"Why?"

"They wanted to remain a small, ground-based team, so they weren't interested in taking on a crewed ship."

She tapped a pencil against her desk blotter. "What makes them think you'll be any different?"

"That's what we have to work out. The boat will be here in a couple of days, and we're going to have a look. We'll do some sea trials and decide if that's the move we want to make."

"What's your gut telling you?"

I smiled. "You always have a way of getting straight to the point. That's just one of the millions of reasons I love you. My initial reaction is to go find my brother and deal with the boat later, but that's not how this works."

She narrowed her eyes. "So, you do want the boat . . . or ship or whatever, right?"

"I do."

She stuck the pencil back into its cup. "So, what's the problem? You want the ship, and it sounds like you're going to get it. Your brother—if he is your brother—has lived in the jungle for thirty years. He's probably not going anywhere. Besides, maybe you can use the boat on the mission to find him."

I leapt from my seat, rounded the desk, and kissed her as if we'd been apart for ages. "Reason number eighty-six thousand that I love you. You always know how to put things into perspective. Now, get back to work. One of us has to earn a living to support me in the manner to which I've grown accustomed."

She gave me a playful shove. "I think we'll be just fine, even if neither of us ever worked again."

"Yeah, but it's good for your brain, so get back to work."

I met Clark in the hallway leading to the library with his phone pressed between his shoulder and ear. In his left hand, he cradled a steaming bowl of something, and in his right, he held a massive spoon. I couldn't resist following him into the library.

Whoever was on the other end of the phone must've answered when Clark least expected it because he'd just filled his mouth with what I assumed to be chili. "Yeah . . . hang on."

I couldn't contain my laughter as he tried to swallow the scalding mouthful, but it was impossible. Finally, he swallowed and shook his head in pain. "Sorry, I was . . . never mind. I'm Clark Johnson, and . . ."

Dropping his name must've been enough to cause some reaction on the other end of the line because he paused and deposited another spoonful into his gullet. When the next voice answered, he was more prepared.

Waving for me to close the door, he pressed the speaker button and laid the phone on the desk.

"Good morning, Clark. How've you been?"

"I'm great, Colonel. I'm calling to check on my baby brother. We need him."

"Of course you do," the voice said. "He's all yours whenever you'd like to pick him up. He's a little beat up, and his brain probably hurts from all the freedom-loving, save-the-world knowledge we poured into it, but he did well, and I have no doubt he'll make a fine addition."

Clark said, "I would've expected nothing less. We'll be there this afternoon to get him, but I've got a favor to ask."

"Anything for you. Just tell me what it is, and I'll make it happen."

Clark laid out his plan for the colonel and finally hung up.

"That's cruel," I said.

He shoved the phone back into his pocket and returned his attention to the bowl. "Yeah, it's cruel, but it's going to be fun. Round everybody up, and let's head for Virginia."

As tightly knit as my team was, we tended to scatter a bit when there was no immediate threat, so it took half an hour to find everyone. Singer declined the invitation so he could fulfill a commitment with his church, and Penny informed me the studio was sending a jet to pick her up for a few days.

"Did you tell them they could land here?" I asked.

She said, "No, I didn't know that was okay. Can a corporate jet use a private airport?"

"When that airport belongs to you, they can. Give them a call and let them know. That way, you won't have to drive to Jacksonville. If they need specifics on the airport, have them call me or Clark."

She grinned. "I guess being married to a spy has its rewards."

Before I could say it, she shook her head. "Yeah, I know . . . You're not a spy."

* * *

Disco set the Citation on the runway at Camp Peary like a butterfly with sore feet, and we taxied to the hangar beside the helicopter pad. Other than a Cold War–era Soviet fighter in pieces at the southwest end of the field, our jet was the only aircraft visible on the tarmac.

Clark crawled from the cockpit, opened the door, and deployed the airstairs. "Let's go have a little fun, boys."

We followed Clark out the door with excitement in our heads, but none of us was as anxious as Skipper. Before we'd taken a dozen steps across the ramp, a tug appeared and towed our Citation into the hangar.

A thirty-something man sporting a buzzcut and the physique of an MMA fighter stuck out his hand toward Clark. "It's good to see you again, Ranger. How've you been?"

Clark swatted away the offered hand and threw his arms around the man. Introductions were made, and hands were shaken.

When the man reached the end of the receiving line, he lowered his sunglasses and pulled off his hat. "Yep . . . now I understand. You must be Skipper. I'm Lieutenant Colonel Bryan Barnaby, and I've heard a lot about you."

She stuck out her hand. "That's me. It's nice to meet you, Colonel, but how did you hear about me?"

Barnaby glanced back across my team, and we all let out a round of knowing laughter. He turned back to our analyst. "Well, ma'am, when you push a young man as hard as we pushed *your* young man, he tends to subconsciously blurt out the things that are most important to him. And your name came up a lot."

Skipper almost blushed. "I don't know if I should be flattered or terrified that he's that easy to crack under pressure."

Colonel Barnaby gave her a wink. "Don't worry, ma'am. There's nothing soft about that boy, and he'd chew off his own tongue before he ever let anything classified come out of his mouth."

"In that case, I'm proud of him. When can I see him?"

Barnaby gave Clark a look of confusion. "Doesn't she know?"

Clark put on that crooked grin and shook his head. "Not yet, but she will soon. Why don't you take her to the, uh . . . reception center, and we'll bring Tony to her?"

Colonel Barnaby threw up a sharp salute, and a second man dressed in all black ambled into the hangar. He said, "Come with me, and I'll point you toward Tuna."

The man instantly had my attention. "Tuna?"

"Yep. We took a few trainees offshore a while back to see how scared we could make them of the cold North Atlantic. It turns out your boy can almost breathe underwater. We were on the verge of believing he was totally fearless in the water, but that all changed when a big ol' bluefin tuna showed up. He was practically pissing himself to get away from that fish, so naturally, we've called him Tuna ever since."

"Oh, that is priceless," I said. "And you can rest assured the moniker will not die with us."

The man said, "I'm Miller, by the way, but there's no use in telling me your names. I won't remember."

We followed Miller into a battered, rusting pickup truck with no doors, and my first day at The Ranch came flooding back. I ran my hand along the top of the tailgate. "I'll never forget the last time I was in a truck like this. I'd been on deck about ten minutes when my training officer bailed out and left me buckled in while the piece-of-crap truck hit the lake."

Miller said, "Yeah, we don't do that one anymore. That little game ended with you."

Mongo shot me a look. "What did you do, Chase?"

"I got rescued and captured simultaneously, but when I tried to play a friendly game of catch with my captors, they chose to catch a pair of baseball-sized rocks with their heads."

"Ahh," came the giant's response.

We bounced through the woods along a well-worn path for five minutes before Miller slid to a stop. We dismounted the vehicle, and our driver pointed through a pine forest. "You'll find your boy about one klick that way trying to defuse a bowling ball."

"A bowling ball?" I asked.

Miller chuckled. "In Tuna's defense, he thinks it's a bomb. Suffice it to say, he's well occupied and laser-focused on the task at hand. He has no idea you or anybody else is coming. I'll leave the truck here for you, and there's a goody bag behind the rear seat. Have fun."

Clark pulled that so-called goody bag from behind the seat and poured out the contents on the bed of the truck. There were two rolls of duct tape, a couple dozen zip ties, a black cloth bag, and an electric cattle prod.

I met Clark's gaze. "Well, they say graduation is supposed to be memorable, so let's go get him."

We crept through the pine-needle-covered forest as if we were walking on pillows. Silent movement on fallen leaves is impossible, but pine needles are a different story. Tony—or Tuna—would never hear us coming.

Hunter took point, and we slowed our pace when a ramshackle lean-to came into sight. Hunter held up a fist and motioned for us to hit the deck. We settled onto the forest floor and watched Clark's brother hunker over a suitcase-sized container in full bomb squad gear. His focus on the task at hand was impressive and exactly the distraction we needed.

We moved in two-man teams with Clark and me on point. Disco and Hunter took the left flank while Mongo moved solo to the right. Mongo's size makes silent movement challenging, and that's exactly what I was counting on.

Clark and I advanced with our eyes trained on the back of Tony's helmet. Any move he made would show itself first with a motion of his head. That's when it happened.

Mongo brushed past a young pine tree and dislodged a pair of pinecones. The cones fell to the ground and made just enough noise to turn Tony's head away from his bowling-ball bomb.

Clark and I lunged, and I wrapped him in a bearhug that would freeze ninety-nine percent of men on the planet, but I hadn't considered the physical training my prey had endured over the previous months. Holding him was like wrestling with a giant anaconda. He was flexible but one hundred percent muscle. I spread my feet, trying to use my weight advantage, but he threw me around like a rag doll. Fortunately, Clark managed to bag his head before he could identify us, and the rest of the team moved in. It took all five of us to subdue him, and by the time we finally had him trussed up like a pig, we were winded and glad the fight was over.

I silently got the team's attention and placed a finger to my lips. Mongo hoisted our captive over his shoulder, and we headed for the truck. Tony never gave up fighting, and we had to pick him back up several times on the way out of the trees. He wrestled with Mongo hard enough to leave the big man exhausted, but we finally got him into the truck and tied to the hard points. I'd never seen anyone fight that hard, but two minutes into the ride back to the airfield, I was afraid Tuna was on the verge of ripping his arms off trying to escape.

We pulled to a stop just outside the hangar door, where Colonel Barnaby waited with a grin the size of Texas. Mongo, Hunter, and I manhandled our newest teammate through the door and slammed him onto a hard wooden chair that was bolted to the floor. Clark laced a rope around Tuna's chest, arms, legs, and the chair until he was securely bound.

Barnaby motioned for the five of us to move to the other side of the table behind Skipper, who sat nervously in a second wooden chair facing the bound, bagged man she loved. Barnaby stepped behind the soon-to-be graduate and yanked the black bag from his head. Tony—now Tuna—shook his head violently and growled like an animal until his vision cleared and he could focus on the five of us and the beautiful young woman waiting impatiently to cut him free and never let him go.

Chapter 10

Practical or Exciting?

Skipper turned into a lovestruck teenage girl, giggling and squirming in her chair. Beckoning up at Colonel Barnaby with anticipation, she asked, "Now?"

The seasoned operator turned training officer gave her a nod, and she leapt from the chair and landed solidly on Tony's lap. The bevy of kisses ended with the former Coast Guard rescue swimmer awkwardly pulling away.

"This would be a lot more fun if somebody would cut me free."

Skipper shuddered and hopped to her feet. In seconds, she had his bindings sliced free and falling to the floor. With her knife folded and stashed back in her pocket, she plunged into Tony's arms, and the kisses continued. When she came up for air, she said, "Oh, by the way . . . congratulations."

Catching his breath, he asked, "Congratulations for what?"

"Graduating, you silly thing."

"But I didn't defuse the bomb. I was just about to—"

Colonel Barnaby laid a hand on his shoulder. "Relax, kid. It wasn't a bomb. It was just a bowling ball with a bunch of circuitry and a timer. Your days of living rent-free in this posh resort and eating our fine cuisine are over. Now you have to go earn your keep, and from the looks of those guys, they could sure use some young blood on the team. They're looking a little long in the tooth to me."

Skipper stood and stepped back as Tony rose and stuck out a hand.

Barnaby shook it. "Oh, I almost forgot. We don't hand out diplomas here. Instead, everybody gets a car *if* they graduate. The valedictorian gets to pick, so, what'll it be? Practical or exciting?"

Tony glanced at Skipper, and she grinned.

"That's what I thought," he said. "I can buy practical, so let's go with exciting."

Barnaby slid a hand into his pocket and retrieved a key on a leather fob. He tossed the key to Tony, but he was too slow.

Skipper snatched it from the air. "Tony, this is a Porsche key! I'm driving. You've got shotgun."

Clark stepped in front of Tony, and they shared a long, mutually appraising look that ended in a hug only brothers can share. "Congratulation, man. I never had any doubt, and I've never been prouder of you. Welcome to the team. Just don't get dead."

Tony threw a pulled jab to Clark's ribs and laughed. "You lived through it, old man. If you can do it, I'm sure I can, too."

We spent several minutes congratulating Tony with good-hearted teasing.

Finally, his face fell blank. "Is it really over?"

Barnaby shook his head. "No, kid. It's just getting started. Get a shower. Get your gear. And most importantly, get out of here. We need your bunk for the next knucklehead who thinks he's got what it takes."

Tony kissed Skipper again and then pulled off his shirt. Her mouth fell open, and I was afraid she was going to chew off her bottom lip. When Tony left Bonaventure, he was in the best shape of any of us, but the time he spent at The Ranch honed the sword to a razor's edge. And Skipper clearly liked what she saw.

He winked. "Give me ten minutes, and I'll be ready to go."

Skipper turned on a heel. "While we're waiting, this would be a really great time to check out the Porsche."

Barnaby motioned toward the door. "It's not just any old Porsche. Go ahead. Check it out."

As expected, Skipper skipped through the door and gasped. "Chase, get out here! You've got to see this. It's a Nine-Eleven GT-Three."

Although I didn't skip, I wasted no time getting through the door, and Skipper was absolutely right. The car was gorgeous.

Before we'd finished admiring one of the world's greatest sports cars, Tony came through the door with a backpack, two pairs of boots, and a duffle. He eyed the car and turned to Barnaby. "Are you serious? That's mine?"

The colonel nodded. "It is."

"Thank you, sir. I don't know what to say."

"Don't thank me. Thank your team. They're the ones who bought you the car. You were getting an F-Two-Fifty from us if you'd chosen practical over exciting."

"Ouch," Tony said. "I'd love to have a truck."

Skipper laced an arm around his waist. "Don't worry, baby. I'll buy you any truck you want as long as I get the Porsche."

Barnaby threw up his hands. "How can you beat that deal?"

Clark stepped in. "That's enough tomfoolery. We've got work to do. You two be at Bonaventure no later than forty-eight hours from right now." He drove a finger through the air at Tony. "We've got a new piece of hardware coming, and we need your license and experience."

Tony's eyes lit up. "New hardware?"

Clark waved a hand toward Skipper. "I'm sure she'll fill you in while you're riding shotgun in *her* new Porsche. You two have fun. Do you want me to take any of your gear with me? Something tells me you can't get that duffle into the trunk of that thing—if it even has a trunk."

Skipper huffed. "It has a trunk, but it's called a boot, and it's up front."

Tony tossed his duffle to Clark. "Thanks. We'll see you in Georgia tomorrow night . . . at the latest."

We made our way back to the airfield while Tony and Skipper left Camp Peary in a cloud of dust.

The flight home was just as uneventful as the northbound leg, except inside my head. The minutes passed like agonizing hours. Knowing—or believing—I had a brother in Central America who knew nothing about me, and whom I had never met, left me anxious to ignore everything else in the world and get to Guatemala immediately. Nothing in the foreseeable future made me believe I'd get there anytime soon.

Hunter slid onto the seat beside me. "You doing all right?"

The words I wanted to say were a lie, so I sighed and shook my head. "No. I don't understand why the ship is more important than my brother."

He pulled a bottle of water from his cargo pants pocket and tossed it to me. I caught it and pulled off the cap. "Thanks. How'd you know?"

He uncapped his bottle and swallowed a long pull. "I know things because I pay attention. I've not seen you drink anything in four hours, and you've been staring off into the distance even longer than that."

"It's that obvious, huh?"

"A little bit. But it's completely understandable. I can't imagine what it must be like knowing you've got a brother out there and not being able to go after him."

I stared down at the carpet and traced imaginary lines with my tortured mind. "That's exactly what I'm feeling. Obviously, the ship is important, but this is a serious struggle for me."

"I know it is. But I think I've come up with a way to make you feel better."

I laid a hand on his knee. "I really appreciate you worrying about me, my friend, but I don't think one of your pep talks is going to work this time. This one is too personal."

He bounced his water bottle off my knuckles. "You might be surprised. I've got an idea how we can go get your brother and still not delay the shakedown cruise on the new boat."

"You have my attention."

He leaned and stared into the cockpit. "We should probably include Clark in this conversation, but I can't think of a better way to shake down the new ship than putting it to use in Central America finding your brother."

I pushed myself from my seat and slid by my partner. "I don't know how the two of you do it, but you and Penny come up with some great ideas."

Making my way forward, I stuck my head into the cockpit. "Hey, Disco, trade seats with me. I've got something I need to discuss with Clark."

Our chief pilot unbuckled and slid from his seat. "I'm glad you're here. I need to make a head call anyway."

I wedged my six-foot-four-inch frame into the captain's seat and turned to Clark.

He pulled off his sunglasses. "What have I done now, College Boy?"

"It's not something you've done. It's an idea Hunter came up with."

He resituated himself in the seat. "Do tell . . . Especially since it's not your idea."

"I've adopted it," I said. "And I think you will, too. We're delaying the mission to find my brother because of the new ship, right?"

He cleared his throat. "I'm not sure I would call it a delay, but go on."

I said, "First, tell me the plan for the ship when it arrives."

He shrugged. "Don't tell the rest of the guys, but I have no idea. This is my first ship. I'm an old, washed-up ground pounder. What do I know about ships?"

"Surely they're not going to hand us a ship and walk away, are they?"

"I wouldn't think so, but who knows?"

"That's a good question," I said. "Who does know? I mean, who's our point of contact on this thing?"

Clark scanned the instrument panel to make sure the autopilot was keeping its end of the bargain. "My POC is the Board. Every assignment we receive comes down that channel. With the rare exception of something coming directly from the White House, the Board is the next link in the chain of command above me."

I raised a finger. "We'll come back to that, but first, why do you think they picked us to get the ship?"

"Don't get excited. We weren't the first choice."

"I know, but why would we qualify at all? I have some civilian boat experience, but outside of that, we're all ground-pounders like you. It doesn't make sense."

He pulled the release beneath his seat and slid backward, creating a little more legroom for himself. "I've been thinking a lot about that, and in order to bring you up to speed, I have to discuss some classified stuff with you."

"Let's have it."

He squirmed in his sheepskin-covered seat and licked his lips. "Okay, here goes . . . There are twenty-seven teams like ours. Well, like yours. I'm not technically a team member. In fact, until last week, I wasn't much of anything."

I frowned. "What are you talking about?"

"It's like this. I was on what you might call a 'probationary period.' When I took over for my dad when he retired, I didn't really take over everything he was doing. I took over the position of handler for your team only. My dad ran four teams before he retired."

"So, did you make it out of probation?"

"I did, and now, I'm handling your team and one other. It'll be a while before I inherit a third team, but that's okay. I've still got a lot to learn. I'm forbidden from telling anyone, on any team, details about another team except in cases like Al Brown's in Montana. That was a mess, but it had to be done."

I narrowed my gaze. "I'm afraid you've started down a rabbit trail."

"I know it sounds that way, but I'm laying some groundwork so this whole thing will make sense when I lay it out for you. Anyway, I have another team. It's Team Seventeen, and there are twenty-five men on it. Five of them are former SEALs."

I interrupted. "If that's true, why wouldn't they get the boat? They're clearly more experienced in marine operations and have enough men to run a big boat."

He squirmed a little more. "Without dancing too close to the out-of-bounds line, suffice it to say they already have access to a big boat. That's not why the Board is sending the ship to us, though."

"So, you do know why they picked us."

"Well, sort of. The truth is this, a twenty-five-man team makes a lot of noise when they show up. Their mission is entirely different than ours. I mean . . . yours. You're getting the boat because of your team size and your ability to work autonomously. Every other team, as far as I know, is headed up by a former special ops guy. You, being a civilian, gives Team Twenty-One a unique flavor. You guys can and will do things that former military dudes won't try. That makes you unique, and that's exactly why I lobbied to get you the ship. She'll come with a skeleton crew to get us trained up, and the crew will likely stay on as technicians until we adopt them permanently or the Board assigns additions to your team to run the ship."

I held up a hand. "Wait a minute. You just said we're the perfect size. I don't know how I feel about adding team members."

"That's not what I said. I said Team Seventeen makes a lot of noise because of its size. I'm not suggesting we bring any more operators on board. We're going to inherit some engineers, crewmen, and navigators who'll be restricted to working on the ship. Of course, they'll all have TS clearances."

I tried to imagine what such an arrangement would mean for our team. "I'm not trying to start a fight, but I feel like you've known about this ship for a long time but kept a lot of details from me."

He swallowed hard. "I know, and I don't feel good about it, but I was under orders to keep it close to the vest."

"I understand, but that doesn't mean I have to like it."

"You're right," he said. "But this won't be the last time it happens, especially now that you're not my only team."

The first pangs of a headache took root in my skull. "So, it sounds like you're saying I'm running the team and making all the operational decisions and that you're stepping farther away to manage Team Seventeen, as well as us. Is that what it comes down to?"

He nodded, perhaps subconsciously. "There's one other element to this that scrambles the bacon."

My headache developed tentacles. "Scrambles the bacon? What does that even mean?"

"I don't know. Just listen. Now that Tony's part of your team, there are some concerns about conflict of interest. The Board is afraid I won't accept risky missions for a team with my brother on it."

"That doesn't make any sense. You were on the team when your father was our handler. What's the difference?"

He groaned. "Apparently, the difference is the fact that my dad is a heartless Cold War dinosaur, and I'm not."

The headache invited some friends over. "I don't see the relevance, but it doesn't matter. Just don't try to protect my team—including your brother—from missions with a side order of gunfights."

"You've got nothing to worry about in that department. I know every one of you guys better than I know myself. I know what you're capable of doing and surviving. You're my go-to guys. Damn the torpedoes. Full speed ahead."

Before the headache consumed my sanity, I said, "None of this is why I came up here to talk with you, but it changes the way I'll phrase the discussion."

"Let's have it."

"I was planning to come up here and *ask* you for a favor, but now that the rules have changed, I'm here to *tell* you what we're going to do. When the ship arrives, we'll meet with the crew and spend a couple of days shaking down the boat and getting to know her."

Clark shrugged. "That's what I assumed we'd do."

"You didn't let me finish. After a couple of days getting our sea legs, we're taking the ship to Guatemala, and we're finding my brother."

Chapter 11

Some Things Never Change

To my surprise, Clark didn't put up an argument.

He scanned the instrument panel and smiled. "Of course that's what we'll do. Why would you think we'd do anything other than that?"

I laid my finger against the altitude ribbon on the EFIS. "You're twenty feet off your altitude, rookie."

He threw a thumb toward the cabin. "Get out of my cockpit!"

I squeezed past Disco as I climbed from the cockpit. "He threw me out."

"He does that," he said. "Let me guess. You called him out on his altitude."

"Some things never change."

The remainder of the trip back to Saint Marys passed without incident, and one of my tormentors in the cockpit made the landing look like child's play.

Back at Bonaventure, I searched the house in vain, having forgotten Penny was being whisked away to Hollywood, leaving the house temporarily devoid of estrogen.

Naturally, the team, minus Skipper, assembled in the kitchen, and Clark was once again shoulders-deep in the refrigerator. He emerged with something that looked like banana pudding, but I had no memory of such an item being placed inside the icebox.

"What are you eating?"

He swallowed an oversized bite and stared down into the bowl. "I don't know, but it's good. Want some?"

"No, thanks. I don't think I could deal with the heartbreak on your face if I took some of your . . . whatever that is."

He waved the spoon through the air in my general direction. "That's love right there, and don't think I don't recognize it."

I sighed. "Yes. Love. That's it. Now, try to focus, Fat Albert. When will the boat be here?"

Clark checked his watch as if it held the answers to all the world's mysteries. "Not sure, but probably by tomorrow night."

"Is there anything we need to do to get ready for the big day?"

He crammed his mouth full again and mumbled, "I don't know. Maybe. What did you have in mind?"

Trying to ignore the mess he was making on his beard, I said, "I would think a boat that size has a stack of manuals taller than this house. Maybe we should be boning up on the ship's systems and performance."

"I guess that sounds as good as anything else. Where are these manuals you speak of?"

I stared at my handler. "Is this a momma bird moment?"

He grinned through pudding-covered teeth. "You're not the quickest bulb in the quiver, but I knew you'd eventually catch on. It's time for you to stop eating out of my mouth and catch your own worms."

"Sharpest bulb in the quiver? Seriously? Do you even speak English?"

"I got my point across, didn't I?"

"Not really," I said. "I've had zero contact with the fairy god-mother who's supposedly delivering this ship, so I have no way to know where manuals are or even if there are manuals. You've hogged all the coordination, momma bird."

He scraped the last bit of muck from his bowl and licked the spoon until it shined. "So I have . . . But this'll be the last time. You can consider me to be Charlie after this mission."

"Charlie? What are you talking about?"

He tossed his bowl and spoon into the dishwasher and glanced over his shoulder. "You know, Charlie from *Charlie's Angels*. You never saw his face. You only heard his voice through that old-school metal speaker on Bosley's desk."

"I guess that makes Mongo, Hunter, and me *your* angels, huh?"

He shuddered. "I was actually thinking about Penny, Skipper, and . . ."

"Do not say Anya!"

"I was going to say Ginger, but clearly, you've got Anya on the gray matter. For the record, I recommend a brain dump to clear that up, angel."

In a blatant attempt to change the subject, I led him into the library and closed the door behind us. "We may not have manuals, but I've got a guy."

Clark parked himself in his preferred wingback. "What kind of guy?"

"A guy who just happens to skipper a boat a lot like ours."

Clark bounced a finger in my direction. "Look at you, thinking like a big boy. I'm proud of you. Get him on the phone."

I dialed the number and pressed the speaker button. Four rings later, a voice said, "Stinnett! Stand by!"

So, we stood by. The sounds pouring from the tiny speaker of my phone sounded like a construction project and Manhattan rush hour rolled into one. Several seconds later, the sound of a metal hatch coming secure echoed through the phone, and a voice growled. "Who is this, and what do you want?"

I cleared my throat. "Captain Stinnett, it's Chase and Clark. If this is a bad time . . ."

His tone softened. "Ah, I thought you two might be calling soon. Did Santa Claus shove a new bathtub toy down your chimney?"

I met Clark's eyes as we echoed surprise between us.

Clark said, "Uh, not yet, but we're expecting the jolly old elf any day now. How did you . . ."

Captain Stinnett chuckled. "Come on, boys. You two have been in the game long enough to know how small this community is—especially the waterborne element. Good news travels fast."

Clark and I shrugged in unison, and I said, "Speaking of boats . . . Are you aboard yours?"

"I am."

"In that case, give us three minutes, and let's continue this conversation on a different connection."

"I'll head upstairs and wait for your ring."

Clark and I traded the library for the ops center and rang the secure line aboard the Research Vessel *Lori Danielle*.

To my surprise, Captain Stinnett answered the line. "Okay, we're all secure on my end."

I said, "Ours, too. Since you already know about our new tool and you were expecting our call, we're all ears."

"From a distance, your new boat and mine look a lot alike, but that's where the similarities end. Yours is state of the art, with weapons systems that didn't exist when they built my tub. You're going to have a steep learning curve, but I've got a handful of gifts that just might make your transition a little easier."

"Easy doesn't come often in this business," Clark said. "We're always open to any ideas that make our lives less complex."

Stinnett said, "That noise you heard when I answered the other phone was the sound of my crane being removed from the stern. They're tearing this old girl to pieces."

"Why?" I demanded.

"She's all washed up, I'm afraid. We put a lot of good miles astern in this old tub, and she never let me down, but she and I are headed out to pasture. I've finally got enough cash buried in the backyard to live out my days without a swaying deck beneath my boots. It's been a long time coming, but both the Lori Danielle and I are ready for it."

I said, "In that case, I guess congratulations are in order, but what about the little gifts you mentioned?"

"I've got a first officer named Sprayberry who's a better skipper than most of the captains at sea. He's a top-notch sailor and a heck of a nice guy. If you don't already have a top dog, he'd make a fine one. And if you do have a skipper already, you could do a lot worse than having my XO on board as a training officer."

"We've got a skipper," I said. "But I like the idea of having your man along for the ride. I'm sure he'd appreciate the steady paycheck, even if it's temporary."

"I'll put the two of you in touch with each other, and you can work out the details. We pay him around sixty thousand and keep him at sea about half the year."

"Thanks for the gift," I said.

"Keep your shirt on, kid. I'm not finished. A captain and an XO are two of the least necessary heads on board. I've got an engineering crew that's second to none. They'll get scarfed up and scattered to the wind, but if you can make them an attractive offer, I'm sure you could get them as a package deal. There's one chief and four wrench-turners who know my ship inside out. From what I hear, yours is a lot like mine at the nuts-and-bolts level but with a trainload of upgrades."

"You know a lot more about my new toy than I do at this point. I saw her once through the windshield of a Citation, but I've not seen so much as a scrap of paper on it."

"Don't worry," he said. "The engineers from Northrop Grumman will have you up to speed in no time. What role do you plan to fill on board?"

I considered his question and admitted, "I don't know yet. I'm not qualified to be captain, so I'll likely be relegated to tactical team lead and leave the shipboard ops to the professionals."

"That sounds like good work if you can get it."

"Regardless of how it comes together, the ship will mean a dramatic mission shift for us. We'll have some growing pains, for sure. Oh, and speaking of pains . . . how about Dr. Shadrack?"

"What about him?" Stinnett asked.

"Is he available? If we become a seaborne force, our injury rate is likely going way up, so I'd love to have an experienced doc on board."

I could almost see Captain Stinnett scratching his chin through his billowing white beard. "You'll have to take that up with him, but medics like him don't come cheap."

"Medics?" I asked. "Isn't he a bona fide MD?"

He chuckled. "Yeah, he's got the sheepskin, but he's still an Eighteen Delta at heart."

"A Special Forces medic?"

"Yep. He wore the Green Beret long before he changed his first name to Doctor."

"I've got a team full of SF guys, so he'll be right at home."

"Just keep in mind that he's worth at least three times the XO's salary. Do you know how well your sick bay is equipped yet?"

I let out a huff. "Like I said before, you know a lot more about my boat than I do."

"Well, they're cutting my boat up for scrap, so if you need or want anything I had on board—like your old friend, the recompression chamber—now's the time to grab it."

"Where are you?" I asked.

"Norfolk, but not for long."

I ran through a mental inventory of what I'd seen aboard the *Lori Danielle*. "I'll see my ship up close and personal for the first time tomorrow. After I get an equipment inventory and crew complement data, I'll give you a call. Will you be aboard for the next few days?"

"I'll be around. It'll take them a couple of weeks to dismantle my boat, so that doesn't give you much time. Get back with me sooner rather than later. There's some warehouse space here if you can't grab what you want right away, so I'll tuck away some of the good pieces until I hear from you."

"Thank you, Captain Stinnett. We'll be in touch soon."

He grumbled. "If you don't start calling me Wayne, I'm going to stop answering the phone."

"As you wish . . . Captain."

Chapter 12
Welcome Aboard

While I was well ensconced behind my desk in the Bonaventure library, my house made a sound I'd never heard. It wasn't unpleasant—merely foreign. It caught my attention but failed to get me out of my chair. A few seconds passed, and the sound made a repeat performance.

Clark's voice boomed through the library door. "Do you want me to get that?"

"Get what?" I yelled back.

"The front door!"

Hmm . . . we have a doorbell, I thought. "Sure. See who it is."

A few seconds later, Clark came through the door of the library with a young Navy officer in tow. "Hey, Chase. The lieutenant says he's here to pick us up. Apparently, we have a package at the submarine base."

I looked up. "How big is your car, Lieutenant?"

"I can carry eight, sir."

I turned my attention to Clark. "Have you heard from our captain and his favorite mermaid this morning?"

"They just pulled up."

I pushed myself from my chair and closed the file I'd been

working on. "In that case, round up the team, and let's go see this package."

The gate guard at the Kings Bay Naval Submarine Base saluted sharply and waved us through the barricades. We wound our way through the base and finally arrived waterside, where my new hardware rested imposingly next to the glistening black topsides of a nuclear submarine. To look up at the wall of haze gray that was the hull of the impressive vessel was surreal.

I was a civilian without a day spent in uniform, and the only sea time I had aboard naval vessels could be counted on my fingers and five remaining toes. Nothing qualified me to be the keeper of such a weapon, but everything inside me was leaping up and down like a kid on Christmas morning.

The seven of us climbed from the lieutenant's van and stood in awe of our ship. From a distance, she appeared docile and unthreatening, but viewed from two dozen feet away, she was a solid wall of steel—cold and harsh.

A pair of sailors clad in the blue camouflage battle dress uniform of the Navy approached, and our driver snapped to attention, rendering a salute.

One of the sailors returned the salute. "Thank you, Lieutenant. That'll be all."

He hopped back into the van and vanished as quickly as he'd appeared.

The older of the two sailors stuck out a hand, and I shook it.

"I'm Chase Fulton."

"I know who you are, Chase. I'm Commander Tapper, and this is Lieutenant Commander LaGrange. Welcome aboard Kings Bay. Are you ready to see your ship?"

In a poor effort to hide exactly how much I wanted to see the ship, I turned on a heel. "It's nice to meet the two of you. This is my team, Hunter, Singer—"

Tapper interrupted. "We know all of you. Let's go aboard."

I gave Clark a look and mouthed, "How?"

He shrugged and turned to follow the officers.

We climbed the gangway, the aluminum rattling with every step, and everyone stopped at the top and turned to me.

Clark held out a palm. "You first, Chase. It's only right."

Of all the thoughts that could have—and probably should have —gone through my head when my only remaining flesh-and-blood foot hit the deck for the first time, none of them came. Instead, I wanted my brother to be the next man to step aboard.

Perhaps sensing the emotion I was experiencing, Hunter—the closest thing to a real brother I'd ever known—landed his boot only inches from mine and gave my shoulder a squeeze.

Commander Tapper furrowed his brow as he watched the exchange. "Is everything all right?"

I threw an arm around Hunter's shoulders. "Yes, everything is exactly right. Let's go see the good parts."

Tapper said, "We'll start at the top and work our way down, if that works for you."

"Fine with me," I said as the commander led us up the ladder from the quarterdeck.

We stepped through the hatch and onto the navigation bridge, and the console looked more like the panel of our Citation jet than the helm of a ship.

I pointed at the wheel that looked like a child's toy. "Is that seriously the wheel?"

"What were you expecting? A mahogany steamboat's wheel?"

That got a chuckle from the team, and I said, "I don't know what I was expecting, but this isn't it."

We spent ten minutes identifying the systems on the bridge before making our way aft.

"This is the captain's quarters," Tapper said.

I pressed open the door and held it for Tony. "Welcome home, Captain Tuna."

Tony shot a thumb toward himself. "Me? What are you talking about?"

"You're the only one of us with a license big enough to manage this thing, so you're the de facto captain."

He turned to his brother. "Is he for real?"

Clark laid a hand on Tony's back and encouraged him through the door. "It's Chase's boat. He can appoint whoever he wants to be the skipper, and it looks like he picked you, little brother."

Our youngest and newest team member stepped through the hatch and took in the relatively small space containing a bed, a desk, two chairs, and a tiny head with a shower. He said, "It's a lot nicer than any berth I ever had on a Coast Guard boat."

"Come on. There's a lot more to see," Tapper said.

We followed him toward the stern.

"That's the helipad. A trusted source told us you have a chopper that'll fit perfectly back there."

I surveyed the pad. "A trusted source, huh?"

Tapper ignored my question and continued down a ladder.

Our tour continued through the onboard ops center, which fascinated Skipper, to the moon pool in the ship's belly, from which we could covertly deploy and recover everything from minisubs to divers. Just as Skipper had been hung up on the ops center, Hunter immediately fell in love with the moon pool.

We strolled through the relatively barren sick bay, and Captain Stinnett's offer of equipment poured through my mind.

We ended our tour in what Commander Tapper called "the beating heart of the ship."

"Welcome to the engine room," he said. "This is where things get interesting. We'll start forward and work our way aft. What you're about to see is a revolutionary propulsion system, making this ship the fastest vessel ever built with this hull style."

Mongo's ears perked up. "How fast?"

Commander Tapper grinned. "You'll see. Follow me."

He led us forward in the engine room, toward a pair of power plants that looked quite familiar.

I said, "Those look a lot like a massive version of the Pratt and Whitney turbine in our Caravan."

Tapper said, "Exactly, but these are a little more advanced than the PT-Six, and over five times the size. They're multi-fuel gas turbine engines capable of producing over thirty-five thousand horsepower each. Their muscle is converted into usable force by a system of gearboxes funneling fifteen thousand RPMs into a pair of controllable pitch propellers. We'll talk more about the props in a few minutes, but are there any questions about the turbines?"

Mongo raised a finger. "What do you do with the bleed air?"

"That's a great question. You must be the engineer."

Our giant shook his head. "No, I just read part of a book once."

"Well, you must've read the good parts. The bleed air—just like in your Caravan—is used for a multitude of things. The most impressive system associated with the bleed air is the revolutionary hull warming system, giving this ship the ability to behave a lot like an icebreaker for arctic operations. The system is capable of raising the hull temperature at the waterline over three hundred degrees Fahrenheit above the water temperature. No other ship in the world has that capability."

"That's a nifty trick," Mongo said. "But I was thinking about more practical applications, like electrical power for the rest of the ship."

"That must've been some book," Tapper said. "Of course, we can provide electricity with the bleed air, but that's not its primary function. We have a pair of smaller turbines, similar to auxiliary power units on airliners, that handle that job so that one hundred percent of the propulsion turbines' power can be used to run from a fight in case you're attacked at sea."

That comment was rewarded with raucous laughter from my team, and Commander Tapper's face distorted in confusion. "Uh, what's so funny?"

Hunter shot me an elbow to the ribs. "Tell him, Chase."

I said, "We're not the kind of guys who run away from a fight. In fact, we have a long history of running *toward* the gunfire when it erupts. As impressive as the speed and horsepower are, we're more interested in just how hard this thing can throw a punch."

Tapper looked at his previously silent partner. "That's Mr. La-Grange's area of expertise. He's a surface and near-surface weapons systems specialist. He not only designed the weapons systems of this boat, but he also worked alongside the research and development team, who created some of the unique offensive and defensive weaponry this old girl has tucked away beneath her skirt. Commander LaGrange—call him Weps, everyone does—will take you through the weaponry later today. For now, let's continue with the propulsions."

Mongo leaned down and stuck his chin beside my ear. "I wish Earl were here. She'd think this is sexier than Cajun Kenny."

I gave him a playful shove, and Tapper continued the tour.

"Okay, so that does it for the multi-fuel gas turbines. Now, let's take a look at the water jet propulsion."

We moved aft and gathered around a pair of futuristic devices that were complex enough to confound even Mongo.

Tapper said, "And here is the mechanical cherry on top." He paused and scanned my team. "Everyone has a TS clearance, right?"

I said, "Yes, as well as signed NDAs, and of course, a need to know."

"Very well. In that case, these are the two water jet propulsion systems that give this ship—your ship—capabilities no other ship at sea can match."

Mongo raised an eyebrow. "There's nothing classified about water jet propulsion systems. They've been in use for decades, and every Jet Ski on the market has a variation of the system."

Tapper's grin made its second appearance. "You're exactly right, but the name *water jet propulsion* is where the similarities end. These units are driven by a hydrogen fuel cell and produce almost twelve thousand horsepower when operating in tandem."

Mongo sighed. "Ah! Nice."

"Just wait," Tapper said. "When used in conjunction with the gas turbines, the vessel's top speed increases by almost fifty percent."

It was my turn to jump into the conversation. "Are you saying we can run both systems simultaneously? I've never heard of anything like that. How are they synchronized?"

"Not only can they all run simultaneously, but the onboard computer system manages the process entirely seamlessly. High-speed ship handling doesn't change from the helmsman's perspective, regardless of how many turbines are spinning or water jets are pumping."

"That's amazing," I admitted. "But what happens *when* that computer fails?"

"That's one of the things you'll love most about this boat. Nearly every system is quadruple redundant. Even if all the computer systems wet the bed, it can all be run by a pair of battery-operated laptops from the bridge, the engine control room, or remotely from your ops center."

Suddenly, Skipper's ears perked up. "Do you mean I can run the whole ship from the ops center at Bonaventure?"

"Yes, ma'am. That's exactly what I mean."

Singer, who'd been silent all day, asked, "Who else?"

Tapper furrowed his brow. "Who else what?"

"Who else has the ability to take control of the ship remotely?"

In an excellent show of federal government tapdancing, Tapper said, "That is yet to be determined."

I met Clark's stare and shared a knowing, barely perceptible nod.

Tapper checked his watch. "I think that's enough overview for the time being. Of course, we'll have the engineers from Northrop Grumman dive as deep into the weeds as you and your crew want after the sea trials. Speaking of crew . . . Do you have one?"

I said, "As we mentioned earlier, Tony will be the captain. We're building the remainder of the crew. Have you ever heard of the Research Vessel *Lori Danielle*?"

Tapper let out a chuckle. "I thought that might happen. If you pick up Captain Stinnett's orphans, you'll have this boat and crew combat-ready inside of sixty days."

I asked, "Did you say sixty days . . . or six?"

"Don't get too anxious," he said. "There are a lot of new systems to learn, even for an experienced crew like that of the *Lori Danielle*. But there will be plenty of time for that. For now, let's take her for a spin around the block."

Chapter 13
High-Speed, Low-Drag Momma

"Are you coming with us?" I asked.

Commander Tapper said, "That's up to you. The Northrop Grumman team is standing by ashore. We didn't want them in the way while we introduced you to the ship. They're a full ship's complement, minus tactical operators."

I chuckled. "I'm pretty sure we've got that one covered, but I have one additional team member I'd like to include in the shakedown cruise."

"This isn't the shakedown cruise. It's just the ship's chance to show off for its new family."

"I like that," I said. "You Navy boys understand how much personality boats can have. We feel the same, but we like to include airships into that feeling."

"That's what I hear. Weps here washed out of flight school. Otherwise, he'd by flying Hornets off a carrier deck somewhere instead of designing weapons systems."

Commander LaGrange held up a palm. "Easy there. I didn't exactly wash out. I was medically disqualified due to the slightest degree of color blindness. I couldn't fly for the Navy after that, but I've got a civilian, multi-engine commercial ticket in my pocket. Call it destiny or fate or whatever name you want to put on it, but

I've made a fine career for myself messing with things that go boom."

I gave him a nod. "I like your way of looking at things. If you ever want to get some time in the driver's seat, we've got a few airplanes over at what used to be the municipal airport."

"I thought that place was closed," he said.

"It's a private field now, so we still keep a couple of hangars and a fuel truck out there."

LaGrange lowered an eyebrow. "How did you work that out with the new owner?"

Clark put on his grin. "One of the new owners is a great guy, but the other one is a real jerk. We just got lucky."

LaGrange mirrored Clark's grin. "Ah, I see. So, if you guys are shopping for a weapons engineer, I just happen to know a guy who's retiring from the Navy later this year."

Clark said, "We'd love to take a look at your . . . I mean, *his* résumé."

"I'll let *him* know."

Tapper reclaimed the floor. "That's enough job interviews for one day. Let's light the fires and cast off the lines."

"Before we go," I said, "I'd like for both of you to stay aboard, and let's plan to pick up my diesel engineer in Cumberland Sound."

"Fine with me," Tapper said. "We'll meet you up in the wheelhouse in half an hour. Feel free to poke around *your* new ship. Just don't touch anything if you don't know what it does."

He and LaGrange disappeared up a ladder and left us in the cleanest engine room I'd ever seen. "What do you think, Mongo?"

The big man leaned back against a workbench so he wouldn't have to continue ducking his head in the tight space. "I'm impressed, but talk is cheap. We'll see if this girl can dance when we get her out on the floor. By the way, are you really going to pick up Earl in the Sound?"

"I really am," I said, pulling my phone from my pocket.

The best diesel mechanic I've ever met answered on the second ring. "Hey there, Baby Boy. What'd you break this time."

"Nothing yet, but the day is still young."

"I'm still pretty upset with you about what you did to the Mark V in Mexico."

"I didn't do anything to the Mark V. I'm completely innocent in that one. Captain Stinnett had the wrong fuel pumped aboard. There was no way for me to know."

She huffed. "I'll bet you don't never let nobody bunker your fuel again without knowing exactly what they're pumping into them tanks."

"You've got that right, Old Girl."

"See there!" she almost shouted. "I've got you. If you would've checked on that heavy fuel instead of trusting them pump-happy gas boys on Stinnett's boat, you could have and would have known. So, there you have it. It *was* your fault, and there ain't nothing you can say to argue about it."

I sighed. "You have me there, but none of that is why I called. I need a few hours of your day. Can you pull yourself away from whatever you're doing to take a look at some brand-new engines like nothing I've ever seen?"

"New engines?" The excitement in her tone said I was on the verge of worming my way back into her good graces.

"Yes, ma'am, and they're all ours. I need somebody to explain them to me in a way that even a dumb old baseball player like me can understand. Believe it or not, they've even got Mongo stumped."

"In that case, I'll be your high-speed, low-drag momma. And I'll have them motors stuck back in the Mark V before you know it."

"Don't get trigger happy yet. These engines aren't for the Mark V. They're already installed in something a lot bigger and a lot sexier."

"Just tell Momma where to be, and I'll be there with bells on. I can't wait to see whatever this is."

"Head over to Bonaventure and put the RHIB from *Aegis* into the water. Meet us in the Cumberland Sound as soon as you can get there."

"Cumberland Sound is a big piece of water, Baby Boy. How will I know where you are?"

"Trust me on this one. You won't have any trouble picking us out of the crowd."

Thirty minutes passed, and we found ourselves on the navigation bridge, but our ship's company had grown. Three men and two women I'd never met greeted us in the wheelhouse, and introductions were made. A man in his fifties with an impressive white beard and lines of years at sea crisscrossing his face eyed me from head to toe and back again. "You the new skipper?"

"No, sir. I'm nobody. Tony Johnson is the captain."

I placed a palm on Tony's back and pressed him toward the weathered man.

Through hidden lips behind mounds of flowing white beard, he said, "Does your mother know you're not in school, young man?"

Tony inhaled a long, deep breath. "No, sir, and I'd appreciate it if you wouldn't tell her I'm a boat captain. She thinks I'm a drug dealer in Tijuana, and I'd hate to disappoint her."

The man's salty demeanor cracked, and he actually laughed. "Get up here, Captain Tony. Let's see if we coax this tub off the dock."

Tony stepped toward the helm, but he did so without his typical confidence.

I laid a hand on his shoulder. "Relax. It's just like commanding your ferry on the Outer Banks."

He glared over his shoulder. "That ferry does fifteen knots and has a crew of four, including me. Trust me. This ain't the same."

"We have faith in you. Otherwise, you wouldn't be here."

Without acknowledging me, he turned back to his bearded mentor and listened intently to every word that fell from the beard.

The rest of us stood in silence as the crew eased the ship away from the dock without any need for a tugboat.

"Well, that was impressive," I said.

Old Whitebeard turned and gave me a wink. "Don't be impressed yet, Mr. Nobody. Just wait 'til you see what she can do on plane."

"On plane? This is a displacement hull, and displacement hulls can't plane."

He chuckled. "Hasn't anybody ever told you that things are rarely what they seem?"

The words of my beloved psych professor and mentor at UGA echoed in my head, and suddenly, he was standing right beside me with those same worn-out, wire-frame glasses and tattered button-down with its threadbare pocket.

Before I could answer, Tony's trainer returned to his task of teaching our captain to transition his new ship from making way astern to coming ahead. The transition was smooth and nearly silent from where I stood on the bridge.

"Why can't we hear or feel the vibrations of the engines?" I asked.

A second crewman stepped beside me and spoke barely above a whisper. "Because I don't want you to hear or feel it. I designed the engine mounting system modeled after a water spider's feet."

The engineer had not only my attention, but Mongo leaned in, as well. "What do you mean, a spider's feet?"

"When a spider runs across the water, he's capable of doing so because of the surface tension of the water and the tiny hairs on his feet. Our main engines are mounted on cushions made up of polymers and filled with liquid silicon."

"Like breast implants," Mongo blurted out.

The engineer paused, examined the mountain of a man, and said, "Yes, exactly like that."

"But how do you manage torque?"

The engineer smiled the broad grin of a proud poppa. "That's why I'm standing here today. I designed a one-of-a-kind torque-management system based on counter-rotating engines. The port engines rotate clockwise while the starboard engines turn counter-clockwise."

Mongo scowled. "That's nothing new, and it doesn't do anything to overcome the torque created by such massive engines."

If possible, the engineer's grin broadened. "It does when the engines are interconnected and run in synchronization, thereby canceling out the torque or twisting moment of the other engine. It's classified, of course, but since the ship is now yours, and you have the clearance, the plans for every system aboard are available, and I'm proud to say my signature is all over the propulsion systems."

Mongo shook his head. "Amazing."

Before we could dive deeper into the young engineer's sorcery, Tony turned from the console. "Uh, Chase. You may want to see this. Somebody's screaming across the Sound on a collision course, and it looks like your RHIB."

"Oh, yeah. I probably should've mentioned that. The screamer would be Earl, and the RHIB is *Aegis*'s tender."

Whitebeard pressed a switch and spoke into a mic. "All crew . . . all crew . . . Prepare for high-speed maneuvering." He looked up and asked, "Can your man, Earl, swim?"

That drew a round of raucous laughter from my team, and I said, "Earl isn't a guy, and what she's made of floats."

Whitebeard took the controls from Captain Tony and brought the speed from twelve knots to thirty-five in less than fifteen seconds.

"Okay, that's impressive," I said, but little did I know that would be one of the least impressive capabilities of our new machine.

At thirty-five knots, we turned hard to port without losing a single knot. Before settling on her new course, the helmsman brought the ship one hundred eighty degrees to starboard, creating a massive wake that must've looked like a tsunami from the deck of the RHIB.

Earl made a turn and headed for the shallows off the shore of Cumberland Island.

Tony said, "Earl's pretty good at evading a deep-water assault."

"Earl's pretty good at a lot of things and downright brilliant at everything else. Let's let her come alongside. She's our senior diesel engineer, and I want her on board so she can explain how this piece of masterful modern warfare works."

The teacher walked Tony through the steps involved in bringing the high-speed vessel back to eight knots on a steady course, then he pulled a radio from his pocket and keyed the mic. "Lower the port side cradle, and prepare to receive a RHIB."

He spun a dial on the face of the radio and tossed it to me. "Have your engineer trail the port stern quarter and mount the cradle when we splash it."

Uncertain what I'd just been instructed to do, I passed the instructions verbatim to Earl via the marine VHF radio. She seemed to understand, so I held the radio out toward Whitebeard.

He took it and said, "You'll want to be on deck for this one. Take your folks outside, and watch over the port rail. You're going to love this."

We did as instructed and headed for the rail outside the pilot-house. A three-man deck crew managed a crane with a long cradle hanging beneath the arm. They lowered the cradle toward the water, and one of the crewmen radioed the bridge. Seconds later, the ship slowed to perhaps four knots, and Earl approached in the RHIB. Easing the tender forward, she navigated into the cradle, shut down the engine, and attached the bow tether. The crew hoisted the cradle back aboard and brought it to rest on its deck-mounted brackets.

All five feet and two hundred pounds of our beloved Earl came tumbling over the starboard tube of the captured RHIB. She slapped away the hands of the waiting crewmen when they offered to help her down, and instead, hopped to the deck and did a little dance as if she represented the Lollipop Guild.

I met her on deck, but before I could welcome her aboard, she threw her hands to her hips and glared up at me. "Chase Fulton, does that skinny, long-legged wife of yours know you bought a ship?"

I threw up both hands in surrender. "I didn't buy it. It was a gift, sort of, and to answer your real question, no, she doesn't know about it yet. She's out in Hollywood working hard to support my bad habits."

Earl shot a conspiratorial glance across each shoulder and leaned in. "Is this thing really yours?"

I whispered, "It's ours, but yes."

She grabbed both my wrists and continued her dance. "Take Momma to the engine room, Stud Muffin."

"I thought you'd never ask. Follow me."

I deposited the best diesel mechanic on Earth into the capable hands of the Northrop Grumman engineers in their white coveralls, hardhats, and headphones.

One of the spotless engineers handed a clear, sealed bag containing Earl's uniform and protective gear of the day. She snatched it from his hands, promptly kicked off her boots, and squirmed out of her tank top. I wasn't sure how far she was going to take her little striptease, but I made my exit before things got hairy.

For the first time in months, I forgot my right foot was still in Western Africa and that I was dragging a robot around at the terminus of my leg. Climbing the ladder without thought or hesitation represented a new pinnacle in my psychophysiological progression toward what Dr. Ham at UAB liked to call *assimilation*.

By the time I made it almost to the bridge, I felt the ship turn to port and knew we'd be through the St. Marys Pass in minutes and on the bounding main of the blue North Atlantic Ocean. Before I stepped through the hatch and onto the bridge, Singer, our sniper, took my arm.

"Step over here a minute, will you?"

I scanned the interior of the navigation bridge, and everything appeared perfectly normal, but something about Singer's tone left me doubting what my eyes perceived.

We stepped to the starboard rail, and Singer chewed on his lower lip.

"What's going on?" I asked.

"Two things. First, you're the psychologist, but something's not right about Tony. Did you pick up on that?"

"I did, but I'm not sure what's going on with him. Do you have any thoughts?"

"It might be that he's a little overwhelmed by the new boat. The only thing this tub has in common with the ferries he ran on the Outer Banks is that they float."

I turned back toward the bridge, but I couldn't see Tony Tuna. "This isn't the shakedown cruise, so we'll only be out a few hours, at most. When we get a minute, I'll pull Tony aside and see if I can figure out what's going on. What's the second thing you want to talk about?"

Singer spent several seconds staring toward Fort Clinch. "This one is a little more personal."

"We're family. We can talk about anything you want, anytime you want."

He licked his lips. "I know, but I don't mean it's personal to me. It's more about you."

"About me?"

"Yeah, Chase, about you. Look, I'm just a sniper—"

I laid a hand on his shoulder. "We both know you're far more than *just* an anything. You're the moral center of this team and one of the best snipers alive. If there's something on your mind, I need to know about it."

He cleared his throat. "What I mean by 'I'm just a sniper' is that I don't have any meaningful role aboard this boat. I'm a shooter, and I'll shoot from wherever you put me. The capabilities and particulars of this boat don't change that."

"I'm not following. Do you not want to be here?"

"It's not that I don't want to be here, but there's no reason for me to be going for a joyride when there's work to be done."

"What work? Is there something you need to be doing?"

His expression told me I'd hit the nail on the head. "Yes, there's something more important I should be doing."

"What is it?"

"Finding your brother."

His answer stopped me in my tracks. "What are you saying?"

"I'm saying I should be in Central America with that Diablo guy doing the groundwork while you and the rest of the guys are out here learning the boat."

I was left bewildered and humbled by Singer's single-minded focus on finding my brother. "Are you saying you *want* to go to Guatemala without the rest of us?"

He leaned in. "No, Chase. I'm saying that's what I *need* to do."

Chapter 14
Where's Your Head?

While Singer's revelation bounced around inside my skull, I motioned toward the navigation bridge. "Let's get back inside and see how the day plays out."

Singer followed, and we rejoined the rest of the team just as we put coastal Georgia astern.

Whitebeard watched us enter and motioned toward the bow. "Get up here, Mr. Nobody. You don't want to miss this."

I stepped beside Tony as he managed the expansive array of controls beneath his fingertips.

He said, "It's pretty impressive already, but watch this."

With the finesse of a seasoned seagoing captain, Tony eased the throttles forward until they froze in place. As the ship accelerated, he glanced toward his instructor, and the man gave him a nod. Tony removed the hinged covers from another pair of previously hidden throttles.

Whitebeard coaxed Tony along. "Easy up . . . Keep it smooth and straight. Don't get anxious. Just wait for it."

Our captain followed the direction as our speed over the water increased through forty knots.

Mesmerized by the speed, I said, "I thought thirty-five knots was the—"

Whitebeard held up a finger and then pressed it to his lips. That made it my turn to obey as the bow of the vessel rose as if levitating.

The man said, "Good. Always fly the bow first and wait for it to stabilize."

Tony watched the prow and held the ship on course as if it were on rails.

"Good. Now, fly the stern."

Tony added more throttle, and the aft section of the vessel rose just as the bow had. A tiny shudder rumbled beneath my left foot and robot, and seconds later, the vibration was gone. It felt as if we were flying.

Whitebeard grinned and tapped the speed indicators. "Watch."

Every eye on the bridge focused on the pair of digital displays as they rose through fifty-five and finally settled on sixty-four knots across the water and sixty-six across the ground.

"We have a couple knots of outgoing tide, but on her foils, she's good for a dependable sixty-five knots in seas less than ten feet. We don't recommend flying on the foils in a sea state above fifteen feet or four and a half meters."

The veins in Tony's forearms bulged, and the man said, "Relax, son. You're flying a two thousand ton waterborne rocket. It's supposed to be fun. Make some turns, and get to know your boat. Push her as hard as you want. She won't let you oversteer."

Tony began his maneuvers with a timid, lazy turn to port, and Whitebeard pushed him aside. "Get up here, Max. Show these boys what this thing can do."

One of the female engineers stepped to the helm and conducted an airshow on the water. She made a three-hundred-sixty-degree turn to starboard and lost only five knots of speed in the sweeping turn. She said, "I don't recommend setting your cocktails on the console before a maneuver like that, but as long as you can hold on, she'll do anything you ask."

Stepping away from the helm, she motioned for Tony to resume control. He stepped back into position and put the boat through her paces with less timidity.

Through his beard, Tony's instructor said, "I guess it's time to teach you to land this thing, huh?"

Tony stepped back. "Yes, sir. I suppose so."

"Stay at the helm, kid. This is complicated, and I don't want you to miss anything. See that amber-colored switch?"

Tony pointed and nodded.

"Leave your throttles where they are and press that switch."

Tony did as he was told, and a second amber light flashed the words "Confirm Descent."

Tony depressed the second light, and the shipboard computers eased the massive hull back into the water in a controlled deceleration that wouldn't have awakened a sleeping baby.

"Have some fun. She's all yours," said the man as he strode away and settled onto an elevated sofa behind the helm.

We took turns handling the ship and learning her personality.

When everyone had spent their time at the controls, Whitebeard said, "Put her back on the dock, Captain Tony."

Our rescue swimmer turned ship captain grimaced and stepped back to the helm. He managed the ship beautifully through the pass and across the sound. With minimal assistance from the engineers, he laid the ship alongside the Navy pier as if he'd done it a thousand times.

Max stepped beside Tony. "We don't conduct the shutdown from up here. We simply advise the engine room of our position and intended length of stay either at anchor or tied alongside. From that information, they'll do the calculations to bring the engines offline safely and slowly to avoid shock cooling or overheating. It's a brilliant vessel, but it'll never be able to fully run itself. It'll always require a human hand . . . or several."

She walked Tony through the process of securing the helm and advising the engine room of their intentions. When the lesson was complete, Tony turned to me and shook his head.

I nodded toward the hatch. "Come on. Let's go for a walk."

He led me through the opening and across the catwalk toward the stern. We took advantage of a deck box that looked like a fine place to park ourselves.

"Tell me where your head's at," I said.

He watched the toe of his boot wave back and forth for a long moment. "It's fine. I mean, I'm fine. It's just that . . ."

I gave him a reassuring punch to the arm. "I know it's over-whelming. Learning a new piece of hardware always is, but we all have faith in you. If we didn't, you wouldn't be where you are."

"It's not that. The ship is complex, but I can learn it without any problem. I've spent enough time at sea to adapt to new plat-forms without missing a beat. But . . ." He paused as if trying to find the words to break up with his high school girlfriend.

"It's okay. Whatever it is, just spit it out."

He sighed. "I know I'm the new guy, and I don't want you to think I'm not grateful for everything. I'm flattered by the confi-dence you and the team have in me. Really, I am. But . . . I don't know. I don't want to . . . I mean, it's not that—"

I laid a hand on his shoulder. "Relax, breathe, and tell me what's happening inside that head of yours. No matter what it is, the team and I need and deserve to know. If we hide things from each other, the team will fall apart. We're one great big well-oiled machine. If one cog stops turning, the whole thing grinds to a halt. Tell me what's on your mind."

He groaned. "Again, I don't want to sound ungrateful, but I spent the last year of my life learning everything from how to kill a man with a Beanie Baby, to defusing a nuclear warhead, and every-thing in between. If all you wanted was a ship's captain, I was qualified to do that before you ever sent me to The Ranch. It just seems like a big waste of time and money if I'm stuck in the wheel-house of some boat, no matter how sexy the boat is."

I leaned back against the bulkhead. "I don't know what I was thinking."

He held up a hand. "No, please don't regret taking me on the team. I'm willing to do whatever you need. I just thought I was go-ing to be on the ground with Hunter."

"Trust me. I don't regret bringing you on board for one sec-ond, and neither does any member of the team. What I meant when I said I didn't know what I was thinking has nothing to do with regret. I should've asked you if you wanted to skipper the ship. I shouldn't have just assumed. A good team leader would never make such a bold assumption. You're exactly right. You've been trained to operate in the mud and muck with the rest of us. If you don't want to run the boat—"

"No, it's not that I don't want to do it. It's just that I don't think it's a good use of my skill set. Maybe we should talk to Hunter about it."

"Hunter? What is it about Hunter that keeps you jumping back to him?"

He shrugged. "He kind of took me under his wing and made me his pet project. He knows more about what I'm capable of do-ing than even me."

I laughed. "You spent a lot of time in the water by yourself when you were a Coastie, didn't you?"

He cocked his head. "What do you mean?"

"I mean, you still don't have the team concept ingrained in your head. We don't keep things from each other. Everything you screwed up and everything you mastered passed through Hunter's eyes and right back out of his mouth. He briefed us on every step of the way. That's how this works. When the bullets start flying, every man on this team needs to know exactly how every other man is going to react. That's why we're so good at what we do. If Mongo burps, Disco tastes it, and Hunter says, 'Excuse me.' That's the essence of a team, and I failed you and the team when I didn't come to you about the decision to put you at the helm."

"No, Chase. You didn't fail any of us. It was a logical assumption, but it's just not where my passion lies."

"Come on. Let's go tell the rest of the guys you chickened out."

He laughed, but it was an uncertain, hesitant chuckle.

"I'm just messing with you, Tony Tuna. I just happen to know where there's a well-qualified skipper who's looking for a job on a boat just like this one."

We joined the rest of the team, who'd assembled on the bow. "I've got some news," I said. "Captain Tony thinks sticking him behind the wheel of this fine machine isn't the highest and best use of his talents. He says he's more suited to playing in the mud with the rest of us swine. What do you think?"

Hunter was the first to speak up. "Good call, kid. Besides, I've spent too many hours getting your head out of a Coast Guard hat and into a Kevlar helmet to watch you throw it all away. You're welcome in my foxhole any time. Just don't forget to bring something to eat. I get hungry in holes in the ground."

Mongo said, "I like it. If we're not doing everything in our power to support the team, we're cheating on our brothers, and that'll never do. I'm with Hunter. I'll fight beside you any day. But what are we going to do for a captain?"

I said, "Captain Stinnett's executive officer from the *Lori Danielle* just happens to be unemployed. We can pick him up for a moderate salary and snag a bunch of bodies from Stinnett now that they're mothballing his boat."

"Are we voting?" Disco asked.

"You can vote if you want," I said. "But unless you vote to cherry-pick a crew from the *Lori Danielle*, your vote won't matter. All in favor, say aye."

Without waiting long enough for anyone to vote, I said, "Good. Motion passes with a unanimous vote. Let's get to Norfolk, ASAP, before somebody else snags our crew. We've got a ship to staff."

Chapter 15
Team Integrity

Skipper took my arm as we headed for the gangway to disembark. "Can we talk?"

"Don't tell me you want to change jobs, too."

She giggled. "On the contrary. I want to double down. I'm still working your brother, but if we're keeping the boat, I need to spend some time in the ops center on board and come up with a shopping list."

"I'm glad you brought that up. Let's head down there now. There's something I need to discuss with you."

She led the way, and soon we were settled into a pair of far-more-comfortable chairs than the ones in the Bonaventure ops center.

I squirmed and adjusted until I felt like I was floating on a cloud. "These are spectacular. We need to upgrade."

"They're nice," she said. "But what did you want to discuss?"

"We're taking on a new crew tomorrow or the next day in Norfolk, so that'll mean a bunch of new people on the payroll."

She slid a notepad and pen from her pocket. "How many more?"

"Maybe twenty or so."

"Okay, that's a lot. But how will that affect me?"

"It won't directly affect you except that we'll need an additional analyst technician. That'll make you the senior analyst with a subordinate, so I'd like for you to go shopping for the right personality. I wouldn't know where to start the search, so I'm leaving it up to you."

"I've already got a list in my head. I'll get right on that."

"Now, here's the real reason I wanted to talk with you. I'm thinking about sending an advance team to Guatemala to start the groundwork on finding my brother. If I do, Singer will be the lead, and we'll send at least one more . . . maybe two. I want your thoughts."

Instead of answering immediately as she usually does, her pause reassured me that she was weighing the pros and cons. She tapped her pen against her pad several times. "We're not in a boss-subordinate situation here, right?"

"What are you asking?"

"Can we talk as Chase and Skipper and not as boss and analyst?"

"Absolutely," I said. "What's on your mind?"

She leaned forward and anchored her elbows on her knees. "Okay, but don't get mad. Would you send an advanced team if we were looking for Michael McMillan's brother in Guatemala?"

I spun my gray-matter Rolodex, but it wasn't coming. "Who's Michael McMillan?"

Skipper leaned back in her chair. "Exactly."

I sighed. "Wow. You have quite a way of putting things in perspective."

"If we treat that mission any differently than we treat every other mission, we'll slip up and do something to get one of us hurt . . . or worse. It's either a mission, or it isn't, and you have to make that call. That's why you make the big bucks."

"How much did you make last year?"

She rolled her eyes. "Okay, I make the big bucks, too, but I'm worth it. Team leaders are a dime a dozen, but a good analyst is worth her weight in gold."

I gave her a wink. "You're worth *my* weight in gold. Thanks for the perspective."

"It's what I do. Oh, and thanks for letting Tony off the hook as captain. He really wants to be in the field with you guys."

"That's where he belongs, and I should've seen that before I put him in an uncomfortable spot. I've been a little preoccupied."

She stood and wrapped her arms around me. "It's understandable, and we're all here to keep your head on straight. But I do have one more thing to say."

"Let's hear it."

She looked around as if making sure no one was listening. "Thanks for not treating it like just another mission when you, Clark, and Anya came to rescue me in Miami."

"We've come a long way since those days," I said.

"Yeah, we've got a ship now."

I knocked on the surface of the console. "We sure do. I just hope she doesn't leave us up one particular creek without a paddle."

She grinned. "We've got Earl and Mongo. If she can't fix it, he can pick us up and carry us back to deep water."

* * *

We reconvened in the kitchen back at Bonaventure, and Earl opened the meeting. "This stings to admit, but I can't be your huckleberry on this one."

I said, "What are you talking about?"

"That new boat of yours is over my head. If them motors laid down, I could make 'em run again if it was mechanical, but that thing is a floating computer, and this dog is too old to learn those new tricks."

"I'm not asking you to come aboard as the chief engineer. I just wanted your thoughts on the propulsion system as a whole."

"It's impressive, but it's complicated. In my experience, the more complex something is, the easier it breaks. I recommend hiring at least one of those Grumman engineers who designed the thing. He'll know it better than anybody else, but I'm not going to be any help at all on that monster."

"Thanks. That's the kind of input I need. Anybody else?"

"I didn't see an armory," Hunter said.

I gave him the thumbs-up. "Let's make a list."

By the time the conversation was over, we had a detailed wish list, including medical equipment, a cook, upgraded commo and computer gear for the ops center, and definitely an armory.

I clapped my hands. "If that's everything, I guess it's all aboard for Norfolk tomorrow."

Singer raised an eyebrow. "All of us?"

"Ah, yes. I almost forgot. I've decided we're maintaining team integrity on this one. If we have to split once we get to Central America, we'll do what we have to do, but for now, we're shaking down the ship as a team."

Singer nodded without a word, but Skipper piped up. "What's her name?"

I cocked my head like a confused puppy. "Whose name?"

"The ship. Doesn't she have a name?"

I turned to Clark and shrugged.

He screwed up his face. "I don't know."

Skipper said, "We can't have a ship without a name."

Hunter threw in his two cents' worth. "I've been through the desert on a horse with no name."

Tony threw a dishrag at him. "You do know you said that out loud, right, old man?"

"Okay, knock it off," I said. "Get out of here and spend some time with the people you love who aren't in this room. We'll hit the deck tomorrow morning at eight, and it's going to be nonstop for a while after that."

Tony and Skipper headed upstairs. Hunter headed to Tina's side. Singer went to church. Mongo left for home, where Irina and Tatiana waited for him.

Clark ambled over and threw his arm across my shoulders. "All right, College Boy. I'm going home to Maebelle and Miami Beach. It's all yours now. I'm just a phone call away when you need me."

"That's it, huh? No ceremony? No last words of wisdom?"

He stepped back. "I taught you how to stay alive and keep the bad guys from doing the same. What more do you want from me?"

I leaned against the sink. "I'm going to miss you. That's all. We've shared a lot of miles and a lot of bad guys over the years."

He wouldn't look at me, and I could've sworn his voice cracked at least a little when he said, "If you're lucky, you'll get old one day, and maybe my little brother will be standing where you are now."

"Maybe so. But I'm still going to miss running and gunning with you. I love you, brother."

He still wouldn't look up, but as he headed for the door, his sentiment floated through the air. "I love you, too, College Boy."

I walked through the back door and across the gallery to the gazebo, where I stared out over the North River and relived the past decade of my life.

Where would I be if Clark Johnson hadn't come stumbling into my life on that dock on Jekyll Island? Would I have lived this long? Would I have met and married Penny? Would I still have my foot? Would Anya have killed me a thousand times over?

My phone chirped, pulling me from the mystical world of what-if. "Hello, this is Chase."

"Chase, Wayne Stinnett here."

"Good evening, Captain."

"So help me, boy, if you don't cut the 'captain' crap, I'm hanging up right now. And trust me, you don't want me to hang up."

"All right. To what do I owe the pleasure of a call from my old friend Wayne?"

"That's better. I've got some information for you, and it's going to sound like a hard sell, but it's the God's honest truth. My XO and most of my crew are being heavily recruited by some outfit in New Zealand. From what they tell me, the offers are strong. If you want them, you'd better put in your bid before the sun goes down."

I checked my watch. "Pick me up at Hampton Roads Executive Airport in ninety minutes, and tell your men to stay where they are until they've heard my offer."

"Done," came his reply, followed by the silence of a dead connection.

I thumbed Disco's speed dial and waited.

"Hey, Chase. What's up?"

"I'm going to Norfolk in the Citation. Wanna come?"

"I'm at the airport now doing some paperwork. I'll have her ready to go when you get here."

"You really need a hobby . . . or a wife."

He chuckled. "I've had both, and I prefer airplanes. They're a lot cheaper and easier to understand. I'll see you in a few."

My robot foot and I hopped aboard the microbus and pulled into the hangar five minutes later. True to his word, Disco had the Citation parked on the ramp.

"Have you done the preflight inspection yet?"

He gave me the thumbs-up. "Yep, and I'm on the phone with flight service right now. Are we going to Norfolk International?"

"No. Hampton Roads Exec."

By the time I was strapped into the captain's seat, Disco had our weather briefing and instrument clearance from Jacksonville Approach. We blasted off with our nose pointed north and settled in for the remaining fifty-five minutes of our flight.

Disco said, "I guess I should've asked why we're going to Virginia."

"Our crew is getting yanked out from under us. We have to get there and offer them a softer spot to land. Some firm out of New Zealand needs a research vessel crew. I hope we can make a good enough offer to keep them here in the up above."

"Up above?" he asked.

"Yeah, that's the opposite of down under, isn't it?"

He chuckled. "If you say so."

We landed at Hampton Roads under beautifully clear skies and light wind to find Captain Stinnett and Doctor Shadrack waiting in the FBO.

I slid a credit card across the desk. "Top off the Citation, and keep the card on file. We'll probably make several trips over the next few days."

The clerk behind the counter keyed the microphone clipped to her collar. "Top off the Citation that just came in."

"Will you be staying overnight, Mr. Fulton?"

"Probably not, but I'll let you know in a couple of hours. Do you have a hangar in case we stay?"

"Sure, but we cut down to one lineman after nine o'clock, so if you could let me know before then, I'd appreciate it."

We climbed into a nondescript white van and buckled in.

Subtlety being one of his weaker suits, Captain Stinnett shot me a look. "There's no time like the present to interview your new medical officer."

"So, what do you say, doctor? Are you up for another hitch on a little newer boat?"

Dr. Shadrack steepled his fingers. "Let's see. I have an offer at Bethesda Naval Hospital to teach as a GS-fourteen with a pension and Blue Cross Blue Shield, and a hundred thousand dollar signing bonus. I could do that, or I could come work for you and probably get shot at, miss every holiday at home, patch up covert operatives in some of the nastiest places on Earth, and eat C rations for every meal. When can I start?"

"How much does a GS-fourteen make at Bethesda?" I asked.

"With the special salary rate and bonuses, somewhere just shy of two hundred."

"I think we can do a little better than that. We'll match the one hundred K signing bonus and get things started with a quarter million for the first year. We can always renegotiate after that. There's going to be some growing pains and a huge learning curve, but working with us is never boring."

Disco let out a laugh. "You can say that again."

The doctor asked, "Do the perks include use of the company jet?"

"Use? Disco will teach you to fly it if you want."

Without another word, Dr. Shadrack stuck out his hand, and I shook it.

Disco seemingly couldn't resist an opportunity to throw a jab. "Nice job, Chase. I know you were willing to go up to four hundred K for the doc. Now we've got extra in the pot to court the future captain."

Shadrack held up four fingers and mouthed, "Four hundred? Really?"

I shook my head and stuck up my thumb. "Higher."

He palmed his forehead. "The food better be good."

Chapter 16

How's the Pay?

We pulled up to the docks where the *Lori Danielle* was being dismantled, and Captain Stinnett sighed. "It hurts to see the old girl coming apart."

"I'm sure it does," I said. "I'll take good care of your crew, though. I promise you that."

"I know you will. I wouldn't have recommended them to you if I didn't believe you'd treat 'em like kings."

"Are there any crew left aboard you wouldn't recommend I pick up?"

"Nope. If they weren't top-notch hands, they didn't last long on the L.D."

"Do you have a wardroom big enough to assemble everybody at once?"

He motioned across the street. "The guesthouse has an assembly room. That's where I put everybody up for now. No one can sleep on a boat that's being cut to pieces around the clock."

"Get them together," I said. "We'll meet you in the assembly room in half an hour."

While we waited for the crew to arrive, I called Clark.

"What? I've been gone two hours, and you're already calling? Seriously?"

Instead of playing his games, I got straight to business. "How much is the crew budget?"

"For the ship?"

"No, Broke Back, for the carnival rides. Yes, of course the ship's crew."

"I guess that would be a handy number to know, wouldn't it? Stand by."

The line clicked. I covered the mouthpiece and said to Disco, "He's checking with the Board."

"Ah . . ."

The line clicked again, and Clark's voice returned. "They think a full complement is forty-five souls. I think that's too many. You'll have people bouncing off each other on a boat that size with the team and forty-five sailors. I recommend—"

"I don't care what you recommend. I want a bank account, not the opinion of a door kicker on how to staff a ship."

"Ooh, they gave College Boy a ship, and he got all uppity. The Board says five point five per year for salaries, bonuses, and benefits."

"I'm not uppity. I'm just trying to corral a crew before they get scattered to the wind."

"Go handle your business, Mr. Uppity, and leave me alone."

I laughed. "I miss you too, sweetheart."

I could almost see him rolling his eyes.

"They said five point five million a year for the crew budget."

Disco stared at the ceiling. "I'm no accountant, but that should be more than enough. How many people do you plan to hire?"

I shrugged. "This is my first time, so I'm playing it by ear. I'm guessing, but maybe thirty crew and five or six officers."

"It might be a good idea to talk to Stinnett before you start throwing money around."

As if out of thin air, Captain Stinnett appeared. "You should listen to the pilot, Chase."

I turned around. "Stop sneaking up on me."

Stinnett laughed. "I'm an old spook. It's what I do. Stop being so jumpy. You're supposed to be some world-class badass, and you're afraid of shadows. Something just ain't adding up."

"Speaking of adding up. How many crew do you have left?"

"You took the doctor already. You may remember Christine Billings. She was my quartermaster, and she's a good one. Don't let her get away. She has six sailors under her that can do everything on the boat that nobody else wants to do. Unfortunately, the cook and galley crew are already gone. They get nabbed up the second they become available, so you'll have to shop elsewhere for a galley team. The XO is a Naval Academy grad named Sprayberry. I know, I know . . . Before you say it, yes, that's a screwed-up last name, but just wait 'til you hear his first name."

"Please tell me it's something like Francis."

"Nope. I'm not going to spoil the surprise. Anyway, the chief engineer and eight of the best wrench-turners you'll ever see are part of the deal. There are twelve able seamen who double as ship's security. I've got four officers, plus the doctor."

I tallied the numbers. "That sounds like thirty-three to me."

"That's what I count." Stinnett slid a thick binder across the table. "You'll find their CVs and salaries in there. Guard that book with your life. It's nobody's business what anybody else makes on payday."

Before he could finish, the assembly room became a cacophony of voices, curiosity, and maybe even some anxiety for a few of the crew as they filed in.

Stinnett gave me a questioning look. "Are you ready?"

I responded with a single nod, and he cleared his throat. That was, apparently, enough from their captain for the crew to halt their conversations and turn their attention to the front of the room.

Stinnett began. "Thank you for coming down. I apologize for interrupting your busy afternoon lounging in a hotel and getting paid for it. I called you down for two reasons. The first is to congratulate you on the offer from New Zealand. If you've not been, you should know it's one of the most beautiful regions on the planet. If you accept that offer, you'll be pleased you did, and you'll be bored out of your minds in six months."

Nervous laughter sounded, and the captain said, "The second reason I asked you to come down is to inform you about another opportunity. It's to continue a line of work similar to what you've done with me for the past years. We've had some adventures, have we not?"

Captain Stinnett motioned toward me. "Some of you, no doubt, remember working with Chase Fulton on a couple of occasions aboard the *Lori Danielle*. Most recently, of course, was the jaunt off the Yucatan Peninsula, when we got to mix it up with the Mexican Navy. I'm pretty sure we came out on top of that little skirmish."

Cheers arose.

"Okay, okay. Calm down. Our old friend, Chase, has been given control over a ship that looks a lot like ours used to before they showed up with torches and wrecking balls to tear her apart. Chase's boat is a little more modern than ours, but it wouldn't take you long to learn it like the backs of your hands—the way you knew the *Lori Danielle*. Chase is going to talk with you for a minute. He's not as eloquent as me, but he's a lot less cantankerous, so listen up." He turned to me. "They're all yours."

"Thank you, Captain Stinnett. As he said, my name is Chase, and I have a small company down in coastal Georgia. What we do is, well, it's not exactly oceanographic research, but we spend a lot of time on the water solving problems other people don't want to deal with."

Captain Stinnett cut in. "They all have clearances, and they know, generally, what you do, Chase."

"Thank you. That makes things a little simpler. In short, I have a boat without a crew, and you are a crew without a boat. I'd like for us to solve both of those problems together."

A voice from the back cut through the air. "How's the food, and what does it pay?"

A gentleman who appeared to be in his mid-forties rose and cast a disapproving eye across the crowd. He said, "It pays a lot better than what you'll be making if you interrupt our new boss again."

That got some laughs and quieted the outburst.

The clean-shaven man who'd come to my rescue held up a hand. "I'm sorry about that, Chase. Please continue."

I turned to Stinnett and mouthed, "XO?"

He nodded.

I continued. "Thank you, Mr. Sprayberry. I'm sorry we couldn't meet privately, but we're under the gun, so to speak, and we need to move quickly."

"Think nothing of it. And call me Barry."

"Barry? Seriously? Barry Sprayberry? Did your mother lose a bet naming you?"

This time, the crowd laughed at me instead of their captain.

Sprayberry held up his hands in surrender. "When you're this good-looking, it doesn't matter if your name rhymes with itself."

"Touché. While you and I are chatting, you come highly recommended by your captain to skipper our boat instead of playing second fiddle to an old, washed-up salt like him. Are you interested?"

He rose back to his feet and glanced backward over the gathered crew. "How's the food, and what does it pay?"

As the crew erupted, I motioned for the XO to come up front. We shook hands, and I said, "We'll match your salary, plus twenty percent, with a ten percent kicker for sea duty. Interested?"

He glanced between Stinnett and me. "You'll match my executive officer salary plus twenty percent, or you'll match the captain's salary plus twenty?"

"You're good at this. We'll double your XO salary, plus ten percent sea pay."

He glanced down at the binder. "You didn't open that yet. You don't know my salary, so how do you know you're willing to double it?"

I gave him an official Clark Johnson crooked smile and stuck out my hand. "Do we have a deal?"

He put his hand in mine and locked eyes with me. "Be generous with my crew, even if you have to cut my pay to do it. They deserve it."

"It looks like we found ourselves a captain."

"It looks like I found a ship."

I held up a hand, and the crew quieted. "Your executive officer has just accepted the helm as captain. I won't tell you what he said about all of you, but you can take it from me, you have a true leader in Captain Sprayberry."

I said, "I'm going to make a similar offer to all of you that I made to Captain Sprayberry. It's a take-it-or-leave-it offer. I don't have time to negotiate salaries and benefits right now. Rest assured that we'll take care of you and your families with good medical insurance and a pension plan. The salary offer is your previous salary, plus twenty-five percent, and a ten percent incentive pay for every day spent at sea."

Murmuring voices filled the room, and one man yelled out, "Where do I sign?"

"We'll get to that in just a moment. In the meantime, if you were an officer aboard the *Lori Danielle*, please raise your hand."

Five hands went into the air.

"Will the five of you come talk with me privately while my associate, Disco, and your new skipper, Captain Sprayberry, get your acceptance or denial of our offer? Oh, and there's one more thing . . . When Captain Stinnett told you that you'd be bored in six months in New Zealand, he was quite right. That gig would've been nothing to write home about. But if you come work with us, I promise it'll be against the law for any of you to write home about the things we do, and boredom will never be in your vocabulary."

As the crew formed a pair of lines to speak with Disco and Captain Sprayberry, the five officers made their way to the corner where I took up residence. The volume in the room elevated a few notches, and it looked like we'd just hired ourselves a crew. Things were falling into place as if directed by the hand of God, until several seconds of automatic weapons fire sounded from the lobby outside the assembly room and screams of panic filled the air beyond the double doors.

Chapter 17
No Next Time

In opposition to the chaos roaring in the lobby of the old hotel, the men and women inside the assembly room took a knee and listened intently.

Stinnett moved to the center of the room and gave the order, "Security team on me, now!"

Disco reached beneath his untucked shirt and drew his Glock at the same instant I drew mine. A glance at Stinnett gathering his security team reassured me that we had at least twelve more trained gunfighters should the evening turn into a train wreck.

Sprayberry silently assembled the crew who weren't armed and moved them to a corner of the room behind a mountain of stacked folding tables. Once he was confident his crew was as safe as possible, he moved across the floor, exactly how Clark had taught me to move. He knelt behind me and whispered, "I need a weapon."

I pulled the small Glock 26 from my ankle holster and stuck it and a backup magazine in his hand. "You and the security team keep the crew alive. I'm going to take a peek outside."

Moving back to join Stinnett and the team, Barry briefed my plan while Disco and I climbed into the acoustic ceiling of the assembly room. We moved side by side and inch by inch until we reached the wall above the lobby. Decade upon decade of battling

East Coast hurricanes and the shifting sands of Norfolk left the old hotel warped and cracked like a massive spiderweb. The layers of plaster over slats crumbled like crackers beneath my fingertips.

After two minutes of digging and prodding, I finally opened a hole large enough to reward one of my eyes with a view of the lobby. I whispered, "Eight gunmen, all masked with gloves and boot covers. They're wearing earpieces and mics."

"They sound like pros. Is it a robbery?" Disco said.

"I don't think so. Take a look."

I moved away from my peephole, and he crawled into my place.

After a few seconds of spying through the hole, he said, "I'm with you. It's definitely not a robbery. What are they doing to the doors? What do you think they want?"

I leaned back and peered through the tiny opening to examine what Disco saw at the doors. My heart fell into my stomach. "They're chaining them shut and wiring them with C4. Whatever they want, they're willing to kill the SWAT team to get it."

"That's not a good sign."

"We need to know what's going on in the hotel," I said. "Get behind that ductwork, and get Skipper on the phone. We need some eyes and ears."

"You got it." He crawled through the insulation and nestled behind the metal duct.

I made my way back to the assembly room and stuck my head through the hole left by the missing ceiling tile. Stinnett saw me first and shuffled closer.

I said, "Eight gunmen, pros. It's not a robbery. They're after something specific. Got any ideas?

He shook his head, but then held up a finger. "Wait one."

He snapped his fingers once, and Sprayberry turned on a heel to face his captain. Stinnett curled a finger, and he crossed the floor in seconds.

Stinnett whispered my question, and Barry looked up at me. He shrugged at first, but recognition flashed in his eyes. He yanked a piece of paper from a nearby table, scribbled furiously on it, and held it up toward me.

I took the sheet and read.

Christopher Abbot, the CEO of Abbot Shipbuilding, is staying in the hotel. He has the whole third floor.

My phone chirped, and I panicked. Hopefully it hadn't echoed through the lobby the way it roared in my head. I thumbed the silent button and stuck the phone to my ear.

"It's Skipper. I'm on it. The only thing I can find is a guy named Abbot."

"Yeah, he's got the whole third floor. Are you in the ops center?"

"I am now. I'm working on satellite and traffic cams, but nothing's coming up. Stand by."

Seconds passed like weeks as I waited for her voice to return. Finally, she said, "I have Norfolk PD on the line."

"Can they hear me?"

"Yes," she said. "It's a multiline call."

"Eight heavily armed gunmen. Multiple shots fired. All lobby doors are wired with C4. Do not rush the doors. At least a dozen innocents on the floor in the main lobby. I have myself and one other operative, and we're backed up by twelve armed maritime security agents. The gunmen don't know we're here."

"What kind of operative are you?" a voice asked.

"The kind who can kill eight heavily armed gunmen if you don't get in our way."

"Stand down," the voice ordered. "SWAT and Emergency Services are en route."

I repeated. "Do not storm the doors! They're armed with explosives that will kill anybody coming through the door, and likely anybody within fifteen feet of the doors on the inside."

"Who are you?" the voice demanded.

"I'm a supervisory special agent with Secret Service, and I'm assuming command of the scene. Do not make any effort to enter the building until I give the okay. Got it?"

The voice said, "I'm sorry, sir, but I can't take your word for who you are. You'll have to—"

I cut in. "Skipper, deal with her, and get the president on the phone if necessary."

Leaving the connection open, I shoved the phone into my shirt pocket and drew a mental picture of our situation. The gunmen in the lobby were the primary concern. Disco and I could outshoot them if we could get into position to create a crossfire, but the necessity of protecting Captain Stinnett's crew remained. I knew nothing of the security team's training or ability, so I focused on Disco and me being the primary problem solvers in the scenario.

While still considering our situation, I slipped the phone from my pocket. "Are you convinced that I'm in charge yet?"

The voice answered, "Yes, sir. Continue feeding intel if possible."

I said, "Disco, if you're on, move to our peephole and situate your camera so Skipper can see the lobby."

He answered immediately. "Roger. Moving."

"When the camera's in place, move to my position over the assembly room."

"Roger."

I met Stinnett's stare, and he must've read my mind. He stepped onto a chair Barry positioned beneath my access hole to the ceiling.

Only inches away, he whispered, "They're good at defending a ship and repelling borders, but this isn't their bailiwick."

"Can they hold this room and repel borders if they come through those doors?"

Stinnett gave me a nod, and I said, "That's good enough. Here are my priorities. One, keep everyone in this room alive and unharmed. I'm leaving that one to you and your security team. Two, stop whatever those gunmen are here to do. Disco and I can outgun them, and we have Skipper and the local EMS dispatcher on the phone. Are you good?"

"We're good. Have Skipper patch me into the comms."

I gave her the instructions, and seconds later, Captain Stinnett was on the line with us.

Skipper said, "Chase, they're on the move. Four of them are moving toward the staircase. I pulled up building plans, so I know the layout."

"And you're sure they're heading for the stairs and not the elevators?"

"Yeah, I'm sure."

"In that case, I'm even more convinced they're pros. They're not willing to bottleneck themselves in the elevators."

"I agree. I found a route for you to get all the way to the fifth floor without exposing yourself, if you want."

"Of course I want, but I don't think we need to get to the fifth floor. I think the action is heading for the third floor. Get me there."

Disco arrived at my side the instant Skipper started talking.

I covered the microphone and whispered to Disco, "We're moving to the third floor. Four of the bad guys are headed up the stairs."

"Lead the way."

We moved as quickly as possible through the ceiling above the assembly room as Skipper directed us. "Keep moving toward the back of the building. You'll see an abandoned shaft. It's huge. It must've been a freight elevator at some point."

"We're there, and we're headed up."

As we climbed the shaft, I listened intently for gunfire or a fight. I didn't know who Abbot was, or why eight armed men would risk their lives to get to him, but my gut told me I wouldn't have to wait long for answers.

Skipper said, "The remaining gunmen in the lobby are flex-cuffing everyone. No one is resisting."

"Let's pray they don't resist. We can neutralize this thing if everybody stays calm."

We reached the third floor, and I pulled on an access panel from the shaft. "The panel isn't moving. Got any ideas?"

I could almost hear Skipper's gears turning in her head. "There's another access panel on the fourth floor."

Voices came through the wall . . .

"Get down! Get down!"

"We don't have time to keep climbing. We're going through this panel."

I tucked the phone away and turned to Disco. "It's time to play Kool-Aid Man."

He nodded, and I said, "I'm going to hit it first. If it gives, I'll go through face-first and hit the deck rolling to the right. You follow me through and move left."

"Got it. Let's move!"

I leaned backward into the open air of the oversized shaft and threw my two hundred twenty pounds as hard as I could toward the panel. To my surprise, it gave way on the first shot, but what followed was nothing like I'd planned.

As the plaster and century of layered paint surrendered to the force of having a human body flung through it, that body—my body—plummeted to the floor five feet below. The fall took me by surprise and left me landing with a thud on my side instead of rolling into a firing position. My right arm absorbed most of the punishment of the fall, trapping my pistol beneath my hip and leaving me gasping for the air that had been knocked from my lungs.

With plaster and dust filling the corridor, two shots rang out, followed by four more in rapid succession. Lying still during a gunfight is one of the best ways to wake up dead, so I dug the heels of my boots into the carpet and propelled myself into an alcove far too small to offer any real cover or concealment. Moving allowed me to raise my pistol into position just in time to see two of the hooded gunmen melt to the floor. Disco's double-taps had been just as precise as his landings. I had yet to fire a shot, but the scene unfolding in front of me said that was about to change.

One of the remaining bandits held a blonde-haired girl of perhaps two beneath an arm as he pinned himself to the wall with his pistol raised toward me. The plaster dust in my eyes left me unwilling and incapable of pressing the trigger. Hitting the child was not a risk I could take.

Two more masked men stepped into position in front of the man with the child and sent a hail of gunfire down the hallway toward Disco and me. Bullet holes formed in the walls, but I didn't feel the sting of a penetrating round into my flesh.

I caught a glimpse of blonde hair flying as the child's captor rounded the corner toward the stairs beyond. I pressed the trigger twice with my front sight centered on the smaller of the two gunmen facing us. The concussion of a pair of nine-millimeter rounds impacting his upper chest sent the man backward and left him dead before he hit the floor. Disco's next two shots were just as accurate as mine, and the second man melted over legs no longer capable of supporting his mass.

I spun to see the opening through which I'd fallen and saw Disco's pistol and hands protruding from the jagged opening. I said, "Are you hit?"

"Not yet. Are you?"

"I'm okay. They're headed to the roof with a little girl. Beat them there. I'm moving to the stairs."

His muzzle disappeared, and his footsteps on the wooden ladder of the former elevator shaft sounded like thunder echoing from the cavity. I straightened my legs and shook the dust from my face and hair. The first two strides felt awkward as I picked up speed down the corridor, but after that, my strides came in fluid, confident motion. Reaching the staircase, I pinned myself to the wall and peeked around the corner in search of more gunmen ascending the stairs.

My mental inventory counted four bodies—three to Disco's credit and one to mine. That cut the opposing force in half, and I prayed for a way to know if anyone else was coming up the stairs. Remembering my eye in the sky, I yanked the phone from my pocket and yelled into the mic. "Skipper! Are you still there?"

"Yeah, I'm here, Chase. What's going on?"

"How many do you see in the lobby?"

"None."

"None? What do you mean, none?"

"None, as in zero. The first four hit the stairs. Two more followed when you started shooting. And the remaining two finished flex-cuffing everyone and hit the elevators."

"They've got a little girl," I said. "Does that mean anything to you?"

"Other than a little girl being kidnapped, it doesn't mean anything specific . . . Wait!"

"I don't have time to wait! I'm going after the girl."

I took the stairs three at a time until a shot rang out and the wall to my right exploded from the impact. I sidestepped toward the inside rail of the stairs and tried to determine how far the shooter was above me.

Fighting uphill is a terrible tactical position and often leads to permanent defeat, but I had no choice. The bad guys were moving toward the roof, and they had a high-value hostage.

Pausing to calm my heart rate, I grabbed my phone again. "Stinnett, are you there?"

"Go for Stinnett."

"Send a team to the lobby. It's empty of bandits, and the innocents are cuffed on the floor. Get the explosive rigs from the doors, and send in the cavalry."

The dispatcher said, "ESU is on scene and standing by."

I yelled into the phone, "Do not shoot anybody in the lobby. They are all good guys. The suspects are headed for the roof."

She began a sentence, but it didn't matter what she had to say. I eased forward and up the stairs, sticking to the interior rail to reduce my visibility from above. I passed the fourth-floor landing and continued up. Two more bullets rained down from above, but they impacted harmlessly to my right.

Passing the fifth floor, I saw the black sleeve of the shooter who'd been taking shots at me, and I stuck a pair of nine-millimeter rounds into his bicep. I knew he might survive the wounds, but his will to fight would weaken as the blood inside his body found its way out.

The distraction gave me the chance to close the distance. As the man's shoulder came into sight, I leapt forward and sent two more rounds into his chest. He crumpled to the stairs and slid toward me. I dodged his descending corpse and continued upward.

The new dead guy made five, and our odds were improving. Gunfire erupted from above, but it wasn't intended for me. I continued my climb and found the remainder of the staircase empty, giving me an unobstructed approach to the door leading to the roof. I dropped my partially depleted magazine from my Glock, pocketed it, and slammed a fresh magazine into the weapon.

Clark's words of wisdom echoed in my head. *"Reload when you want to instead of when you have to, College Boy."*

With a fresh magazine and rekindled drive, I sent a front kick to the door, sending it exploding outward onto the roof of the old hotel.

It is possible to overload the human brain with more information than it can process, and that's exactly what I did as I tried to take in the scene on the roof. A black helicopter waited at a hover near the western edge of the roof. Disco was in the gunfight of his life with two black-clad forms tucked behind an air conditioning unit. The man with the child beneath his harm was sprinting toward the chopper like a running back with his human football tucked beneath his left arm.

As my brain filed away everything my eyes were seeing, I squeezed the trigger four times, dispatching the two men who were trying to punch holes in Disco. Without waiting for their bodies to hit the ground, both Disco and I sprinted toward the chopper. Each of us had our pistols raised, but taking a running shot was far too risky. Instead, we poured on the coals in a life-or-death effort to out-run the one remaining bad guy carrying the child.

Realizing the distance and speed made it impossible for either of us to catch the man before he made it to the chopper. I aimed low and cracked off four rounds. At least one of my shots found its mark, and the man stumbled. Only feet from the chopper, he forced himself farther forward as the muscles and bone of his lower leg grew weaker with every stride.

Disco had at least three paces on me, and he was closing the distance between himself and the wounded would-be kidnapper. Believing I could put two more rounds in his calves, I squeezed the trigger twice more. He bucked and twisted with his now useless legs folding beneath him. As one final act of defiance and determination, he threw the child toward the chopper. Her petite form flew through the air and toward the open door of the flying machine. I couldn't believe the man's final act of treachery actually worked. The child landed on the deck of the chopper, and the pilot banked hard away from the building.

Leaning back, I arrested my forward motion before I tumbled across the knee wall at the edge of the roof. Disco made no effort to stop himself. He left the roof in a giant stride, landing one foot on top of the knee wall and propelling himself through the air five stories above the street below.

His lunge ended with him hanging by his arms from the left skid of the escaping chopper, and he swung wildly beneath the machine until he could throw one foot over the skid. Disco forced himself up and into the cabin of the chopper as it made its escape.

The black helicopter spun one hundred eighty degrees, and the pilot forced the aircraft between a pair of buildings at least twice as tall as the hotel on which I stood.

With nothing else to do, I grabbed my phone. "The child and one of my commandos are aboard the chopper. The pilot is escaping to the northeast. All eight gunmen are dead."

"Did you say Disco is on the chopper?" Skipper asked.

"Yes, he's on the helicopter with the little girl and the pilot."

She stammered, "How did he . . ."

"It doesn't matter. Just don't shoot him down!"

"Freeze!" came a booming voice. "Drop your weapon, and get on the ground!"

I turned around and saw six men in full SWAT gear with weapons trained on me. Without hesitation, I laid my pistol on the ground, hit my knees, and threw my hands into the air. "I'm Special Agent Fulton! Don't shoot!"

"Where's your partner?" one of them yelled.

I pointed toward the fleeing chopper. "He's on the helo with the little girl and the pilot."

The man motioned for his team to lower their weapons, and they followed his direction. "Show me some ID, Fulton."

I slowly reached for my credentials pack and produced the badge and ID.

"Toss it over," he ordered, and I obeyed.

As he inspected my ID, I yelled. "Get somebody on the horn who can track that chopper. My man and an innocent little girl are on that helo."

The SWAT commander folded my cred pack and approached. He tossed the pack back to me and said, "We're tracking them, and they're coming back."

"Coming back?"

He held up a finger toward the east. "Yeah, they're coming back."

I looked up to see the chopper coming to a hover just inches above the roof. One of the SWAT team members pulled the child from the chopper, and Disco gave a little salute from behind the controls. I grinned and returned the salute. Sixty seconds later, the helo touched down in the parking lot of the hotel, and the blades whined to a halt.

The SWAT commander offered me a hand and helped me to my feet. "Nice job, Agent Fulton. But next time, let us do the shooting."

As I stood, I said, "What are you talking about? You and your team *were* the shooters. My partner and I were never here."

Chapter 18
Choices . . . Choices

With my phone pressed to my face, I said, "Skipper, it's time to fire up the spin machine. Keep us off the six o'clock news."

"Consider it done. The locals will be more than happy to take the credit for rescuing the granddaughter of one of the wealthiest men in America."

"What are you talking about?"

"It turns out the little girl you and Disco saved was Tiffany Abbot, the granddaughter of Christopher Abbot—owner and CEO of Abbot Shipbuilding—and this isn't the first attempt. We'll probably never know the whole story, but I'm sure Mr. Abbot would like to shake your hand and buy you a small country somewhere."

"I'm glad the girl is safe, but I'm not interested in shaking any hands. I have to get back downstairs to the crew."

"I'll do what I can to keep you and Disco out of the spotlight. Let me know what else you need. Ops center, out."

She was gone, and her line was dead.

Captain Stinnett's connection was clearly alive and well. "Good show, son. You've got a roomful of shipmates who can't wait to get on your boat after that performance."

"I'm on my way down, Captain. In the meantime, can you send someone up into the ceiling to retrieve Disco's phone? It's propped against the wall facing the lobby."

"Consider it done."

Retrieving Disco from the parking lot turned out to be an exercise in badge-flashing. Getting out of the building was more challenging than getting back in, but I made the retrieval, and we were soon back inside the assembly room. A bevy of questions shouting from every corner of the room sounded like an approaching freight train.

Captain Sprayberry called the commotion to order with two fingers in the corners of his mouth and a shrill whistle. "That's enough. Knock it off."

The crew quieted, and Sprayberry turned to me. "If there was anybody on the fence about whether to join your crew, they're not straddling that fence any longer. After that show, these guys would come to work for you for free, just so they could watch the show."

"I'll take them up on that offer. That'll dramatically reduce our payroll expenses."

That got a chuckle, and we returned to the task of signing up new officers and crew.

With the process complete, I pulled our captain aside. "The crew obviously respects you, so that stands to make this transition a lot smoother than I expected."

"It's mutual respect," he said. "Being second under a skipper like Captain Stinnett is a master class in personnel management. He's hard on the outside, so that gave me the opportunity to play good cop over the last few years. I've built relationships with the crew from the inside out. You just bought yourself a remarkable bunch of shipmates, Chase."

I checked over my shoulder to ensure no one was within earshot. "What happened here today is pretty common in our world. We have a knack for stumbling into gunfights, so if you or any member of the crew isn't okay with that, now's the time to exit stage left."

He shook his head. "Thanks for the option, but we're in for the long haul. Oh, one more thing. The crew has already been briefed that none of this happened. They all hold clearances and take the old adage about loose lips sinking ships extremely seriously."

"Thank you for that," I said. "Here's what comes next. You and I are headed to Saint Marys. Bring your second-in-command, your chief engineer, and the yeoman, if you have one. We'll bring our ship to Norfolk in the next couple of days to pick up the crew, stock the medical bay, and start the shakedown cruise."

"I thought that might be your first order, so I've already briefed the crew, and we're ready to go."

News reporters, vans sporting satellite dishes mounted on telescoping poles, and every law enforcement agency within a hundred miles of Norfolk surrounded the hotel, so waiting for the circus to end wasn't an option. We wormed our way through the crowd, desperately trying to appear meaningless until we were clear of the mayhem. To my surprise, a crew-cab, four-wheel-drive truck approached and came to a stop only feet from us as we approached the *Lori Danielle*.

A young man rolled down the driver's window. "Hop in."

I turned to Barry, and he said, "It's okay. He's one of ours."

We mounted the truck and headed for the airport.

I gave our chief pilot a slug to the arm. "All right, hero. Tell us about the chopper."

"I don't know why I did that. I just couldn't stand the thought of something happening to that little girl. I've got a niece about her age, and I couldn't stop thinking about what I'd do to save her."

"The jump was amazing, but how did you get control of the helo?"

"It all just sort of happened, I guess. Once I realized I'd survived the jump, I stuck the little girl on a seat and strapped her in. She was crying and screaming, but I finally convinced her I was one of the good guys, and she calmed down a little. Dr. Glock and I had a conversation with the pilot and made him understand he was no longer the pilot in command."

"Did you kill him?" Barry asked.

Disco shook his head. "No, but he's going to have a monster headache when he wakes up."

"Good thinking," I said. "Being the only survivor of the kidnapping attempt, he'll be the sole source of info during the interrogation."

Disco said, "That was my thinking, exactly. At one point, I wished we were close enough to Guantanamo Bay to drop him off with our old friend, Van Halen. If anyone can do it, he'd be the guy to get pilot-boy to talk."

"Maybe we should make that suggestion to the Norfolk PD."

Barry lifted an eyebrow. "You guys are a trip. Is it always like this?"

"No," Disco and I said in unison. "It's usually a lot more exciting, and we're rarely this serious."

We pulled through the airport gate, and I pointed toward our plane. "That's our Citation."

Our new captain let out a long, low whistle. "Nice."

"It's no Gulfstream, but it's not a bad ride."

Barry said, "Do you keep full-time pilots on staff, as well?"

Disco chuckled. "Yep, around the clock. But they're some real jerks."

With Captain Barry, Chief Engineer Big Bob, Probationary Executive Officer Greg, and Yeoman Purser Ronda nestled into the plush leather seats, Disco and I wriggled our way into the cockpit.

He pulled the checklist from the pouch, but before we fully assumed the role of charter pilots, I laid a hand on the checklist.

"All kidding aside, that was some real hero stuff you pulled back there. You probably saved that girl's life, you know."

He slid the book from beneath my hand. "We've got a plane to fly."

The southbound flight was short, thanks to a nice low-pressure system off the East Coast, generating a ninety-knot tailwind for us at thirty-six thousand feet.

We marshaled our ship's officers onto the ramp, and Disco tugged the Citation into the hangar.

Barry gave me a playful shove. "Your pilots are jerks, huh?"

"Oh, we are. Give it time. You'll see."

Skipper met us in the ops center, and introductions were made. She took the floor. "Welcome aboard the crazy train, guys. Your baptism by fire earlier today was just the tip of the iceberg. Now, let's get down to business." She scanned the room. "Forgive me if I get your names wrong. You're Ronda, the purser, right?"

Ronda nodded. "Yes, that's me . . . Ronda, no H. I was a CPA in the real world, but January through April fifteenth made me want to kill everybody in the office, so I jumped ship and jumped *on* a ship."

Skipper sighed. "That's so good. Whatever the opposite of an accountant is, I'm that. It's going to be great having you around. You and I will spend some time together privately to go over the mind-numbing process of getting everyone paid and keeping the ship's finances out of the red."

Ronda said, "That's a dream-come-true for me, just as long as I don't have to file anyone's taxes next spring."

Skipper flipped a page in her notepad. "So, for the rest of you, you'll see the ship for the first time tomorrow morning. From the dock, she looks like the *Lori Danielle*'s twin, but that's where the similarities end. I think you're going to love the interior. Any questions?"

Barry's eyes scanned the room. "Oh, yeah. I've got about a billion questions, but we'll start with this one. How long will the Northrop Grumman team be aboard with us?"

Skipper pointed at me. "That's a question for the boss."

I said, "They'll stay until we don't need them anymore. Once your team is up to speed and has the design team's phone numbers memorized, we'll kick them off the boat and go to work. We have an urgent mission pending, so I expect your team to climb that learning curve at full speed. We don't drag our feet around here."

Skipper couldn't resist. "Well, in your case, Chase, we don't drag our *foot*."

I ignored the jab. "Come on. I'll show you around the house, and you can pick a bedroom."

Big Bob, the chief engineer, spoke up for the first time. "You mean we're not sleeping on the boat?"

"Not tonight," I said. "You'll get a real bed for the night, but don't get used to it."

He chewed on his upper lip. "When can I see the library?"

I thought about the odd question. "Right now, if you want."

Big Bob grunted. "Yeah, I want."

His size made me push the elevator call button, but he didn't stop to wait for the ride. He started down the stairs behind me, mumbling something about ships not having elevators.

I led the seasoned marine engineer down the hall and into my favorite room of the house. "All right. Here it is."

"Here what is?"

"The library."

He shook his head and huffed. "What kind of jackass would want to see a room called a library? I need to see the specs, the service manuals, the design sheets, and anything else you've got about the engines." He waved his arms around the library. "Nobody cares about all this."

"In my defense, you did say you wanted to see the library."

"I did, but I guess I need to get used to picking my words a little more precisely. Say, are you an Agency guy like Stinnett?"

"Nope. I'm a nobody from nowhere who knows nothing."

"That's what I thought. Why ain't you the captain?"

I gave him a wink. "We covered that. I'm nobody from nowhere who knows . . . "

"Yeah, yeah, I get it. I guess I'll take that rack now. I'll need some sleep if I'm going to put up with you, and people like you, for the rest of my life."

I installed Big Bob in a bedroom and showed the rest of the team the house. With the tour complete and everyone situated in their own rooms, it was time for a call to the West Coast.

Penny answered on the second ring and immediately burst into action. "Have you seen the news? Can you believe it? Who would do such a thing?"

When she paused to take a breath, I said, "I've not seen any news today. What's going on?"

"Somebody tried to kidnap the daughter of some shipping tycoon from an old hotel in Norfolk."

"Oh, yeah. I heard about that. I think it was the guy's granddaughter, though. From what I hear, it all worked out, but a bunch of the kidnappers got shot."

"The world is a scary place. Anyway, how are you? What have you been doing today? How's the new boat?"

"It's been a boring day for the most part. We picked up the new officers and brought them home with us so they can be on board for the trip north. The ship is impressive. I can't wait for you to see it. How's the make-believe world in California?"

"Still make-believe. I can't wait to see it, either. Where did you have to go to pick up the officers?"

The word fell out of my mouth before I could stop it. "Norfolk."

"Norfolk? That's where the kidnapping happened."

"*Attempted* kidnapping."

I silently hoped she hadn't put it together, but hoping something slipped past Penny's brain was like hoping the world would stop turning.

She gasped. "Chase, no! Was that Disco in the helicopter?"

"We didn't volunteer. We were victims of circumstances . . . Wrong place, wrong time."

"It sounds to me like the right place, right time, as far as that little girl is concerned."

"We got lucky again."

"Who did you have with you?"

"It was just Disco and me, but that's enough. The odds were heavily in our favor."

"Eight dead bodies and one unconscious pilot sounds like nine against two."

"See? I told you the odds were in our favor. I just wanted to call and tell you good night. We're heading to sea tomorrow morning, so it might be a couple of days before we get to talk again."

"Okay. I understand. Please be safe. I love you."

"I love you too, sweetheart, and we're always safe . . . mostly."

* * *

Morning yawned and stretched its way across the Atlantic and shone its light on a kitchen full of people at Bonaventure. By the time I poured my first cup of coffee, everyone had been introduced, and conversation ensued.

With breakfast behind us, I called Commander Tapper for a ride to the base. Instead of sending a subordinate, the commander himself picked us up in a crew van that was only slightly undersized.

"We may have to strap Mongo to the top," Hunter said.

The giant snatched Hunter from his feet in a massive bear hug. "You can sit on my lap, little man."

The antics continued, but we finally poured out of the van as if we were a troop of clowns exiting a tiny car in the center ring.

"There she is," I said with my arms outstretched toward our ship.

The ship's new officers took in every inch of the haze-gray behemoth, and Greg, the executive officer, said, "You were right, Chase. From here, she looks a lot like the *Lori Danielle*. Has she been christened yet?"

"Not yet. But I can't think of a reason *Lori Danielle* can't live on. Can you?"

Greg turned to Captain Sprayberry. "You always said you were going to command the *L.D.* if Old Man Stinnett would ever die. It sounds like you're getting your shot before the captain kicks the bucket."

Commander Tapper said, "I'll call the painters and inform Congress."

"Congress?" I asked. "What do they have to do with this?"

He spent the next ten minutes explaining the politics of christening a ship paid for by the American taxpayers. I stopped listening thirty seconds into his dissertation.

Once aboard, Big Bob vanished down a ladder to find his domain— the engine room. One of the Grumman technicians escorted Ronda No-H to her new office, and Barry and Greg sidled up to the console on the bridge.

I said, "How about we knuckle-draggers find someplace to play while the learning curve is being climbed up here on the bridge?"

My suggestion was well received, and my team headed for the stern deck. Hunter extended his arms, made airplane noises, and circled the helipad like a dying bird.

I laughed. "What are you doing? You look like an idiot."

"What? I'm playing Huey. The chopper is going to look great out here."

Disco sighed, and that caught my attention.

"What is it?"

He studied the pad for a while. "I don't know. The Huey would take up a lot of space out here. Is there any money in the budget for something smaller?"

Mongo said, "Something smaller? That's a terrible idea."

"Not necessarily," Disco said. "Are you guys familiar with the 'Loach' that the Night Stalkers at the One-Sixtieth Special Operations Aviation Regiment fly?"

I said, "I've seen them, but I've never been in one. It's based on the Hughes Five-hundred, right?"

"That's right," Disco said. "There are a lot of upgrades for the special ops version. It's officially designated as the MH-Six Little Bird. They added an extra blade to the main rotor, and they even hang guns on them. They make a variant that can carry the Hellfire or the FIM-Ninety-Two missile."

Mongo's eyes lit up. "I'd like to rescind my earlier objection. The Little Bird sounds great."

Every eye turned to me as if I could conjure a special ops chopper out of thin air. "I'll see what I can do, but no promises."

We explored the ship and finally ended up by the moon pool.

"This may be my favorite part," I said. "I still don't know what we'll do with it, but it's going to be fun."

The rocking motion of the ship told me we'd left the protected waters of Cumberland Sound for the North Atlantic.

Hunter said, "They're going to fly on the foils again, aren't they?"

"Probably," I said. "I can't wait to see it from this perspective."

Mongo explained, "They can't run high-speed ops or fly the hull with the moon pool open. The opening in the hull would cause too much turbulence and resistance."

Just as his physics lesson concluded, the bay doors of the moon pool moved slowly into place.

I said, "Once again, it looks like the big guy is correct."

Disco shot a thumb toward the ladder. "Let's go up on deck and see how it looks from up there."

By the time we reached the open deck, the bridge crew had the new *Lori Danielle* soaring across the water like a flying fish. With the massive vessel nearly matching the speed of the Mark V, the capabilities the ship gave my team were practically limitless.

Mongo pulled off his hat and leaned over the rail. "At this speed, we'll make Norfolk before dark."

I said, "Surely we won't stay on foils for six hundred miles."

* * *

Mongo's prediction wasn't completely accurate, but he didn't miss it by much. We laid alongside, just astern of Captain Stinnett's partially dismantled boat in Norfolk, ninety minutes before midnight.

The next two days were spent initiating the crew and taking on any piece of the original *Lori Danielle* we thought we might be able to use. To my surprise, the loading and set up of the medical equipment went flawlessly, and our deck crane proved to offer more than twice the hoisting capability as the original.

Chief Engineer Big Bob finally found the library he wanted so desperately, and Ronda, our yeoman purser, had her office in ship-shape with the initial accounting organized in pristine order.

All in all, everyone on and around our ship seemed to have discovered their life's purpose . . . except me.

Chapter 19
The Cruelty of Time

By the end of day two on the pier, I proved to be nothing short of a hindrance on deck, so Mongo said, "Let's go below. I've got something for you."

I followed the mountain of a man down the series of ladders until we reached the moon pool, where the bay doors lay open, giving us a perfect view of the filthy black water of Willoughby Bay. I stared into the water and wondered if it was filthy enough to walk on.

Mongo obviously noticed. "Don't worry. The tide is coming in. It'll look a lot better in an hour."

"It certainly can't look any worse."

"Forget about the water for a minute and have a seat."

Trusting Mongo completely, I plopped down on an aluminum seat welded to the bulkhead. "Whatever you say."

He pulled two large, zippered bags from a rack and unzipped the first one. From inside, he pulled out a single swim fin identical to the ones I'd dived with for years.

"That looks familiar," I said.

He laid a hand on the upper half of the fin. "From here down, it looks familiar, but take a look at this." He revealed the upper portion of the fin with a neoprene bootie protruding from the binding.

"Let me guess. The neoprene isn't really neoprene."

"Good guess. It's a flexible polymer-coated sock guaranteed to keep the delicate electronics of your ankle bone-dry."

"Really? *Bone*-dry? That's what we're going with?"

He shrugged. "It wasn't intentional, but it was apropos."

I snatched the sock from his hand and shucked off my boot. The sock was far stiffer than neoprene, but I managed to wrangle it across my robot foot and several inches up the prosthetic.

Mongo inspected the fit. "How does it feel?"

I grabbed the fin and bounced it off his head. "Bone-dry was bad enough, but now you want me to tell you how a rubber sock *feels* on my metal foot?"

He palm-slapped his forehead. "I guess that was a bone-headed question, huh?"

"You're worse than Clark."

Mongo grabbed his chest. "Ouch! Right through the heart. And I thought you cared . . ."

"Everybody knows you don't have a heart. You left it with Irina and Tatiana."

He almost blushed. "Well, maybe."

I uncrossed my legs and placed my socked robot on the deck. "That's a new look for you, my friend. How serious is it with Irina?"

He stared down into the moon pool for a moment, laid the fin on the deck, and joined me on the metal bench. "It's not just with Irina."

"There's someone else? I didn't see that coming."

"No, not like that. It's Tatiana. I'm in love with both of them. Irina is everything any man could want. She's smart, funny, beautiful, and loyal."

"I know that feeling, big guy. I married one of those, too, and she gets better every day."

"I know you did, but mine comes with a bonus. Little Tatiana makes me believe in humanity. You and I see the worst the world has to offer, but when that little girl looks up at me and knows I'll never let anyone hurt her, that's indescribable."

The smile came and wouldn't leave. I said, "She's not a little girl anymore. She'll graduate in a couple of years and probably head off to college."

His eyes glazed over as if imagining a future without Tatiana "Little Anya" Volkovna. "Yeah, but your timeline is a little off. If she were the typical American high school student, she'd graduate in a couple of years, but she's anything but typical. She'll graduate later this year, and she's already been accepted into schools all over the world. She chose Juilliard in New York City."

I raised an eyebrow. "Juilliard? That sounds expensive."

He grinned. "Not when you're the best amateur ballerina in the country. They offered her a full scholarship. Every school she applied to made the same offer, but none were as prestigious."

"Please tell me you're not moving to New York City."

"Don't be ridiculous," he said. "New York City would drive me to drinking. You know how I am when it comes to crowds."

I wiped my brow with a make-believe handkerchief. "Whew. That was a close one."

Out of the blue, he blurted out, "I'm going to ask her to marry me."

"Wow! Does she know you're going to ask?"

He shrugged his enormous shoulders. "Tatiana knows. I talked to her about it, and she swore she wouldn't tell her mother, but I doubt she could keep the secret. Irina hasn't said anything, but Tatiana probably told her."

"Congratulations, my friend. That's fantastic news. Are you planning to live in the house in Athens?"

He seemed to consider the question. "Probably not. That's one of the things I wanted to talk about with you. I want us to move to Saint Marys to be close to the team."

"I think that's the best idea you've had in a long time. When are you going to pop the question?"

He held up a pair of island-sized palms. "I don't know. With the new ship and the mission to find your brother, it may be a while."

"Do you have a ring yet?"

He chuckled. "Yeah, I have one, and it's the most expensive thing I've ever bought. Thanks to you, I can afford stuff like that now."

I shook him off. "It's not thanks to me. You earned every penny and then some. I do have an idea if you're up for it."

He cocked his head. "Let's hear it."

I patted the bulkhead of our new weapon of war. "We have to christen the boat. You know, break the champagne bottle over the bow and officially name her."

"Yeah, I know. I've seen it done a couple of times. Is Penny going to break the bottle?"

"Not exactly. I thought maybe Tatiana could do it."

His typical expression of happiness doubled in intensity. "Are you serious? She'd love that. And her mother would love it even more."

"Oh, yeah. I'm serious. But that's not where the idea ends. What better time to ask Irina to marry you than when she least expects it?"

His expression grew. "That's a fantastic idea. When we get back from Guatemala—"

"No, don't wait. Do it before we leave."

The grin on his face was impossibly infectious, and I almost forgot about the rubber sock on my prosthetic.

He yanked me from the bench as if I were a rag doll and pulled me into a hug from which neither man nor beast could escape. When he finally let go of me, he said, "Let's get back to work. You have to see the fin I built."

I glanced down at the device. "What do you mean, you built it? It's the same fin I've used for years."

"It may look like the original, but it has a few features the boys at ScubaPro never thought of." He patted his leg. "Put your prosthetic foot up here."

I awkwardly turned and put my robot on his thigh. "This feels a little weird."

"Relax. I knew you when you had two feet, so we go way back. Now, point your toes as if you were swimming."

The neural transmitter surgically implanted just above my knee received the signal from my brain to point my imaginary toes. It then sent the instructions wirelessly to the receiver built into my prosthetic, setting the servo motors in motion. The metallic foot tilted away, but only about half the required angle for proper swimming with fins.

"That's the best I can do."

He lifted the fin from the deck and slid it onto my robot. The angle looked unnatural and awkward.

"That's no good. I'll never be able to produce any thrust at that angle."

Mongo held up a finger. "Just watch."

He squeezed a pair of recessed buttons near the binding, and the blade of the fin fell another thirty degrees. "How does that look?"

I lifted my finned foot from his leg and examined the work. "That's perfect."

"There's no way to know if it's perfect until we get in the water, so suit up."

I shot a look into the moon pool that had previously looked more like coffee than clear water. "I guess you were right. It *is* clearing up."

We donned wetsuits and scuba gear, and Mongo pressed the intercom on the forward bulkhead of the space. "Bridge, moon pool."

A disembodied voice came through the speaker. "Go ahead, moon pool."

Mongo said, "Splashing two divers. Expected recovery in twenty minutes."

The speaker announced, "Roger. Control locks in position. Report divers aboard."

"Roger."

We pulled on our full face masks with internal comms, and Mongo slid into the water. "Have a seat on the edge, and let your feet dangle into the water."

I did as he instructed, and he made small adjustments to the fin. When he finished, he slapped the edge of the foot God gave me. "All right, come on in. The water's fine."

I pressed off the deck and slipped into the water. The feeling of taking breaths underwater again was like freedom from prison. I had forgotten the peaceful solace of being engulfed by the ocean and experiencing a whole new world on the same old planet.

After several minutes hovering motionless beneath the ship, Mongo's voice filled my ears. "I thought you might need a minute to just enjoy being wet again. How does it feel?"

"I can't describe it. Thank you for making it possible."

"Let's start with some range-of-motion exercises to make sure your Electro-Foot Two-Thousand works under pressure."

I chuckled. "I think we just christened my robot."

"I think you're right. Now, let's see you wiggle it . . . just a little bit. Hey, that could be a song."

I drew my foot upward and back down in full range of motion. Although the left and right rotation of the ankle wasn't necessary for swimming, I wanted to know it still worked, so I turned the foot through the few degrees of rotation, and it worked just as it did above the surface.

"Looks good," Mongo said. "Let's go for a swim."

"Let's go," I repeated. "I'd like to see the foils near the bow."

Mongo held out a hand. "After you, sir."

I kicked for the front of the ship, and Mongo fell in behind me. The swimming came easily and felt almost natural. Reaching the forward foil, I examined the wing and tried to imagine how it would look in the fully extended position.

"What do you think?" Mongo asked.

"It's fascinating. Let's go have a look at the props and the aft foil."

He repositioned himself behind me again. "Lead the way."

I finned for the stern and rolled onto my back as we passed the moon pool. Seeing into the belly of the ship from the depths was an eerie sight. I continued aft and examined the retracted hydrofoil. Its design was vastly different from the forward foil, and it was retracted almost flush with the hull. The Azipods containing the massive propellers loomed above us and appeared to belong to a much larger vessel than our ship.

Mongo said, "I'll race you back to the moon pool."

Without a word, I kicked with all my strength and tucked my hands against my body to improve my streamlined position. My initial burst of speed put me several feet in front of Mongo, but his strength and oversized fins allowed him to quickly catch me. He grabbed my biological ankle and yanked me backward as he swam past. As his right foot passed my shoulder, I reached out and unfastened his fin. It slipped from his foot right into my hand, and I kicked away from my dive partner with three times the number of fins he had left.

Having cheated, I arrived back at the moon pool several seconds ahead of my competition. When the big lug finally climbed from the water, he was grinning from ear to ear.

"What's so funny?" I asked. "You lost the race."

He shucked off his buoyancy compensator and laid it on the deck. "I may have failed at winning the race, but I succeeded in making you forget you were wearing a robotic foot. Welcome back! We missed you underwater."

I stared down at my feet, still shod with matching fins, and I saw no difference between the two limbs. Beneath the plastic, rubber, and neoprene, all things were equal, and I was temporarily whole again . . . at least physically.

Time doesn't heal all wounds; it only offers more snares and strokes, causing us to forget the pain of the original blows. No, healing doesn't happen. We merely harden and grow more calloused until the cruelty of time finally pours out more than our fragile bodies and minds can endure, and our presence on Earth realizes its end.

The sound of Mongo's voice yanked me from my momentary foray into the depths of my psyche. "Bridge, moon pool. All divers aboard. Mission complete."

Chapter 20
What's in a Name?

"What are we doing here?"

Although I believed I'd spoken the words only in my mind, they seemed to fall from my mouth, and suddenly, I had the whole team's attention.

Hunter said, "We're wasting time, as far as I'm concerned."

Heads nodded, and groans of agreement rose.

"Why didn't any of you say something?" I asked in disbelief.

Tony said, "I didn't bring it up because I'm the new guy, and my opinion ain't worth squat."

I held up a finger. "First, that's not true. You *are* the new guy, but you've just been through fourteen months of some of the most intense training anyone ever endures. We've all been there, but it's been a while. That stuff is still fresh in your head. That alone gives your opinions merit, but that's not all . . . All of our life experiences are different. Yours was in the water in life-or-death scenarios. We don't have that on our résumés. When something comes up that doesn't smell right, speak up. Nobody's going to yell at you."

Hunter jumped in the mix. "Easy there, Chase. There's a better-than-good chance I'll yell at him."

"Okay, I'll give you that. But it's not like you matter. You were in the Air Force."

It was Disco's turn to pile on. "Hey! That's, well . . . true. Never mind."

I tapped my heel on the deck. "Does anyone have a good reason why we should be here?"

A chorus of silent shrugs resounded.

"In that case, it's time for me to repeat the same speech I give before every mission. I'm going to Guatemala to find the man who is, likely, my brother. Every one of you has a skill set that offers something meaningful to that mission. I'm asking you to come with me, but you are under no obligation to do so. If you're in, roll up your gear, and let's go. If you're out, we'll see you when we get back."

Singer eyed Mongo and said, "I guess now that Clark is gone, you and I are the senior guys since we've been here longer than anyone else."

I'll never know the point Singer was about to make when Skipper stopped him in his tracks. "You two may be the senior *men* on the team, but I was here long before we ever knew you two existed. So, that means I'm the senior person . . . next to Chase, of course."

Singer curtsied. "Of course, your highness. We yield back the balance of our time."

"Thank you, peasant. Now, as the *real* senior member of the team, I'd like to say that we are officially tired of that speech. We're all in, all the time, every time, so just tell us where we're going and who we're chasing."

I slapped my knees and stood. "In that case, that's the last time you'll hear that speech . . . today. There is one thing we have to do before we head for Central America, though."

I did my best Vanna White impression and motioned toward our quarter-billion-dollar warship. "This young girl needs a name, and naming a ship takes a ceremony. Since we aren't ready to take our ship to the ceremony, we'll have to settle for the next best thing and bring the ceremony to the ship. I've arranged for the people we care about the most to be here tomorrow morning, so by noon, the second Research Vessel *Lori Danielle* will get her first taste of champagne and broken glass."

Tony wrinkled his brow. "Research vessel?"

That earned a chuckle from the team, and Hunter threw an arm across his shoulders. "You'll learn soon, kid. In this business, things are rarely what they appear to be. Look at you, for example. You look like a combat-hardened freedom fighter, but underneath it all, you're just a soft little Coastie."

Tony stood. "Come on, old man. Get in the water with me, and we'll see who's soft."

Hunter waved him off. "I'll pass. Chase likes you, and Skipper loves you, so I don't want to hurt you again."

Even though I was amused by the banter, I called it to a halt and pulled Tony aside. "I know you don't want to be captain, but I want you to have at least the basic skill to move and dock the ship. You have more ship-handling experience than the rest of us combined, so that duty falls to you. In time, we'll all learn it, but I need you up to speed now. Are you okay with that?"

"Absolutely. I've been sitting in on the bridge for the past couple of days while Captain Barry and the XO are training on systems and procedures. I'll head up there now and shadow them for the rest of the day."

"Excellent. We'll get you some actual hands-on time as we go along. The more we know, the more capable we are. There's one more covert operation I need from you."

He cocked his head. "Covert op?"

"Yes, I need you to watch Barry and Greg, the XO. If you pick up on anything you don't like about how they operate, I need to know about it. They're going to be in command of the ship, but we are in command of the missions. If you get the slightest hint that either of them can't handle that power structure, I want to head it off before it becomes an issue."

"You got it, Chase. I'll keep my eyes open, but so far, I don't see anything to worry about from either of them."

He bounded up the gangway for his assignment that was less of a mission and more of an attempt to keep him out of Skipper's hair. Young love is far too much distraction for two people who are critical to the success of an operation.

* * *

With the arrangements made and loved ones delivered, the small but distinguished crowd gathered near the bow of the United States' most recent attempt at a masquerade. The deceptively demure-looking ship lay alongside the pier at Kings Bay Naval Submarine Base, looking out of place among the pair of surfaced nuclear submarines also resting beside the pier.

The classified operation of the base made access challenging, even for a team of tier-one operators with some of the highest security clearances anyone could hold. Getting a former Russian national and her teenage daughter aboard the base nearly took an act of Congress. Thankfully, I had such an act practically in my back pocket.

Congressman David Solomon of Tennessee and Congressman James "Jimmy" Paige of Pennsylvania pulled the requisite strings to hustle the unknowing guests of honor through the checkpoints staffed by highly trained, extremely well-armed security officers, who seemed still a bit dubious of the congressmen's demand.

Congressmen Paige and Solomon had been abducted by an international team of terrorists two years before, and my team did what we did best: we captured or killed the entire team and recovered the hostages—including the congressmen—relatively unharmed. It would be a long time before those particular lawmakers forgot the team of ragtag operators who snatched them from the jaws of near-certain death. Having friends in high places tended to transform a great many denials into approvals with the drop of a name and the wave of a hat.

Although not officially a member of our team, Tatiana "Little Anya" Volkovna took the temporary stage constructed specifically to allow access to the sharp-pointed bow of the warship hiding behind the demure veil of a research vessel. In her slightly Russian-accented English, Tatiana raised the bottle of Dom Pérignon and declared, "As prescribed by the Congress of the United States of America, I christen this vessel R.V. *Lori Danielle* and commend her into the service of this great nation."

With that, she swung the bottle as if swinging on a hanging curveball and driving it over the leftfield wall. The four-hundred-dollar bottle of champagne exploded in a flurry of flying green glass and white alcoholic foam. We cheered, and from somewhere, a recording of a brass band played its ceremonial refrain.

The officers and crew who'd become members of our team, as if delivered from on high, shook hands and exchanged the age-old expression of accepting a ship from her previous crew. The engineers and technicians of Northrop Grumman wore the expressions of men and women who were proud to have delivered a weapon that possessed the potential to change the world in the coming decades, and our crew willingly stepped into the armor of such a noble edict.

As the cheers diminished to a dull roar, Tatiana looked down and caught my eye. I gave her a knowing wink and turned to Mongo, the mighty oak of a man who was wrapped like a ribbon around the pinky finger of a tiny ballerina and her mother.

I said, "Take your Russian queen up there with your princess to get their pictures taken by the bow."

A bead of nervous sweat rolled down the giant's face. In all the years I'd worked beside him, I'd never seen him show any outward sign of fear or anxiety.

I reached up and wiped the bead of sweat from his face. "It's not that hot, big man. Why are you sweating?"

He gave me a shove and ushered Irina up the temporary stairs to the platform where Tatiana stood. Captain Sprayberry stuck two fingers into the corners of his mouth and blew the long, shrill tone he'd mastered so well. The whistle hushed the revelry and sent every head turning to the stage.

With the crowd hushed, the captain said, "There's one more thing we need to take care of before we take our ship to sea. The *Lori Danielle* isn't the only beautiful girl getting a new name this morning. Mongo, the stage is all yours."

The most physically powerful man I'd ever known took a shaking knee before the two women he loved more than anyone on Earth and pulled a small velvet box from the pocket of his cargo pants. The gentle voice that had stricken terror into the minds of evildoers all over the globe cracked and trembled as the words he'd practiced dozens of times left him, and he was reduced to pure loving emotion.

"Irina Volkovna, I would like . . . I mean, if you would . . ."

Irina pressed her lips into a thin line, and tears rolled from her eyes like fountains. Involuntarily, she bounced on her toes as if beseeching the man she loved to finally find the words and ask the question.

The frozen mammoth shook and flashed every shade of red imaginable. Tatiana stepped forward, leaned to Mongo's ear, and whispered something. Whatever it was, it worked.

Mongo cleared his throat, held out the glistening diamond ring, and spoke in flawless Russian. "Irina Volkovna, *ty vyydesh' za menya zamuzh?*"

Irina leapt into his arms, completely ignoring the ring. "*Da! Da!* Yes, yes, a thousand times, yes!"

If the cheers following the christening of the ship were loud, the roar after Mongo's proposal could be heard on the moon.

Chapter 21

A Real Job

When the guests scattered and only our great big family remained behind, Irina spent an hour with her left hand sticking out in front of her so everyone could marvel at the unbelievable diamond Mongo had chosen. "Is perfect, yes?"

Penny took Irina's hand in hers, inspected the ring, and then eyed me as if I needed to step up my game. "Yes, it is. Mongo always does everything bigger and grander than everyone around him."

The eyes returned, and I looked away.

Penny hugged Irina. "Congratulations, and welcome to the family. I've never been a bridesmaid, but I'm up for the task. I know some great party planners in L.A. I'll make sure you have the best bridal shower, ever."

"I hate to break up the party," I said, "but some of us have a real job."

Penny turned and threw her arms around me. "You know I love my ring. I'd never even entertain the idea of replacing it. But . . . I wouldn't be mad if you bought my diamond some friends to play with."

"We all need friends," I said.

She kissed me and whispered, "I'm sorry, but I have to get back to L.A. I've got a deal working that you won't believe."

"I can't wait to hear about it. Be safe, and try not to get any Hollywood on you."

She giggled. "Try not to get any Guatemala on you."

It took ten minutes to gather the team and our two top sailors into the ship's ops center.

"By the way, you landlubbers," Captain Sprayberry began, "it's not an ops center aboard a ship. It's a CIC—combat information center."

The space was cramped, but we managed to pile inside, and I started the briefing. "Gentlemen and ladies, this will be a two-part mission briefing. The first half is for the ship's officers, and the second is for everyone. Any questions before we get rolling?"

None came, so I continued. "Captain Sprayberry will conduct the shakedown cruise with the Northrop Grumman team on board. I want you to shake it 'til the bolts rattle loose. If you don't break something on the shakedown, you didn't push it hard enough. The boat has flaws. All vessels do. It's up to you to find them, fix them, and retest them. Got it?"

The captain nodded in silent understanding.

"Where's Big Bob, the engineer?" I asked.

The grizzly curmudgeon poked his head around Mongo. "I'm back here, and meetings are a waste of time when there's work to be done."

"Thanks for the input, but this one is necessary. I want you to push every system on board this ship beyond its designed limits. I want to know her real capabilities—not the limits the engineers wrote in that library of yours."

He grunted. "Like I said, meetings are a waste of time. I was going to do that before you said it, but now that it's an order, I'm not responsible for melting anything down. That one's on you now. But you'll have your hard limits."

"There's one more issue I want to cover before moving on to

part two. We don't have a weapons officer, but we have a nice stable of things that go boom. Commander LaGrange designed the weapons systems, so there's nobody on Earth who knows them better. He'll retire from the Navy in less than sixty days. I'm considering bringing him on board as our weapons officer. Any objections?"

The executive officer raised a finger. "I was weps aboard a destroyer and a missile frigate before the Agency recruited me out of the Navy."

I studied the XO. "Is that an objection?"

"No, sir. I'm only saying that I'm a qualified weapons officer until Commander LaGrange comes aboard."

I turned to Barry. "That one is yours to figure out. You're the captain. If you want LaGrange, he's yours. If not, you can start shopping for a weapons officer or demote your XO. It's up to you."

Captain Sprayberry shook his head. "There's no decision to be made there, Chase. I want LaGrange, but I want Long John to back him up."

"Long John?"

"Yeah, that's what we call Greg Silver, the XO."

"I like it. I'll send LaGrange to talk with you. I'm going to stay out of your way when it comes to the operation of your ship, but when the mission dictates, the application of the ship's capabilities is my decision. Are there any questions about that?"

Heads shook, so I said, "Very well. That brings us to part two. From now on, to avoid confusion, I'll refer to the officers and crew as 'the ship's complement' and the rest of us as 'the tactical team.' The tactical team is departing today. We have a real-world mission in Central America. The details of the mission aren't important, but you'll be briefed in when you have a need to know. For now, plan to rendezvous with us on the Caribbean Coast of Guatemala in Amatique Bay at Puerto Barrios. Are you familiar?"

Barry said, "There aren't many Central American ports I'm not familiar with. The port commander at Barrios smokes Cohibas and drinks Canadian Mist."

"Canadian Mist? Don't they have some rancid water or something out of a toilet bowl to drink down there?"

Captain Barry shrugged. "It's what he likes."

"In that case, I recommend taking on a couple of boxes of Cohibas and a case of Canadian Mist. I'll let you know when to pick us up."

The captain pulled a notepad from his pocket and scratched a couple of lines. "Will it be a hot exfil?"

I stared at the overhead for a moment. "I don't know yet. Depending on how things go in the jungle, it could go either way."

Barry made more notes. "In that case, we'll rig for a hot exfiltration and have a plan for a covert exit if necessary."

"I'm starting to understand why Captain Stinnett holds you in such high regard, Captain."

Ignoring the compliment, he said, "Godspeed, guys. We'll be ready when you need a ride. Oh, and from what I understand, we're capable of softening a target up to fifty miles inland."

My interest was instantly piqued. "Fifty miles, you say . . . Statute or nautical?"

He lowered his gaze. "We're sailors, Chase."

"Nautical it is. Skipper will be in touch to set up comms. Consider her to be the CIC ashore and aboard."

He put on a smile. "I picked up on that. She sounds handy to have around."

"You have no idea how right you are, but you'll soon see just how irreplaceable she is." I let the statement hang in the air for a moment before saying, "That's all I have. Does anyone have anything for me?"

No one spoke up, so I said, "Enjoy the ship. We're off to see the Lizard."

* * *

Back at Bonaventure, the mission load-out continued, but so did the uncertainty. I watched the indecision as every member of the team pulled weapon after weapon from the racks and replaced them, exchanging each for something lighter, until I stepped in.

"I wish I knew what to tell you about what we're up against in Guatemala, but it's a huge mystery to all of us. I want Singer to bring something long and accurate. I want at least three M-Fours in case we get pinned down. I'm taking a pair of Glock Nineteens and two hundred rounds. If you want something heavier than an M-Four, be willing to hump it all over the jungle. We may find my brother the day we put boots on the ground, or we may run out of beans, bullets, and fresh water before we see any sign of him. Take what you need, but nothing more."

"How are we getting in-country?" asked Hunter

"The Citation," I said. We'll have to leave off some fuel and make at least one stop. If the wind is in our favor, we'll make Cancun and then hop to Guatemala."

Disco asked. "Are we still meeting that Diablo guy?"

"I've got Skipper and Ginger working on that right now. We were originally supposed to meet him in Puerto Grande on Bahía de Chismuyo in Honduras near the border with El Salvador, but that was a week ago. If they can find him, they'll arrange a new rendezvous, and we'll go wheels-up."

It took two vehicles to carry our gear and supplies from the Bonaventure armory to the airport, but we soon had everything loaded, and Disco was wearing out a calculator determining how much fuel we could carry with the cabin loaded to the gills.

He finally tossed the calculator over his shoulder. "We need a bigger airplane."

"That's not an option right now. How much gas can we take?"

"None. In fact, we can take negative one thousand pounds of gas, and I still don't think we'll get off the ground."

"So, how much gear do we need to offload?"

Disco wiped the sweat from his brow. "At least twelve hundred pounds."

I studied my team and played guess-my-weight like a carnival conman. "Hunter, Mongo, Singer, Tony . . . The four of you are flying commercial. Disco and I will bring the Citation and the gear."

Disco sighed. "As much as I hate to split up the team, I can't see another option. We could always take the Caravan, but then we'd have two airplanes twelve hundred miles from home."

I scratched my head and wiped a gallon of sweat from my neck. "That's not a bad idea. Having the Caravan dramatically increases our mobility in-country."

Hunter said, "That gives us a few extra pounds of gear, too."

I raised a hand. "No. Thirty seconds ago, all the gear you needed was on the Citation. What changed between then and now to make you need another piece of gear?"

He stammered. "Well, we . . . we have more room now."

I pointed toward his pants. "Tell me something. If I sewed an extra pocket on those pants, would you go find something to put in it?"

He shook his head and surrendered. "Fine. No more gear. But an extra pocket might be nice."

Doing some flight planning in my head, I said, "I want you to make an extra stop in Key West. I don't like the idea of you being over the middle of the Gulf of Mexico on fumes. Add a couple hundred miles to the trip, and make a fuel stop at Key West International. That'll be the cheapest insurance policy we can buy for crossing the Gulf."

"Sounds good to me. When do we leave?"

I pulled out my phone, and Skipper answered almost immediately. "We found him. I was just about to call you."

Before she could finish, I almost yelled into the phone. "You found my brother?"

She groaned. "Would you let me finish? We weren't looking for him. We were looking for Diablo, and we found him."

"Sorry. I'm a little anxious."

She sighed. "I understand. We'll get there, but step one is getting you and Diablo in the same room. There's a town on the southwestern coast of Guatemala called Puerto San Jose. It has a sixty-five-hundred-foot runway."

"That's plenty of concrete. We're taking both the Citation and the Caravan. We're too heavy with our load-out for the Citation alone."

"Thanks for letting me know. I'll include the Caravan in the mission parameters. Anyway, when you get to Puerto San Jose, I have you booked in the Gran Océano. Diablo will find you there. When are you going wheels-up?"

"As soon as this conversation ends. What else do you have for me?"

The sound of papers rustling wafted through the phone. "I took care of Immigration and Customs for you, and I have some satellite access, but the jungle canopy renders the satellites useless except for position tracking."

"Sounds good, Skipper. As always, you're the best."

She let out a sound that could've been a squeaky door hinge, and I asked, "What was that?"

"I was just thinking that maybe you need to take one more look through the armory to make sure you have everything. You know . . ."

I laughed. "How about I send Tony and let him take one last look before we leave?"

"Thank you, Chase."

Chapter 22
The Devil Is in the Details

A "sterile cockpit" is what the airline pilots call it, but Disco and I simply called it "smart flying." Once we lit the fires in the pair of turbines designed to push the Citation through the atmosphere at five hundred knots, we didn't talk about anything except flying the airplane until we reached cruising altitude. There's simply too much to do during the first few minutes of a flight to let our minds wander for even a few seconds.

From the right seat, my role was radio operator, navigator, and monitoring pilot. That would leave Disco having all the fun in the left seat by doing the hands-on flying. These roles were interchangeable and had nothing to do with our abilities in the cockpit. The division of responsibility served only to efficiently manage the demanding, high-tech flying carpet beneath us.

Disco's experienced hand pressed the throttles to the takeoff setting, and the turbines whistled their beautiful cry, starting our accelerating roll down the runway. Scanning the instrument panel, I gave the call, "Airspeed alive and building . . . seventy knots."

Disco checked his airspeed indicator and returned, "Crosschecked," confirming that both my instrumentation and his agreed.

Our acceleration down the long yet quickly vanishing runway ahead increased, and I made the speed calls. "V-One." The speed at which we were committed to flying changed with environmental and loading variables, but essentially, even if an engine failed above that speed, we would leave the planet and deal with the failure in the air rather than shutting down the engines and skidding off the end of the runway.

I called, "Rotate," and Disco pulled his right hand from the throttles and gripped the yoke to initiate our nosewheel's departure from the runway. An instant later, I called, "V-Two," indicating the airplane had built enough speed to safely and successfully climb with only one engine should the second one fail. Some pilots refer to this as the "takeoff safety speed."

At Disco's urging, the wings assumed the task that had previously been the burden of the landing gear, supporting the weight of the airplane, its cargo, and occupants.

When no usable runway remained in front of us and the airplane was climbing, Disco called, "Gear up," and I raised the landing gear handle. That small switch set a complex dance in motion. The electronics and hydraulics required to lift and stow the heavy landing gear were impossibly complex, yet one of the most critical and reliable systems on the airplane. A great many systems can fail on such a flying machine and never affect the safety of the flight, but the valves, hoses, hydraulic pumps, and switches of the landing gear system don't fall into that category.

Disco ordered, "Flaps up," and I raised the trailing edge blades of aluminum designed to increase the lifting force of the wings during times of relatively slow airspeed. As the speed increased once clear of the ground, the wings no longer needed any help from the flaps.

We continued our all-business process until reaching our cruising altitude of thirty-eight thousand feet, and the Citation lost her need for input from either of us. Aircraft of the complexity of our jet are nearly autonomous in cruise flight.

We touched down at Puerto San Jose long before the Caravan carrying the remainder of our team reached Key West for their first fuel stop. Just as promised, Skipper had already greased the wheels of customs and immigration. We were neither detained nor searched as we deplaned and stepped into the back of the waiting limo.

The Gran Océano looked like every tropical resort's advertising flier. Palm trees and tiny umbrellas atop rum drinks swayed in the constant breeze off the Pacific Ocean.

Disco spun in slow circles, trying to take in the beauty of the luxurious surroundings. "Why don't we run more missions in Guatemala?"

"I'm starting to think we should," I said.

A young hostess hired specifically to catch the eye—and the tipping instinct of every man on the property—led us to our expansive suite. My tipping instinct was impressed enough to do exactly what the young lady expected.

"Gracias, sir. Your luggage will arrive soon."

She closed the door behind her, and Disco and I stood in awe of the palatial suite.

"Skipper has done it again," I said.

Disco poured a pair of cocktails from the wet bar and handed one to me. "She always does."

We made our way to the balcony overlooking the acres of winding swimming pool and lazy river.

"You should bring Penny back here. She'd love this place."

I took the first sip of my bourbon. "Bring her? I'm thinking about selling Bonaventure and moving into this place."

We sat in silence for several minutes as the cubes of ice lost their fight with the warmth of the whiskey and we breathed in the sea breeze from what was, to us, a foreign ocean.

The doorbell chimed, and Disco pushed from his chair.

I put a hand on his forearm. "Relax. I'll get it. It's probably just our luggage."

He put up no argument, and I headed for the door. My guess was correct except for one small issue. The bellman rolled his cart into the suite and kicked a rubber stopper beneath the door. In local Spanish, he said, "Here is your luggage, sir."

I examined the four soft bags and discovered the zippers in precisely the same position we'd left them, but the one detail out of place still rested on the bellman's cart.

"Where would you like the trunk, sir?"

"The trunk isn't ours," I said, in Spanish more suited to Calle Ocho in Miami than the Pacific Coast of Guatemala.

The man nodded with great energy. "It was delivered for you, sir. They said you were expecting it, so I assure you it is yours and nobody else's."

Even though he didn't share the attributes of the hostess, I placed a folded bill in his palm, and he and his unladen cart vanished.

I stuck my head through the sliding glass door to the balcony. "Hey, Disco. Are you expecting a trunk?"

He looked up from his drink. "A trunk? What kind of trunk?"

"What difference does that make? You're either expecting one or you're not. Which is it?"

He placed his tumbler on the side table and rose from his lounger. He circled the trunk, eying every corner until he'd apparently seen all he needed. He pressed a knee against the edge of it and seemed surprised by the absence of excessive weight. "What is it?"

"I don't know," I admitted, "but the bellman insisted it was delivered for us. Open it up."

He leapt backward. "No! You open it."

I chuckled. "This is starting to feel like a Life cereal commercial. Let's get Mikey. He'll open anything."

I lifted my shirttail across my holster and gripped the handle of my Glock before manipulating the latch with the toe of my boot. Disco followed suit and drew his pistol to the low-ready position. I turned to him with questioning, raised eyebrows, and he nodded. I kicked open the lid and raised my pistol simultaneously, ready to destroy anything unfriendly.

The lid of the trunk flew backward and slapped against the side of the trunk. My finger flew to the trigger as the bright-white teeth of an impossibly wide grin shone on the brown-skinned face of the small man sitting cross-legged inside the trunk.

The urge to press the trigger diminished immediately, and I said, "Disco, meet Diablo de Agua."

Diablo leapt from the trunk and dusted himself off. "Hello, my friend. It's wonderful to see you again. It has been too many years."

His English was immeasurably better than my Spanish. I stuck out a hand. "It has, indeed, been too long. This is Disco."

He shook my hand and turned to examine the seasoned pilot.

Diablo shook Disco's hand with some obvious hesitation and turned back to me. "He is too old to do these things."

I laughed at the little man's lack of a filter. "Don't let the lines around his eyes fool you. Those lines are experience, not age. He's a gunslinger just like the rest of us."

Diablo said, "I am not a gunslinger."

"No, my friend, you are not. But that's only because you're more deadly than any gun ever built."

He waved a dismissive hand. "You flatter me, old friend. I also have such lines."

Disco frowned. "How long have you been in that trunk?"

Diablo glanced back at the box as if he'd never seen it. "I don't know . . . Maybe a long time, maybe not."

That was the best answer Disco would ever get from Diablo, and the look on his face said he had just reached the same conclusion. He shook off the non-answer and motioned toward the bar. "Would you care for a drink?"

Diablo asked, "Are you having one?"

"We are."

The Water Devil glanced between me and Disco. "I didn't ask if we are having a drink. I asked if *you* are having a drink."

"So you did," Disco said. "I guess it's true what they say about the devil. He really is in the details."

Diablo's grin returned. "I am alive all these years because of such details. I asked if you were drinking because this room is too big for only two people. This probably means there are more men to come before we begin finding the Lizard. If you are drinking, this means I am correct and you are waiting for the rest of your team. If only you and my old friend Chase are here and no more are coming, you would not be drinking. We would already be working."

Disco offered a barely visible nod of respect. "I'll pour you a drink."

Six hours later, after grilling Diablo about his dealing with the man who may share my DNA, my phone chirped. "Hey, Chase. It's Hunter. We're safe on deck, and there's a limo driver here at the airport who says he's here for us. Is he for real?"

"Consider it your last taste of civilization for a while. I know you're sensitive to spiders, snakes, and ingrown toenails. Just get in the limo. We'll see you in a few minutes. Oh, I almost forgot. The devil is among us."

The confusion in his tone was abundant. "What are you talking about?"

"You'll see soon enough, but there's no reason to be afraid of this particular devil . . . unless you're one of the bad guys."

The four remaining members of the team came through the door with disbelief and fascination in their eyes. "Is this really where we're staying?"

Disco handed each of them a tumbler and raised his own. "It's where we're *temporarily* staying, courtesy of Skipper."

Glasses were raised, and Hunter said, "Thank you, Skipper!"

Diablo materialized, and I jumped. "You've got to stop doing that."

"Doing what?"

"Showing up out of thin air."

Back came his toothy grin, and he pointed toward Mongo. "Can he fight?"

"That's quite an introduction," I said. "Guys, meet Diablo de Agua. Diablo, meet Hunter, Singer, Tony Tuna, and Mongo."

The Central American ninja seemed to ignore the introduction and asked again, "Can the big one fight?"

I studied the look on Diablo's face. It appeared to be sincere concern. "Yes, he can fight. All of us can fight. Why do you ask?"

He looked up at me, doubt filling his eyes. "You weren't so good at fighting last time you were here."

I hung my head. "I've learned a lot since then."

"We'll see. Fighting will be necessary. Mongo isn't the only one who'll be tested. He's just the biggest and most obvious threat. I hope you've learned the rule about eliminating the threat that appears most dangerous."

I gave our Southern Baptist sniper a wink and turned back to Diablo. "Mongo may be the biggest, but he's not the deadliest among us."

Diablo's trademark toothy grin returned as he surveyed my team. "You and I know this, my friend, but the people we are pursuing do not."

Chapter 23
The Big Picture

"There's no reason to keep everyone standing," I said. "Stow your gear, and we'll brief everyone in."

The team scattered and returned minutes later, devoid of their bags.

Surprisingly, Mongo was the first to speak. "Tell me about these people who are so anxious to mix it up with us."

Diablo situated himself on a cushion on the floor. "They aren't looking for a fight—at least not with us directly. They're always ready to fight, but they don't know about any of you yet."

"What about you?" I asked.

The Water Devil said, "Oh, yes, they know me. Or at least the part of me I want them to know."

"How hard will they be to find?" I asked.

"This depends on many things. First, we are talking about the Lizard as if he were a group of men. Of course, he is not. He is only one man, but he rarely works alone. His loyalty isn't to a team, though. It's to the money, drugs, and women his masters provide."

"His masters?"

Diablo nodded. "Not one master, but several. He will work for anyone and for any cause as long as the money, drugs, and beautiful women keep flowing."

"So, he's not an idealist?" Singer said.

"If you are asking if he has a political agenda, the answer is no. He is not an idealist except to the extent of his own hedonism."

Hunter tossed a bottle of water to me. "This guy sounds like your alter ego, Chase."

Diablo said, "Not alter ego. More like, evil twin. I knew this man the instant I saw him. It was like looking directly at you, my old friend, with one exception . . ."

He had everyone's attention. "He has a darkness about him. I don't say these things to discourage you or hurt you. It is important that you understand what kind of man the Lizard is. You will not walk up and shake his hand. We will track him like a panther tracks his prey and seize him when he least expects it."

"How?" I asked.

Diablo furrowed his brow. "How what?"

"How will we track him? Do you know where he is?"

The little man scratched the back of his hand and inspected the skin. "This is an omen here in the jungle. If the palm itches, soon come riches, but if it's the back, beware the attack."

"I never pegged you as the superstitious type."

Diablo glared into my soul. "Watch the hair on the neck of the cat or dog when danger approaches. It stands on end because their senses are heightened." He waved his arms around the room. "All of you live a life of comfort in places like this, so your senses aren't the same as mine. I live among the cats and monkeys, where instinct is often the only thing separating me from the carcasses rotting on the jungle floor."

The air in the room suddenly felt heavy and humid against my skin. "I have to admit I may have come down here a little less prepared than I should've been. We're a strong, capable team, but I wouldn't trade the life of anyone in this room for my brother—if he is, in fact, my brother at all."

Diablo sighed. "This is the decision you must make, my friend. I cannot make it for you. I will not promise I can bring all of you back from the jungle, but I will try." His words trailed off, and he locked eyes with our newest recruit. "You are Tony, correct?"

Tony nodded. "That's right."

Diablo crossed the room and took our rescue swimmer's hand in his. "These are not the hands of a killer. These are hands for healing. You are the medic?"

Tony pulled his hand from Diablo's and turned to Hunter as if begging to be rescued from whatever he'd fallen into.

Hunter threw up his hands. "I'm not pulling you out of this one, Tuna. Good luck."

Tony said, "I was a rescue swimmer in the American Coast Guard. I am a well-trained medic, but no more well trained than any of the other guys."

"This is the difference," Diablo said. "You find people who desperately need your help, and you save them from peril. The rest of your team is exactly the opposite. They find men who are not in peril, and they leave them either dead or dying. This is now what you are. You must decide."

"Decide what?"

"You must decide to either turn away from what you are on the inside, or you must embrace it."

Tony leaned back, creating distance between himself and Diablo. "This is getting a little too hocus-pocus for me."

Diablo patted his knee. "Relax. I am merely telling you what I see so every man will know what he is when we leave the concrete and comfort of the city for the world of predators and prey. We too often think of ourselves as predators, when we are, in fact, the hunted. Learn to feel, taste, and smell the difference, and do not hide from yourself, Tony."

In a feeble attempt to rescue his understudy, Hunter said, "All right. We've all held hands and sang "Kum Ba Yah," so break it down for those of us who *are* the trigger-pullers."

Diablo returned to his cushion. "I know a place where we can find people who can tell us where the Lizard is, but getting them to tell us may not be easy."

Mongo chuckled. "We're pretty good at convincing people to talk."

"These people will tell you what you want to know, but they are for sale."

"For sale?" I asked.

"Yes, when they tell us their secrets, they have a new secret that is very valuable in the jungle."

Hunter huffed. "A little less cryptic, please. What are you talking about?"

"I will show you, and you will see. For now, it is not important. We must first eat, sleep, and then find these people."

Steps one and two were simple, and we proved to be masters of both. The morning sun dusted the nighttime shadows from the Central American paradise that would soon be in our wake as the real mission of finding one man officially began.

I was the first to the kitchenette, but I wasn't alone for long. The rest of the team poured from their rooms, demanding coffee and wiping the sleep from their eyes.

"Morning, Chase. How'd you sleep?"

I handed Singer his first cup of the day. "Surprisingly well, considering the fire we're about to jump into."

He sipped the first taste. "This is real coffee. Not the swill we're forced to drink at home."

I poured and tasted mine. "Maybe we should move to Central America."

He rolled his eyes. "Maybe we should take a thousand pounds of this stuff home with us instead."

Hunter lifted his cup from the counter. "Is everybody up?"

"I think so," I said, counting heads.

Mongo should've counted as two humans, but my count came up one short. "Where's Diablo?"

Instinctually, everyone looked down, but the Water Devil was nowhere to be found.

Tony said, "That's one weird little dude. What's his story?"

I topped off my cup. "His story is simple. He's the deadliest predator in this part of the planet, and I'm thankful he's on our side."

"You may think he's on our side," Hunter said, "but he's clearly gone AWOL. I, for one, don't think that's much of a display of teamwork."

A knock sounded at the door, and just like the team of tier-one operators they were, everyone found cover and drew sidearms.

I said, "Relax, guys. It's just breakfast."

Ignoring the peephole, I swung open the door, and a waiter rolled a pair of carts into the suite. In the local Spanish, he said, "Good morning, sir. Your breakfast is here. Shall I set the table for you?"

I answered in my best Spanish. "Thank you, but no. We'll set the table ourselves."

He disappeared with an American twenty in his palm, and my team—my family—tore into the carts.

We ate for fifteen minutes before Tony said, "If Diablo is gone, how are we going to pull this off?"

"He's not gone. He's just somewhere else, probably waiting to pop out of a birthday cake. He'll turn up. Trust me."

Tony wiped his hands and the corners of his mouth. "If you say so. But I'm sticking with my initial assessment. That's one weird dude."

With breakfast astern, we took the resort's fifteen-passenger van back to the airport to claim our gear.

I unlocked the Citation and lowered the airstairs. "Get what you need. The plane will be our resupply point for now. I don't know how far into the jungle we're going today, but take enough to survive for four days. If it becomes necessary, a couple of us can hump our way back out of the bush and move the jet."

Ten minutes later, we looked more like an action team than a gang or tourists, and I raised the stairs and secured the hatch. Stepping back from the plane, I caught a glimpse of something unexpected, and I leapt aside, drawing my pistol as I moved.

Hunter and Disco reacted exactly like me, but Tony became the voice of reason.

"Take it easy, guys. It's just the Devil."

"You're going to get shot if you keep doing that," I warned, but Diablo only grinned.

"Are we ready to go?"

"We are," I said. "But are we going to hoof it off the airport or just teleport into the jungle like you?"

Diablo motioned toward an ancient four-wheel-drive truck with a canvas cover over the bed, making it look more like a Conestoga wagon than a truck. "We're taking that as far as it will go. Load your gear and bring everything."

"Everything?" I asked. "Are we moving too far to use the airplane as a resupply point?"

"Everything. You will not see this airport again until we have accomplished our mission or we've given up."

Hunter, having anticipated Diablo's answer, was already sprinting for the truck. He parked it alongside the Citation. With bucket-brigade precision, we had every piece of our gear stowed on the truck in minutes.

We climbed aboard the ancient relic of a vehicle, and Diablo crawled onto the front passenger seat.

Tony motioned toward the vacant driver's seat. "Uh, aren't you going to drive?"

Diablo shook his head. "I don't drive, but I will tell you where to go."

With his weird-little-dude theory fortified, Tony climbed behind the wheel and ground his way through the gears. As we navigated the narrow streets leading away from the town of Puerto San Jose, the temperature inside the back of the truck soared easily above a hundred.

Mongo looked the most uncomfortable of all of us with his legs wrapped around a pair of duffle bags and his enormous shoulders wedged against the cab of the truck.

I yelled over the roar of the truck. "Are you okay up there, big man?"

He groaned. "That depends on how far we have to ride like this."

I leaned through the space that had once been occupied by the rear glass of the truck, although decades had obviously passed since there had been anything in that space. "Where are we going, Diablo?"

He opened his eyes and glanced over his shoulder. "*Iglesia católica encima de la montaña.*"

"Church?"

"This is where the truth can be found."

I was on the verge of losing patience with Diablo's cryptic answers and behavior, but I forced down my rising anxiety. "Okay, how long will it take? We're pretty uncomfortable back here."

He stared through the windshield at the rising terrain in front of us. "Maybe two hours. Maybe two days."

I bit the flesh inside my jaw and focused on breathing. "Let's try to communicate without the word games. Can we do that?"

"There are no word games. If your truck does not run out of gasoline and does not break down, it will be two hours. If your truck does stop, it may take two days to walk there."

"My truck?" I said with more grit in my tone than intended.

"Yes, your truck."

"This is not *my* truck. It's *your* truck."

He shook his head. "No, it's not my truck."

Through gritted teeth, I said, "*You* brought it to the airport."

"No, I didn't. I only pointed to the truck when you asked how we were going to travel. You stole the truck . . . not me."

It wasn't exactly anger boiling inside of me. Perhaps it was a twisted hodgepodge of respect blended with frustration, but yelling at our only link to the world in which my brother lived would do nothing other than increase the tension and weaken the communication, so I withdrew from the area that should've held the pane of glass. "Did you hear that?"

Mongo grunted. "No, I'm twisted up like a contortionist. I think I may have a couple of my toes stuck in my ears. What did he say?"

I leaned back through the opening. "Tony, stop the truck. We've got some rearranging to do."

Tony continued wrestling with the steering wheel. "Can't you rearrange while we're moving?"

Hunter awarded Tony with a solid slap to the back of his head. "When the boss says stop the truck, it's not a negotiation."

He covered the brake pedal with one foot and the clutch with the other. Downshifting resulted in little more than backfiring and the engine revving out of control, and the brakes appeared to have even less effect, but Tony finally wrangled the truck to a stop on the winding mountain road.

With dust encompassing our vehicle, I gave the order. "Scoot over, Diablo. Mongo's coming up front."

With the emissaries of each end of the human size chart occupying the front seat, Tony coaxed the old workhorse back into motion, and our trek continued.

As we bounced and swayed across what apparently qualified as a road in the mountains of Guatemala, Hunter leaned toward me. "Sorry about the kid sassing you. I'll straighten him out."

"In his position, I would've likely put up an argument, as well. Did you see how much work it took to stop this hayride?"

"That's no excuse. I'll get his mind right. We don't have time for stuff like that."

"Don't beat him up too badly. We were all rookies once."

Hunter leaned back against the billowing canvas cover and closed his eyes.

Hunter wasn't the only member of the team with his eyes closed, but I suspected Singer wasn't trying to sleep. When his lips stopped moving and he raised his head, I asked, "Did He say everything was going to be all right?"

Our sniper grinned. "Eventually. Don't forget that we aren't promised riches and comfort on Earth, but those of us who believe get all the milk and honey we can throw down our gullet when our work is done."

"Now, that's big-picture thinking, my friend."

He nodded. "What's on your mind?"

"It's probably nothing, but I'm not feeling great about being led through the jungle without knowing what's around the next bend."

Singer caressed the barrel of his rifle. "How often do we know what's waiting around the corner?"

"I guess you're right, but Diablo said we're going to church because that's where the truth can be found."

Singer shrugged. "He's not wrong as long as it's a good church."

"Something tells me we're not going to find spiritual edification at this particular church."

He pulled a bottle of water from his pocket and enjoyed a long pull. "Big picture thinking, my friend. Don't get so wrapped up in the *right now* that you lose sight of the real goal."

"Milk and honey?"

"Not quite that big. Let's think about why we're piled into this rickety rattletrap of a truck."

"We're here to find my brother."

"Is that really what we're looking for, or are we combing the jungle in search of a part of you that got left behind here twenty years ago?"

Chapter 24
Novia de Cristo

I didn't have time to explore Singer's question, but my gut said it would churn inside my head for days to come.

We bounced for the balance of Diablo's two-hour prediction and rattled to a stop on ground that may have once known vegetation but had long since been trod bare by parishioners hungry for the truth.

Diablo hopped to his knees on the seat of the truck and faced the team. "Stay here, and don't kill anyone. If they are ready to talk, I will come back for you."

As abruptly as he'd turned to address us, he spun away, but I caught his arm. "And if they aren't ready to talk, are you still coming back for us?"

His grin didn't come. "Amigo, if they are not ready to talk, there will be no reason for me to come back for you."

"In that case, I believe I'll come with you."

Against his protest, I slid from the truck and followed the jungle's deadliest predator toward the dilapidated church. What had once, no doubt, been a magnificent pane of stained glass, lay in a red and gold glimmering heap beneath a boarded-up window with rusting nails protruding in various directions.

"It looks like they could use a carpenter around here."

Diablo examined the botched repair. "Jesus was a carpenter, wasn't he?"

He clearly wasn't expecting an answer from me, so I followed him around the building toward a second structure that was, if possible, in worse condition than the sanctuary. Two women wearing plain cotton dresses emerged through a doorway with only a curtain for closure. The first woman carried an axe in her left hand and a well-worn basket in her right. The second woman noticed us first and held out a hand, stopping the first in her tracks.

The axe bearer dropped her basket and crossed herself with her eyes cast towards the heavens.

Diablo took my wrist. "Stay here."

Something kept me from arguing, and I took a knee on the barren earth. Diablo closed the distance to the women in an instant and spoke in rapid-fire Spanish with a tone of respect and humility.

The dialect was impossible to identify, but I caught enough of the conversation to understand that the Devil was well outside his comfort zone.

The women glanced at me periodically throughout the discussion, but neither showed any expression. With Diablo's back to me, I could only pick out pieces of the women's responses to his approach.

The first said, "Does he know of la Fiera?"

Her question turned Diablo's head and sent him studying me. I tried not to react, but asking if I knew of the wild beast was an impossible question to ignore.

The second woman quickly turned back twice toward the ramshackle building behind them during the conversation, and that caught my attention. Her nervous reaction turned what I thought was a conversation with two women into a potential confrontation with far more than a pair of Guatemalan women with an axe.

I stood and moved back around the sanctuary within sight of our chariot. I should've known my team wouldn't wait in the vehicle like impatient children. As the rank structure dictated, Mongo had taken command in my absence and deployed the team in perimeter security.

When I met Mongo's gaze, he turned his eyes to the belfry of the church, and I followed his line of sight to see our sniper building his nest in the highest available spot, giving himself an unobstructed view of the opening around the church. Whatever the encounter would become would not catch us on our heels.

I turned back toward the women, and Diablo motioned for me to join him. The small, leather-skinned women gazed up at me as if they'd never seen an American. Towering over the three of them, I made the psychological play to take a knee, hopefully decreasing my imposing presence.

The woman with the axe bounced the tool against the ground in rhythmic thuds, and I couldn't resist the urge to watch the glistening blade rise and fall in two-inch motions. The sound and motion were almost hypnotic, like the tick-tock of a metronome, only deeper as the iron head struck the compacted earth beside her foot.

Her narrow, dark eyes pierced my flesh and scored my soul. "*¿Eres cristiano, muchacho?*"

The question caught me off guard, but I managed to answer in Spanish. "Yes, I'm a Christian, but not Catholic."

The lines around her eyes deepened in what I perceived as disappointment. She took a small step toward me. "It is not too late, my child. This is no place for you."

I turned to the Devil and to English. "What's she talking about?"

Without looking at me, he spoke, and I was momentarily lost. His words came in German. "She is confused and doesn't understand that you are Protestant."

My German wasn't fluent, but it was strong enough to hide our conversation from the two women. "Does she understand what we want?"

"She does, but she is concerned for your soul."

It was time to end the games. I stood, stared down at the axe bearer, and spoke her language. "My soul is in good hands, ma'am. Just tell us what we need to know, and we'll leave you alone."

As if my words had been the spark igniting an inferno, Diablo sprang forward, ripping the axe from the woman, and yelled, "Protect the nuns!"

Nuns? What nuns?

I stood in frozen disbelief at the scene unfolding around me.

The two women hit their knees and yanked ancient wooden rosary beads from beneath their dresses. Their cries into the heavens shook me from my stupor, and I caught each of them beneath an arm only an instant before a phalanx of men poured from the shack behind them.

Half-carrying and half-dragging them, I moved as fast as flesh and prosthetic could carry the three of us, clearing the line of fire between Singer high above and the aggressors still coming from behind the worn curtain covering the crude opening.

The two women found their feet at the same instant and relieved me of the burden of their weight. They ran, still clutching their rosaries and crying out to God in their native tongue. I wrangled them in with a sweep of my arms and hefted them behind a stacked pile of roughly cut firewood. Parking them behind the cover, I took each of their faces in my hands and prayed the words about to explode from my mouth were Spanish for, "Stay here, stay down, and keep praying!"

By the time I burst back into the fight, Diablo had turned at least half of the mass of warriors into bloody remains of previously treacherous fighters. The ones Diablo hadn't decapitated or otherwise shredded with the nun's axe, Singer sent into the afterlife with perfectly placed .308 rounds through their chests. Hunter and Tony ran into the melee with M4 rifles pressed to their shoulders, orange fire and scalding lead exploding from their muzzles. With my pistol raised, I was careful to avoid putting myself between Singer and the fight as I powered toward the shack. Only steps short of the ragged opening into the back of the structure, a massive shadow overtook me, and I spun to engage whoever or whatever was closing on my six.

Fully prepared to destroy my pursuer, I raised my Glock, only to be met with a massive sweeping hand. The pistol didn't leave my hand, but the swatting paw knocked me off-balance, leaning onto my prosthetic. My unbalanced position left me powerless to stop Mongo's momentum toward the structure. Without missing a stride, he caught my arm, restoring my balance, and thundered through the jagged opening.

I sent up a silent prayer, thankful I hadn't put two rounds into the big man's chest, and then followed him into the shelter. A pair of double-taps from his pistol silenced the coming crack of two rifles aimed at our heads.

Motion from the semi-darkness drew my muzzle, and I pressed my trigger twice in rapid succession. Blood and torn flesh filled the air, and I yanked my flashlight from my left pocket. The beam cut through the air like a razor, and Mongo yelled, "Clear!"

I echoed his call, and we retreated through the opening we'd come through. Rounding the corner, Diablo came into view. He knelt with the blood-covered axe at his feet and crimson stains streaking his skin.

"Diablo! Are you hurt?"

His soft, somber tone wafted on the silence of the midday heat. "Only on the inside, amigo."

As the adrenaline waned and the reality of the moment washed over us, Diablo crossed himself and stood. "Where are the nuns?"

"They're safe," I said.

He wiped his face and sighed. "No, they have never been safe, but they will not leave. The priest has been dead for more than two years, yet the sisters remain."

"Why doesn't the diocese send another priest?" I asked.

He whispered, "This is *Central* America, my friend. Not *your* America."

I tried to understand the reality of his words of wisdom, but the jungle would forever remain a chasm of mystery for me. "Who were those guys, and what set them off?"

Diablo hung his head. "I made a terrible mistake. Sister Maria Angelica is left-handed, and I didn't heed her warning of the axe in her right hand. Sister Maria Isabella was nervous, but I thought it was because I brought someone she didn't recognize to her door. I should have seen the signs. I was . . ."

I laid a hand on his shoulder. "It's not your fault. You wouldn't be here if it weren't for me."

Mongo stepped in. "It doesn't matter who's to blame. We have a mess to clean up. My question is this . . . What were these guys doing here?"

Singer sounded his shrill whistle from the belfry, and every eye turned skyward. He pointed toward the woodpile where I'd hidden the nuns without habits. We turned to see the pair making their way back to the shack, and Mongo stepped to intercept them.

Diablo said, "Let them come. This is their home. They know the price for what they do."

"What do you mean, the price for what they do?"

"They are las novias de Cristo. They know only love. The sins of men can't stop their love. They will feed, shelter, and care for anyone who calls on them." He took a long breath before saying,

"They will care for the bodies left behind by the departed souls." He turned and motioned toward a sloping hill bearing dozens of wooden crosses. "Those two nuns, along with one other, dug every grave in that field."

"What happened to the third nun?"

"Maria Angelica and Maria Isabella dug her grave after the man you believe to be your brother ran a machete through her heart."

Chapter 25
Meine Schwester

My team wiped the sweat from their brows and then cleaned and stowed their entrenching tools after covering graves and driving nine simple wooden crosses into the blood-soaked earth.

The nuns drew water from a well with a wooden bucket on a hemp rope and dipped metal cups into the leaking container. They placed a cup in each of our hands and called down Heaven's blessings on each of us. I couldn't allow my eyes to meet theirs. The thought of their sister's corpse rotting in its earthen grave because of the cruelty of the man who likely shared my bloodline was more than I could bear.

Sister Maria Isabella knelt in front of me and slowly unlaced each of my boots.

The look on my face caught Diablo's attention, and he leaned toward me. "Relax and let her do it. This is important to her."

Still unsure what was happening, I tried to follow Diablo's direction, but the thought of having the Devil tell me to let a Guatemalan nun do anything she wants to me was well outside my comfort zone.

The sister cupped her hand beneath the heel of my left boot and slid it from my foot. She carefully folded the laces inside and placed it by her knee on the hard ground. My sock followed and was treated with equal attention and care before being placed inside my sweat-stained leather boot. Then, she reached for my right foot—or where my right foot had once been—and I panicked. My eyes shot between Singer and Diablo as Sister Maria Isabella slid my right boot from my robot and repeated the ritual of tucking and placing. Mortified, I froze in horror at what the nun was about to see, likely, for the first time in her life.

To my surprise, she slipped my sock from the metallic implement protruding from my stump and showed absolutely no reaction to the state-of-the-art medical miracle in her palm. With my terror turned to wonder, I watched in amazement as she lifted the hem of her dress to her lips and tore an inch-long separation in the worn cotton fabric. She repeated the bite and tear until she held a rectangular piece of cloth in her hands. She bowed her head and whispered too softly for me to hear or understand what she was saying, but I had little doubt as to the intended recipient of her whispers.

With her prayer complete, she pressed the cloth into the bottom of the wooden pail, soaking it with cold, clear water from the depths of the well. She lifted my feet onto her thighs and ran the cloth over the filthy flesh of my left and the gleaming smooth surface of my prosthetic.

The care with which she reversed the ceremony outshined the effort she'd shown in removing my boots. My socks followed her gentle hands, and then she placed each boot back on my feet. For the first time, her hands faltered as she fumbled with tying the knot back into the shape she'd undone only minutes before.

Taking my hand in hers, she pressed the still-damp cloth into my palm and folded my fingers around it, then looked up into my eyes. I was lost and mesmerized. Words wouldn't come, until finally, "Why," fell from my lips.

She squeezed my hands in hers, smiled, and in perfect German, said, "Because Jesus told us to."

No matter how hard I tried to keep it from appearing, my smile came. "You speak German."

She bowed her head in humility. "Yes, and eleven other languages, plus more dialects than I can count. Thank you for allowing me the privilege of washing your feet. You are a brave man and a leader of brave men. You probably saved our lives today, which means my work here on Earth isn't complete, and I must continue in service to our Lord."

I spoke softly. "Sister, we can take you away from this place to somewhere safe with running water and churches that aren't falling down around you."

She tilted her head. "These places you speak of, are they free from evil? Do people only love and never harm each other in these places? Is there no hunger, no disease, no pain in these places?"

"I'm sorry, Sister, but I don't know of such a place."

She smiled, apparently pleased with her argument and confident in her faith. "Then I shall remain here in this place where I know the land and the people, and where I can hear God softly whispering through the trees when night falls. The world is so big, and I am so small. Leaving this place where I can do little to change things would only take me someplace where I could change even less. Thank you, brave soldier, but I will stay here where my calling has brought me and where you have preserved my life."

Diablo delivered us into the hands of un-habited nuns and onto the tips of angry swords, but for reasons I'll never understand, I wasn't angry or frightened or discouraged.

Sister Maria Isabella stood, straightened her torn dress, and turned for her shack. "Come. You must eat, and we must tell you what we know."

I had almost forgotten why we'd come so far into the Guatemalan mountains, but the confidence in the nun's tone left me revived with hope for accomplishing our mission.

Inside the crumbling shell of a home, the two nuns rolled out a threadbare carpet and placed woven baskets of bread, sliced fruit, and seven tiny pieces of cheese.

"Please sit and enjoy. I am sorry we have no meat, but this is the last of our cheese instead."

As we ate in silence, it occurred to me that no one could ever believe what we'd encountered in the previous hour. We'd been attacked by enraged warriors and left unharmed. We buried the dead. And a Catholic nun washed my feet in the middle of the jungle. Even Penny, the best screenwriter I knew, couldn't write a script so fantastic.

When we pretended that we'd eaten our fill, Disco and Hunter rolled the carpet and returned the cheese to the wax paper wrapper from which the nuns had taken it. I wanted to find a way to initiate the conversation that would lead to finding my brother, but every thought that passed through my head sounded ham-fisted.

Since I couldn't do it, Diablo opened the door. "Sisters, we came here for information because no one in the jungle, not even the monkeys who see everything, know more than you about the men and animals in these trees."

Sister Maria Angelica folded her hands in silent prayer before saying, "The man you want to find is the most dangerous kind of animal. He is driven only by lust and hunger. Such a man is unpredictable and impossible to control. If you are here to capture or kill him, you will likely fail. If God smiles upon you and you achieve what you've come to do, it will not come without unimaginable sacrifice. You are fighting a viper inside the darkness of his own den."

"We don't want to capture or kill him," I said. "If he is who we believe him to be, I have to see him and talk with him. That's all I want."

"This isn't true," she said, looking almost ashamed for having spoken so boldly. "Forgive me, but it is clear you do not only want to talk with him and see him. You want a brother, but this man isn't what you are. He is loyal only to himself and those who give him what he wants. But even that loyalty is short-lived. When he has devoured what he desires, he turns to the next hand to offer him a fistful of crumbs or thirty silver coins. We will tell you where to find this man, el Lagarto, but before you pursue him, perhaps you should dig the graves for yourself and your true brothers."

I swallowed hard and choked out, "Thank you for the warning, Sister, but please just tell us where we can find him."

She crossed herself and kissed the wooden cross hanging from her rosary beads. "There is a sacred place to the Maya called Uaxactun in the northern lowlands in the Petén Basin. Do you know this place?"

I was instantly mesmerized. "No, I've never heard of Uaxactun. I'm sorry, but I don't know—"

She patted my hand and smiled toward Diablo. "It's okay. He will take you there." Not pausing to hear Diablo's response, she continued. "Twelve kilometers north of Uaxactun is a small village. Not really a village—more of a *camp* in English. There is fresh water there from the earth."

I asked, "Like a river or stream?"

"No, from inside the Earth. Like a well, but on the surface."

"A spring?"

"Yes, a spring. It doesn't produce water in the winter months, but in summer, it is plentiful. Enough to provide for several men. This is where you will find el Lagarto if he is not doing his evil work for evil men."

I made a note in my book and tucked it away. "If he isn't there, where should we look next?"

Her smile faded. "If he isn't there when you arrive, you should wait. If he is alive, he will come back to that place. It is his home."

"I have just one more question, if you don't mind."

She folded her hands and listened intently.

"Do you know anything about this man's family or where he came from?"

She fingered her rosary beads. "The rain forest is a mysterious place for those who don't understand its ways. The Maya believed in and worshipped many gods—false gods, of course— and believed people and things often came from these gods. This place I described to you was called Siaan K'aan in the ancient Mayan. This means 'born in Heaven' in your language."

"What does that have to do with my brother?"

She closed her eyes. "Some say el Lagarto fell from the heavens as an infant and caused the earth to tremble when he landed. I don't know what that means, but legends such as these are common among people like him."

"That legend actually makes sense, but I don't have time to explain it to you. I'd like to ask you one final question. Have you ever seen him?"

She swallowed hard. "I have seen him twice, and until you spoke, I believed today was the third. You have his same spirit, but that spirit obviously does not control you. You are a man capable of pressing back the things that haunt you. El Lagarto cannot do this."

I took her hands. "Thank you for everything. I'm sorry about what happened this morning. I will be back, and I will find a way to make your life better."

She kissed the backs of each of my hands and turned away.

Back inside our "borrowed" truck, I gave Diablo a shake. "What was that back there? Why did those people try to kill us? And she washed my feet! What was that about?"

He shook his head. "Those men didn't try to kill *us*. They tried to kill *me*. I did not know they were there. I'm sorry about that, but I am thankful you were with me."

I wanted to know what Diablo had done to those people to leave them looking for an opportunity to kill him, but a fear of the truth kept me from digging further. "You're the wild beast the nuns were afraid of, aren't you?"

He looked away. "Perhaps. As they said, legends are everywhere in the jungle."

"Okay, none of that matters anymore. But why did she wash my feet?"

Singer answered before Diablo could. "The practice originated in ancient Palestine as a show of respect for guests who walked in sandals on dry, dusty paths. Its Christian origin began at the Last Supper when Jesus washed the feet of his disciples as an act of service and love before his arrest, trial, and crucifixion. The nun washed your feet—or foot—for the same reasons."

"But why me?"

"Even women of God recognize you as our leader. It's that simple."

"It's not simple. It's strange. I'm honored, but it was weird."

Hunter jumped in. "Washing your prosthetic was weird, but other than that, I thought it was pretty cool."

Diablo said, "Today's action was unexpected, but we got the information we needed."

"How far is this Uaxactun place?" Tony asked as he continued his losing battle with the steering wheel.

Diablo said, "Maybe four hundred kilometers, but there is no road for the final fifty kilometers."

Chapter 26
Giving it Back

I gave Tony, our overworked driver, a slap on the shoulder. "I know it's a lot of work, but see if you can find a spot to get us stopped. We've got some decisions to make before we get too far north."

Instead of the protest he made the first time, he stood on the brake. "Yes, sir."

Hunter grinned. "I told you I'd get his mind right. A man who gets his feet washed by the only pretty girl in Guatemala deserves a little respect."

"She's a nun, Hunter. Calm down."

"She's still pretty, regardless of her nunnism."

"Nunnism? Really? That's what you're sticking with?"

"Why not? With Clark gone, somebody has to pick up the slack in the linguistical arena. It might as well be me."

Eventually, Tony managed to get the truck stopped on a gravel-covered shoulder of the goat trail of a road, and we climbed out of what had become an oven on wheels. Disco spread the map over the hood and pointed to a spot where he reckoned we must've been. Diablo climbed onto the front bumper and examined the map. His nod of agreement gave me confidence in Disco's spot.

I said, "Show us where we're going."

Diablo traced a finger from our position winding to the northeast through dense jungle and rugged terrain.

Mongo leaned in and studied the route. "It's a shame there isn't a lake about a mile long up there."

Diablo furrowed his brow. "Why do you want a lake?"

"We've got a seaplane," I said. "That would be a much more comfortable—and faster—insertion."

Diablo touched the map near our destination. "There is one lake large enough for a seaplane in the north. It is called Lake Petén Itzá, but it's very busy. There's no way to land on the water and unload the gear without being seen by dozens of people. It's too bad the plane is only a seaplane because there's a runway about two kilometers to the east of the camp the nuns mentioned."

That earned grins all around, and Diablo backed away. "Why's everyone smiling like that?"

"Our Caravan isn't *just* a seaplane, my friend. It's amphibious and loves runways cut out of the jungle."

Diablo shook his head. "Oh, no. It's not jungle where we're going. It's lowlands with lush vegetation, but your airplane shouldn't care."

I jabbed a finger through the air to the south. "Back to the airport we go! If it makes it back, we can give this piece-of-junk truck back to its rightful owner. He'll probably be furious with us for bringing it back."

With everyone crammed back aboard the Beverly Hillbillies Special, we bounced our way south, and Tony couldn't stop whistling and grinning.

Diablo studied our driver. "Why are you suddenly so happy?"

Tony drummed out his version of "Wipeout" on the steering wheel. "I'm happy that I only have to drive this contraption for another couple of hours. Nothing could make me happier than seeing this thing burst into flames as soon as we dismount."

Diablo wore a look of confusion. "Is this not better than walking?"

Tony gave him an elbow. "Barely."

To our surprise, the truck made the trip, and we rolled to a stop beside the Caravan.

Diablo said, "This one is yours also?"

"This is our version of a flying truck."

We offloaded gear and humans from the ancient vehicle and carefully loaded only the bare essentials onto the Caravan. I ran the weight and balance calculation through my head, but I didn't like the math. "We're too heavy. We'll never get off the ground."

Disco eyed the gear and shook his head. "Tell us about this runway in the jungle. Is it paved? How long is it? Do they have any jet fuel lying around in fifty-five-gallon drums?"

Diablo shrugged. "It's been a long time since I've seen it. It is not paved, but there is gravel on the part that stays wet in the rainy season. The rest is dirt and grass. It's maybe a thousand meters, but I can't be sure."

I gave Disco a groan. "I like what you're thinking, but it's not going to work. Even if we could get the Citation on the ground, we'd never get it out of there. I've got to be honest . . . I'm a little nervous about getting in and out with the Caravan."

He grimaced and scratched his temple. "If only there were some way to get our chopper down here, this would be a milk run."

It hit Diablo only slightly before the idea slammed into my head, and our answer came out in stereo. "Leo!"

Hunter suddenly became the spokesman for the team. "Are you going to let the rest of us in on this little mystery of yours? You two clearly know him, but the rest of us are in the dark."

I said, "Leo is a former . . . Well, maybe not former. Maybe he's still on the payroll of some OGA."

Hunter said, "None of us cares what other government agency this cat Leo works for. Who and what is he?"

"He's the most insane helicopter pilot who's ever lived. He can do things with a Huey that even Disco won't try."

Hunter rolled a finger through the air. "Keep talking. Where and how do we find this guy?"

That shut me up, and I surrendered the floor to Diablo. In his typical style, he stood there grinning from ear to ear.

Mongo finally had enough. "If you don't start talking and stop grinning, I'm going to—"

That was enough for Diablo to come out of his glee-induced trance, and he pulled a satellite phone from his pocket. Seconds later, he tossed the phone to me, and I stuck it to my ear.

"Is this the world's worst underwater bomb tech?"

Half a decade earlier, Clark and I worked a mission at the southern end of the Panama Canal near the Bridge of the Americas. Leo and his Huey had been our ride to work. I pulled a bone-headed trick and blew myself out of the water while trying to defuse a bomb I didn't understand.

"That's me," I said. "Please tell me you're sober enough to get yourself and your chopper to Guatemala."

"Sober enough?" he said. "I'm offended by such an implication. I haven't been sober since nineteen sixty-seven in Da Nang. Sobriety is for quitters, and I'm no quitter. What are you doing in Guatemala? I hope to high heaven you're not dealing with a bomb."

"You might call it a bombshell," I said. "We're looking for a guy they call the Lizard. Ever heard of him?"

Sounds of him scratching his beard crackled through the phone. "Maybe. There are so many characters in these jungles, it's impossible to keep up with them all. What did this guy do to get you and Clark on his tail?"

"Clark's out of the game. He got busted up pretty good in Afghanistan, so he got himself promoted. I'm running a full team now. There's six of us, and seven if you count Diablo."

"Nice job of sidestepping my question, but I'm not buying ten thousand dollars' worth of jet fuel just to chase some guy I've never heard of. You've got to do better than that."

"I'll buy the fuel, Leo. Just get down here . . . or up here. Where are you?"

"It doesn't matter where I am. Guatemala is a big place. You'll need to give me a hint where to find you."

"How long will it take you to get to the airport in Puerto San Jose?"

"You're buying the gas, you say?"

"Yeah, I've got that covered. What's your daily rate?"

"I'm a grand a day, and the helo is a grand an hour."

"A grand an hour *plus* gas?"

"No, since it's for you, kid, I'll eat the gas bill. But it's a five-day minimum for me."

I said, "Nice job dodging my question."

"Oh, yeah. I can be there in three hours. Throw some beans down your gullet, catch a nap, and rustle up my cash. I'll be there before the beans kick in and the nap is over."

Before I could ask anything else, the line went dead, and I gave the phone a look. "He hung up on me."

Diablo said, "He does that. It means he's coming."

I motioned toward the truck. "Get the rest of the gear out of that thing, and shove it aboard the Caravan for now. We'll deal with the loading when Leo gets here with his chopper."

Tony held up a finger. "I've driven that thing the last mile I ever plan to, so somebody else can put it back where we found it."

Hunter shot him a look. "You'll drive when Chase tells you—"

I cut in. "I get it. I'll take care of the truck."

Tony was right. Driving the truck was like wrestling a mountain lion. It required both feet and both hands. I finally got it parked somewhere near the spot we'd found it, and I was less than certain I'd won the wrestling match.

A well-equipped team of covert operatives is anything but covert on a wide-open airport, so we took Leo's advice, secured the airplane, and headed for cover.

Diablo led us to an open-air cantina, where we saddled up to a high table and devoured piles of tamales and *caldo de res*.

Spooning the rich soup into my mouth, I mumbled, "This is amazing. What is it?"

Diablo wiped his mouth. "It's a very common dish here in Guatemala. It's a simple soup of meat bones, broth, and vegetables."

After wiping out the cantina's inventory, it was time for the siesta Leo suggested.

Diablo said, "We can go inside the airport if you want, but the wind is nice, and the shade will keep us cool if you don't want to draw attention."

I surveyed the surrounding terrain. "I think we'll take the breeze and the shade."

"Good call, amigo."

Diablo led the way down a winding path to an opening where a dozen hammocks waited in the tropical paradise.

I said, "This place is great. Why are we the only ones here?"

Diablo looked toward the rising terrain to the north and east. "Sometimes, there are some not-so-friendly people here, but you have nothing to fear. Sleep, my friends. I will see that no one interrupts your siesta."

I was the only hesitant member of the team. "What do you mean, not-so-friendly people?"

He waved a hand. "Don't worry. Everything will be fine. I'll hear Leo when he lands, and I'll wake you."

Still unsure, I climbed into a hammock and prepared myself for an hour of fighting losing battles inside my head that would never let me fall asleep, but I was wrong. Sleep took me in minutes as the gentle breeze wafted through the trees and the sounds of distant howler monkeys echoed on the wind.

Sometime later, I awoke to Diablo poking my back with a stick. "Leo is here, amigo. Let's go."

I forced my eyes open and spent a few seconds wondering where I was. The confusion quickly cleared, and the team was on their feet.

We met the chopper on the ramp only a few steps from our Caravan, and I stuck out my hand. "You've not aged a day, Leo, but that shirt has seen better days. That's the same shirt you were wearing the day we met."

He tugged at his threadbare tropical print shirt that had, at some point, been new . . . and clean. "Hey! Lay off this old thing. It's my lucky shirt. I've worn it every time I crashed, and I haven't gotten dead yet."

I made introductions, and Leo pretended not to care. "I won't remember your names, but I will put you in a hot LZ if that's what you're looking for."

Diablo said, "The insertion shouldn't be hot, but getting out may be a little tricky. We're headed for a camp a few kilometers northeast of Uaxactun."

Leo grimaced. "Uaxactun? That's some sacred ground up there." He took off his hat and wrung it between his hands. "There's about a million dead Maya floating around that place. I'm scared of only two things . . . getting shot in the face and ghosts. If this mission of yours is what I think it is, we're likely to deal with both."

Chapter 27
All Grown Up

Diablo briefed Leo on the mission while the rest of us sorted gear.

"Here's what I want to do," I said. "Rebuild your three-day kit. Keep it light. The Caravan will be the resupply point at the airstrip up north. Hunter and Tony will fly the Caravan, and the rest of us will take the Huey with Leo. Any questions?"

Singer raised his chin. "Are we staggering departures to arrive at the same time since the Caravan is fifty knots faster than the Huey?"

"Yes, we are. Hunter and Tony will hang back for an hour. That'll give us time to put boots on the ground and set up a perimeter to protect the Caravan in case we get any more resistance like the guys at the church."

Disco said, "Just give Diablo another axe, and turn him loose."

I checked over my shoulder to make sure Diablo and Leo were still absorbed in the conversation. "That's not a bad idea, but we can't forget that those guys aren't part of this circle. I trust them both, but if we find ourselves up against a wall and either of those two guys has to decide between saving themselves and saving the team, we have to be prepared for the real probability that they'll escape alive and leave us to fight it out."

Singer asked, "If you can't trust them, why are they here?"

"You weren't listening. I trust them to get us to where we need to be, but we're brothers. There's not a man here who wouldn't give his life for the rest of us. That's something beyond trust. That's . . . well, I don't know what to call it, but that's what we have."

"It's called family, Chase."

"Yeah, that's exactly what it is, Mongo. Thank you. When we go home, those two will still be in the jungle doing whatever it is they do when we're sitting in the gazebo daydreaming about the next mission."

Disco said, "I've got a question, and it's not me second-guessing your call, but why Hunter and Tony in the Caravan?"

"Good question. And I knew somebody would bring it up. Hunter's doing the Caravan driving because he's just as good as me in that cockpit, and I want mine to be the first feet—or foot—on the ground in the spot we're going to find my brother. Tony's going with him because he's earned it. I drove that truck a thousand yards, and it kicked my butt. Tony drove it for seven hours. He needs a break."

"That's why you're in charge," Tony belted out.

I ignored him. "And here's the answer to your real question, Disco. I want you in the chopper because Leo likes to take little naps while he's flying. I like the idea of you being in the left seat to pick up the slack."

Disco nodded. "That's good enough for me."

The team went to work picking through the gear piled aboard the Caravan, and I jogged over to Leo and Diablo.

Before I came to a stop, Leo said, "You think he's your brother? Are you serious?"

"It looks that way."

He shook his head. "You've kept yourself alive for the past seven or eight years, so you must have some sense, but going after your own brother? That's too close, man. You're not going to be objective, and that kind of thinking has gotten a lot of good men killed."

"That's exactly why I'm not calling the shots when we hit the ground. I'm just another trigger-puller. Mongo will be in command as soon as we hit the airfield up north."

Leo peered over my shoulder toward the team. "What's his background?"

"As solid as they come," I said. "Green Beret, combat medic, one-eighty IQ, impossible to shake."

Leo seemed to be examining the giant. "Does he know he'll be in charge?"

"Not yet, but I'll brief him on the ride up. Disco, retired A-Ten driver turned gunslinger, will be up front with you. Singer, the sniper, will be on the door. Mongo and I will work through the plan on the ride up."

Leo frowned. "That's only four heads, and I count seven, including Diablo."

"Diablo will be with us on the chopper, but Hunter and Tony will lag behind and bring the Caravan up about an hour after we launch."

Leo pulled a flask from his pocket and uncapped it.

I caught his arm. "Let's keep this one dry."

He jerked away, recapped the flask, and tossed it toward me. I caught the cold metal container, and he said, "Give that a whiff and a taste."

I unscrewed the cap and waved it beneath my nose. With no discernable smell, I touched it to my lips and poured a drop onto my tongue. I instantly laughed, recapped the flask, and tossed it back. "Why are you carrying water in a whiskey flask?"

"To see if you've grown up enough to call me out on drinking before a mission." He raised the flask toward me. "You've come a long way, kid. Let's go find this guy."

I jogged back to the Caravan and quickly reassembled my kit and inventoried what remained on the airplane. "This should be enough supplies for two weeks, at least. Is there anything left on the Citation?"

Disco said, "No, the jet's empty, but while the fuel truck is out here, it wouldn't hurt to top her off."

The lineman insisted that we stay away from the helicopter while he refueled it, so we obeyed, and I put in the order to top off the Citation and Caravan.

Leo hustled toward the lineman and stuck his Colt Government forty-five beneath the man's chin. I couldn't hear the exchange over the noise of the fuel truck, but it was obvious the man fully understood Leo's position . . . whatever that position was.

With the forty-five holstered, Leo ambled over to the team. "Are you ready to go?"

I pointed my chin toward the fuel truck. "What was that about?"

Leo smiled. "I was just making sure he understood that we know precisely how much fuel our tanks need. They have the reputation of selling you five hundred gallons in a three-hundred-gallon tank, if you know what I mean."

"There's nothing like a forty-five under the chin to improve a man's math skills," I said.

Before climbing aboard the chopper, I pulled Hunter aside. "You can find the airfield, right?"

He pulled out Diablo's map. "Piece of cake, boss. Be careful up there. We'll be hot on your tail."

I slugged him on the arm. "And we'll cover your arrival with a little suppressive fire, if necessary." I spun on a heel and shot a finger toward Tony's chest. "Don't let him get lost."

He returned a wordless nod, and I climbed aboard the chopper behind the rest of my team. Before I was fully aboard, Leo pulled pitch, and the skids of the helo left the concrete of Puerto San Jose.

The noise inside a Huey with both doors open is something akin to the inside of a tornado.

I grabbed Mongo's vest and pulled him toward me. "When we hit the ground, this is your show. I'm just a grunt. You're in charge. I'm too close to be objective."

He leaned in. "Whatever you say. Does everybody else know I'm in charge?"

"Yep. I told everyone."

"I'm always the last to know," he yelled over the wind and rotor noise.

Two hours into the flight, Leo turned, held up three fingers, and yelled from the cockpit. "Three minutes! No bandits so far."

I held up a trio of fingers and repeated his call. We press-checked our chambers and retied our boots.

Diablo yelled, "We shouldn't expect any resistance while we're airborne. If we're going to get hit, it'll happen when the rotors spin down. If they start anything while we're still in the air, it's too easy for us to escape."

"That's comforting," I said.

Singer leaned toward the center of the aircraft from his sling at the door. "I've got one technical and at least four men at ten o'clock."

I stuck my head into the cockpit. "Singer spotted a truck-mounted heavy weapon and at least four men at ten o'clock."

Disco leaned left and scanned the trees. "I don't see anything."

"That's why you're not a sniper," I said. "Take us around the LZ once before touching down. I want Singer's eyes on the terrain from the sky before we step into a fight with a vehicle-mounted big gun."

Leo banked hard to the right and started a wide, sweeping turn around the airfield. Singer studied every inch of the terrain, and I focused on the airfield. Diablo's assessment was solid. I saw at least three thousand feet of relatively clear airstrip. Hunter would have no problem putting the Caravan on the ground as long as no one shot him down first.

I shuffled toward our sniper. "What else do you see?"

"There were a couple dozen noncombatants off to the east, the technical I mentioned, and a two-man team about a click north of the airfield."

"Spotter and sniper?"

"Probably, but there's no high ground except the Mayan ruins to the southwest. If they're a hunter-killer team, they chose a bad perch. Do you want me to take out the technical?"

"Not yet," I yelled. "We don't know if they're hostile yet."

"That's at least a fifty-cal," he said. "If they turn hostile with us on the ground, fighting back is going to be a losing proposition."

I reached behind me and grabbed Diablo's shirt, dragging him to the door. "There's a vehicle-mounted heavy weapon with at least four crew in those trees."

He hopped to his feet and leaned into the cockpit. I couldn't hear what he said to Leo and Disco, but they banked the chopper away from the tree line and slowly arced back around the target.

Diablo lay on his stomach with his head and shoulders outside the door as we overflew the threat.

"What do you think?" I yelled.

Instead of answering, he pulled a grenade from his belt, pulled the pin, and dropped it into the trees. Mesmerized by what he'd done, I watched the scene below play out in slow motion. The explosion belched orange fire and sent shrapnel flying in every direction.

Mongo pointed to the south of the explosion. "We've got a runner." He pulled his rifle to his shoulder and leaned farther outside the chopper, only seconds away from stopping the runner forever.

Diablo leapt to his feet and grabbed Singer's shoulder. "No! Let him go."

"Let him go?" Singer asked. "Why?"

"Because he will tell everybody he knows about the men from the sky who aren't afraid to start a fight."

Singer planted himself on the deck of the chopper. "Won't that send everybody in the camp running for their lives?"

"That's what you don't understand about the men here in the jungle. We respect animals more dangerous than ourselves, so we watch and learn from them."

"Then why is that guy running?"

Diablo turned to watch the man sprinting to the south. "Because he's afraid and probably smart. We destroyed his vehicle and his heavy gun. He might have a pistol, a machete, and a stick. Wouldn't you run if you were on the verge of a fight with a team like us and that's all you had to fight with?"

Singer raised an eyebrow, accepting Diablo's premise, and I asked, "How many will he bring back?"

Chapter 28
Party Time

I kept my eyes outside the chopper as we descended to the deck, but I didn't have to look into the cockpit to know Leo was on the controls. We dove into the LZ with far more speed than any corporate pilot would attempt. As Leo brought the chopper to a hover only inches above the ground, Mongo, Singer, Diablo, and I launched ourselves from the helo as if we'd been fired from a cannon.

A four-man perimeter is barely better than no perimeter at all, but when the team is constructed of tier-one operators, that four-man barrier against the bad guys feels a lot more like a whole platoon of ground-pounders.

Leo snatched the chopper back off the ground and climbed away to the southeast. With the noise of the Huey well in the distance, we listened intently as the sounds of nature slowly reclaimed the environment around the airfield. Nothing sounded out of place, and the only movement in the trees seemed to be the breeze rustling through the leaves.

No one took any shots at the chopper, so Diablo pulled a small radio from his pocket and keyed the mic. Thirty seconds later, Disco and Leo put the chopper in the grass to the left of the makeshift runway and climbed from the cockpit.

We moved to the tree line on the western edge of the airstrip, and I said, "What was that all about?"

Leo said, "I'm harder to hit in the air, and I'd rather take my chances crashing that chopper than getting in a gunfight on the ground."

"Good enough for me. Now I know the playbook."

Leo laughed. "Kid, there ain't no playbook down here. There's just a play page, and all it says is 'don't get dead.'"

"I like that play. Did you hear from Hunter and Tony?"

Disco said, "They're ten minutes out and planning to fly a random steep."

I shot a look into the sky. "That should be fun to watch."

Singer said, "I've never heard of a random steep. What is it?"

I checked my watch. "You'll see in nine minutes."

The sound of the Caravan's turbine and spinning prop showed up a full minute before the airplane was in sight. When they appeared, Hunter had the airplane in the perfect position for the approach.

I pointed skyward. "Watch. He's got the flaps set for the approach, and as soon as he's over the landing threshold at five thousand feet, he'll roll into a bank of at least thirty degrees. I suspect he'll be closer to forty-five. Then he'll push the nose over and fall out of the sky, losing at least a thousand feet for every ninety degrees of turn. If he gets it right, he'll roll out on a half-mile final fully configured for landing."

Singer watched with the fascination of a child as Hunter executed the maneuver flawlessly and stuck the Caravan to the ground as if it was tired of flying. After the rollout, he taxied the plane back to the approach end of the strip and parked it on the opposite side of the runway from Leo's Huey. It was perfectly poised for a hasty departure—should it become necessary.

Tony and Hunter climbed down the ladders and slung their gear across their shoulders.

"Welcome to paradise," I said. "Nice job on the approach."

Hunter gave Disco a fist bump and said, "That's how it's done in the Air Force."

"Right," I said. "Just how many airplanes did you fly in the Air Force?"

He closed one eye and glared at me with the other. "I may not have been in the cockpit, but I put more steel and fire on targets with my voice in six years than most fighter pilots dish out in a career."

Disco came to his defense. "He's right. Without the combat controllers, ground targets would be a lot safer."

Singer chimed in. "Hmm, I never had any trouble finding ground targets without a combat controller."

I said, "All right, that's enough interservice rivalry. We've got work to do. Will the terrain look like this all the way to the camp?"

Diablo eyed the tree line. "No. The first kilometer will be easy-going, but the rest will be thicker vegetation. If we go now, we'll make the camp before sundown."

"Let's get the airplanes covered up and hit the road."

Leo grunted. "I don't think so."

I asked, "What do you mean, you don't think so?"

"First, I'm not doing a ruck march through the bush, and second, I ain't leaving my chopper on the ground and unguarded in the middle of the jungle. If you've got any sense, you'll feel the same way about your Caravan."

Suddenly, I missed Clark's boots-on-the-ground wisdom, but the decision was left to me. I turned to Leo, "If I leave one man with you, will you stand watch until we get back?"

He put on the grimace that said I was about to write a check. "I can do that, but the daily rate I quoted you was for flying duty, not guard duty. That's another grand."

"Fine. You and Disco guard the hardware. We'll be back by sunrise. If we're not, wait longer."

Mongo took me by the elbow and whispered, "I don't disagree with your call. Disco is obviously the only reasonable choice since he can fly either machine, but you seem to have forgotten that I'm in command now that we're on the ground."

I gave myself a mental slap to the forehead. "Of course. I'm sorry. It's your show."

He took a knee. "Here's the plan. We'll check in with Skipper first. Then, if everything looks good, Diablo will walk point, and we'll trail in five-to-seven-meter intervals depending on terrain and visibility. I want Singer in the rear on guns and Chase up front behind Diablo."

Mongo's infantry training, and especially his jungle warfare experience, gave him the expertise to manage small-team ops in environments just like ours.

He scanned the team. "Anybody have questions?"

Heads shook, and he pulled the sat-phone from his pocket as the rest of us donned our earpieces and mics.

Skipper answered exactly as I expected. "It's about time. Is everybody okay?"

Mongo said, "We're good to go. I just sent our coordinates, and we're ready to move on the camp. Do you have anything for us?"

"I have some satellite imagery from about twenty hours ago if you want it."

"Is there anything we need to know in the images?"

"Not really. The only noteworthy item is a technical situated not far from the airstrip."

Mongo smiled. "Diablo took care of the truck and the gun on our way in."

"Of course he did. Okay, so we're on satellite comms for the duration of the mission, right?"

Mongo said, "Affirmative. Disco and Leo are remaining behind to guard the equipment. You'll be our only relay to them should something come up, so make sure you have solid comms."

"I just did a commo check with Disco, and we're loud and clear. What's your ETA to the camp?"

Mongo turned to Diablo, and he looked up to our gentle giant. "Three hours, but no contact until after sunset. We are at a disadvantage because they know the terrain and we do not."

Mongo relayed the message to Skipper, and I felt completely helpless. I didn't see myself getting accustomed to my new role, but I understood the temporary necessity of the arrangement.

"That's all for now," Mongo said. "Do you have anything else for me?"

She said, "Yeah, I've got something extremely important. Stand by."

Mongo frowned and stared down into the sat-phone. When he glanced at me, I shrugged.

An instant later, a pair of Russian-accented female voices filled the air. "We love you! Come home safe."

A tear came to the big man's eye, but he shoved it away with a knuckle. "I love both of you, as well. I'll be home soon." He thumbed the end button and chewed on his bottom lip. "How do you do it, Chase?"

"Do what?"

"Leave Penny behind every time we deploy."

I swallowed the lump and patted my chest. "I don't leave her behind. She's always right here. But it is hard."

He cleared his throat. "I'm figuring that out. This is the first time I've ever really had anyone . . . you know . . ."

"Yes, I know, and I'd love to tell you it gets easier, but it doesn't. When those two have your last name, it's going to be even harder."

He flushed pale. "I hadn't thought about that. I don't know how to do that."

I leaned in. "Do what?"

Give little Tatiana my last name. Just because I marry her mother, that doesn't change her name, right?"

"No, but I think it's a relatively simple thing. You find a lawyer and have him draw up the adoption paperwork, and then get a judge to sign it. Surely, we can get that done."

He pulled a small spiralbound notepad from his pocket, and the pages looked minuscule in his hands. I'd never seen him with a pad before, but I didn't interrupt. He wrote a few lines of notes and tucked it away.

When he caught me watching, he said, "What? I've got a lot on my mind, so I write the most important things down so I don't forget them."

I held out a hand. "Give me that book."

He hesitantly pulled it from his pocket and handed it over. I opened it to the first page and pulled a pen from my pocket, then I scribbled in the book and handed it back.

His sausage-sized fingers fumbled with the thin cover. He examined my note and looked up like a confused puppy. "It just says Irina and Tatiana."

"That's right. Keep them on page number one . . . always. Everything else we do is meaningless compared to them, and don't you forget it."

He folded the pad and slid it next to his heart. "Let's go to work."

Diablo withdrew his machete and gave a nod toward the west. "Here we go, amigos. If you hear this blade strike anything other than grass or vines, it's time to party."

Chapter 29
Darwin Was Wrong

I thought coastal Georgia had the patent on flying insects, but the low country couldn't hold a candle to Guatemala. I could've sworn I saw a pair of pterodactyls in formation around my head. "What kind of bugs are these?"

Diablo grinned. "I don't know, but they taste good when you're hungry enough."

"I'm not sure I could eat a whole one by myself."

"Don't worry. It'll get much worse before it gets better."

We trekked through the bush with Diablo cutting a trail.

After crossing a well-worn path twice, I asked, "Why aren't we following that path?"

He stopped hacking long enough to say, "We are following it, but we're not walking on it. There are too many other people on the trail, and we don't want any extra players in our game."

"Fair enough."

We continued our slow progress through the environment that was completely foreign to me.

Another hour passed. and Diablo spoke softly into his microphone. "Quietly come to me."

We followed his instructions and carefully made our way to his position. We found him perched twenty feet from a small stream with a pair of monkeys drinking from the water.

He said, "Those are howler monkeys. They know we're here, but they're not concerned."

"How can you tell?" Tony asked.

"If they were concerned, they would be screaming like crazy to warn everyone else. As long as we don't approach them or show any signs of aggression, they'll stay quiet."

Tony said, "How are we supposed to know what a monkey considers aggressive?"

Diablo looked up at him. "Put yourself in the monkey's position. We are intruders. How would you perceive six armed men intruding in your home?"

"Good point. Do you think they'd consider it aggression if I drank from their creek?"

"Yes, they would, but if you can wait until they are finished, we can drink all we want."

I asked, "How do you know the water's safe to drink?"

"Darwin was wrong," Diablo said. "The monkeys are far more evolved than us when it comes to life in the rain forest. We can learn so much from them if we will just watch, and we have nothing to teach them."

I whispered, "Darwin was wrong about a lot of stuff—not just monkeys."

Suddenly, both howler monkeys stood straight up and snapped their heads to the north. The hair on their shoulders stood on end, and they looked like statues standing by the water's edge. I had the overwhelming urge to follow their gaze to the north. For the first time, I felt inferior to the primates. They were clearly capable of sensing a danger I couldn't detect.

Diablo pressed a finger to his lips and motioned for us to get down. We followed his order and nestled into the tall grass. The

Water Devil pawed at the ground, scooping moist soil into his palms and smearing it onto his face. We followed suit and camouflaged our skin just as the pair of monkeys lived up to their names and howled like air raid sirens. As quickly as they'd taken notice of the coming intruders, they disappeared into the trees. What didn't disappear was their howls. They seemed to set off a chain reaction of screeching primates for miles in every direction.

Diablo slowly twisted the machete in his palm until he had the precise grip he wanted. "Get ready. They are coming for us."

I had a thousand questions. *Who's coming for us? Why us? How many? How close?* And perhaps most of all, I wanted to know how Diablo knew.

Two of my questions were answered when a dozen men appeared through the broadleaf grass and shrubs less than a hundred yards away. My mouth went dry, and my heartbeat thudded in my ears. Part of me wanted to react just like the howler monkeys, but having a soul instead of a tail, I pressed myself deeper into the soft earth.

The hunting party continued south, prodding and inspecting the banks of the stream. Their intent was clearly to find the point where my team crossed the stream. Crossing without leaving evidence would've been impossible, so I was instantly thankful for Diablo's agonizingly slow pace.

The dozen men became ten, and I wasn't certain if I'd miscounted or if two had broken off to search farther away from the water. They spoke in a Spanish dialect I'd never heard, and I could only pick out a few words and phrases.

I shifted my focus to Diablo's machete and silently celebrated my choice to bring a rifle. His fingers vibrated on the wooden handle of the tool as if preparing for the fight of his life. Our slightly elevated position gave us a small advantage, but if the squad of ten men caught sight of us and attacked, we would be outnumbered almost two to one. We were likely better trained and possibly better armed, but our true ace in the hole was the warrior with the death grip on his machete.

The men continued their patrol, seemingly more interested in laughing with each other than finding us, so we lay motionless as they made their way south, clearly oblivious to our presence.

When they were out of sight, Diablo turned to me and whispered, "I don't like it."

"You don't like what?"

"I'm not sure, but something isn't right. Now is the time to cross the stream. I will go first. When I am invisible in the bushes on the other side, I want Singer to follow. He will set up overwatch for the rest of you. Cross one at a time and as quietly as possible."

"What about our tracks?" Hunter asked.

"Don't worry about them. There is nothing we can do to prevent us from leaving evidence behind. Just cross as quickly and as quietly as possible."

Without another word, Diablo leapt into a low crouch and sprang down the slope. He was across the stream and deep into cover on the opposite side in less than half the time it would take me to make the crossing.

Mongo motioned for Singer to move, and the sniper followed Diablo's lead and crossed the open space in seconds.

Thirty seconds after he left my side, Singer's voice appeared in my earpiece. "Overwatch is set. Move out."

Hunter tapped Tony, and the younger man sprang into action, moving without a stumble. Hunter followed and made short work of the crossing.

Mongo tapped my shoulder. "I'll go next. You bring up the rear and check both directions for anything that doesn't look as it should."

"Like what?"

"I don't know, but I'm with Diablo. Something about this doesn't feel right. Just get a picture in your head of how the stream looks in both directions. I'll see you on the other side."

Despite his size, there was nothing clumsy or lumbering about Mongo. He moved like a man half his size and age. To avoid the slick slope where Hunter crossed, Mongo took two full strides to the north before building speed to leap the flowing water. His footfalls were louder than anyone else's, but his quickness paid off as his broad form melted into the vegetation.

I eased myself forward toward the break in the tall grass so I could see in both directions before beginning my run. The sound of the stream changed ever so slightly, and just like the monkeys', my attention was piqued. Anything downstream wouldn't have changed the sound, so the action had to be to the north. I listened intently and detected another change in the water's sound.

Mongo's voice appeared in my earpiece. "What are you waiting for, Chase? Move!"

I whispered into my mic so quietly it had to be barely audible. "Something's happening upstream."

"How far?"

"I can't tell, but it's definitely something or someone in the water."

"Hold your position, and report any movement."

I pressed my chin to the ground and let my ears become my eyes. I wouldn't see the intruders before Singer spotted them, but from my position, I would likely hear them first.

I opened my eyes just in time to watch a muddy disturbance waft by on the surface of the stream. I whispered, "Floating mud."

"Roger. We're moving to intercept. Report changes."

I continued to focus on both the water's color and the sound it made as it cascaded across the exposed roots and muddy bottom. I saw glimpses of movement across the stream as my team moved northward. Whoever was wading in the stream clearly had no fear of exposing themselves. I silently wondered if it could be children playing, but I shook the idea from my head when I pictured the map of the area. No villages were close enough to grant access to the stream for playing children.

Whatever was in the creek was big enough to be a concern but not loud enough to be a covert threat. Whatever it was, my team would soon have it neutralized.

Singer's voice rang from my earpiece. "Contact. Seven men. Rifles and sidearms. Should I put them down?"

Forgetting I wasn't in charge, I opened my mouth to call him off, but Mongo beat me to the punch. "Stand by. If they see us and make any moves our way, we'll cut them down."

Singer whispered, "Roger."

The closer they came, the more noises they made, almost as if they wanted to be seen and heard—almost as if it were a diversion. With the lead man now clearly in sight, I watched his every move with laser focus. Just as the monkeys had done, the man stood erect and turned to the west, holding up a fist to stop his team. They froze in place and followed his gaze into the trees.

I hadn't heard or seen what caught their attention, but it had apparently been enough to stop them in their tracks. I watched as every man in the squad drew his weapon and climbed the opposite bank in pursuit of some unseen threat.

I reported their action, and Mongo returned, "Roger. In sight. Cross at will."

I replied, "Moving now."

I never heard Mongo's reply—only the echoing report of multiple gunshots and the sound of every cubic inch of breath in my lungs exploding through my mouth and nose.

Chapter 30
The Warrior's Dance

The weight crashing down on me felt like a steamroller pressing me into the earth, and I gasped hungrily in a wasted effort to refill my lungs with air. No matter how desperately I begged my diaphragm to force my lungs into submission, I only gagged on the emptiness.

Have I been shot? Is this the feeling of a scorching rifle round having torn through my lungs? Is the burning in my chest more than hunger for life-giving air? Is the crushing mass descending on me the weight of death itself?

The weight drove my face into the hot ground, both blinding me and destroying any hope I had of drawing air through my nose or mouth. Regardless of the source of the agony, I was seconds away from eternity, and panic crept into the corners of my mind. I felt as if I were lying beneath myself in an endless press that was determined to crush the life from my body, but my fingertips moved at the limits of my arms, and the five remaining toes I possessed pressed against the insole of my boot. I was alive, even if only temporarily. My left hand was twisted and pressed beneath my abdomen, but I could feel no warmth of blood or fluid. Perhaps I wasn't shot, or perhaps I was delirious from the shock.

My rifle lay an eternity away, yet only centimeters from the fingertips of my right hand. Powerless to move, breathe, or resist, I dug the toes of my boots into the softness of the earth and propelled myself forward an inch. The motion sent the crushing weight above me clawing forward, and a hammer pounded into the flesh and bones of my hand that was desperately grasping for my rifle.

Unable to thwart my endless quest for the weapon, the force above me made its first mistake. The old familiar feeling of a human fist driving against my ribcage told me I was still alive, still in the fight, and still a threat to my attacker. The second and third blows from the fist did something my body had refused to do for itself: they rolled my body to the left, barely enough to expose the corner of my mouth to the air. It sent a shuddering convulsion through my abdomen, forcing my lungs to draw the breath of life back into my previously dying cavity.

I no longer wanted my rifle. I only wanted to continue rolling and somehow get my back against the ground. Defeating an animal that fights from the flat of its back is nearly impossible. The full force of my legs, and the hammerlike construction of my right foot gave me advantages my attacker would never consider. I kicked and thrust at the ground like a man possessed until my hip rotated through ninety degrees and I was unstoppable. In less than a second, I would be on my back with my legs wrapped around my attacker and my fists free to do their terrible work. Giving me the inch I needed would prove to be my opponent's fatal mistake. I wouldn't lose the battle, and he would pay the ultimate price.

The final ninety degrees of my roll should've left my opponent vulnerable and off-balance, but he moved like a cat, leaping to his left and throwing a massive descending elbow strike to my face. The blow set fireworks exploding behind my eyelids and blood pouring into my mouth. Inhaling through my nose served only to suck blood and torn flesh into my throat. I gagged on the warmth and spat toward what I hoped was my attacker's face. My blood in his eyes would hopefully open another window for my counterattack. The pain I expected didn't come. It was, no doubt, arrested by the adrenaline rushing through my veins.

I reached to my right and continued rolling as my vision slowly cleared. A form hunkered just out of reach, and I lunged toward the darkened shape with my knife protruding from my clenched fist. The shadow fluttered sideward and sent me thrusting through nothing. I stumbled and fell back to the grassy earth. Barely in time, I tucked a shoulder and turned the energy of my fall into the force required to return to my feet. The fall and ultimate roll served to build at least six feet of distance between me and the man bent on killing me.

My vision continued to improve with every heaving breath, and I threw my blade into my left hand at the same time I snatched my Glock from its holster on my right hip. My opponent hadn't initially meant to kill me; otherwise, he would've stabbed or shot me long before I'd reclaimed my feet. If shots were to be fired between us, I would be the reason for the escalation.

I scanned the tall grass, watching every blade for unnatural movement. My blurred vision didn't allow for precise observation, but even out-of-focus motion would warn my brain of impending danger, giving me the opportunity to end the fight someone else had started.

As my mind focused, I remembered the earpiece and microphone. Help was only a call away if they weren't in a gunfight of their own on the other side of the stream.

"I could use some help over here." I realized the microphone that was once beneath my chin had long since become a casualty of the battle. Not only was my radio gone, so seemed to be my attacker. My ability to focus on large objects returned, and I could once again tell the difference between a bush and a crouching fighter.

Spinning in a constantly widening arc, I hoped to find my aggressor before he attacked from a distance. I felt the heightening grass brush against my hips as I managed to calm my breathing and listen for movement over the screams of the howler monkeys.

The sound I'd been hoping for rang in my ears like a tolling bell, and I spun to face the man who was determined to take me down without a weapon. He moved like the monkeys, and his form flashed into my vision only long enough to feel his booted foot strike my wrist and send my Glock tumbling toward the stream.

I lunged for the pistol, but the same boot that had kicked it from my hand landed sharply against my ribs, knocking me from my feet and rendering my lungs once again struggling to do their job. The ground caught me in its soggy embrace, and I refused to hold still, continuing the roll toward the flowing water as the man's boots sopped in the increasingly soft terrain around me.

Perhaps it was a streak of luck, or maybe my guardian angel, but I managed to get both hands wrapped around the man's ankle only inches from the water's edge. I clamped hard against his boot and twisted with every grain of strength I possessed. His leg buckled at the knee, and I took advantage of the instant of weakness. Releasing the ankle, I drove a powerful elbow into the back of the bending knee, continuing its fold and throwing the man off-balance. As his body hit the shallow water, I got my first dependable glance of my foe. He was bigger than me, tall and thick with long, lean muscle. I wanted to cry out for Mongo to jump into the fight, but I didn't have time. Ignoring the collision with the water, the man threw a wild fist toward my face. I turned to avoid the blow and managed to take only a grazing shot across my jawline.

I caught his fist and forced him facedown into the water. Drowning in a tablespoon wasn't possible, but maybe I could get enough water into his lungs to even the playing field.

Rifle fire filled the air to the north and west, but I couldn't fight two battles at once. I had my hands full of all the fight I wanted, and I had no intention of losing the upper hand again. My right knee in the small of his back and my left relentlessly pounding his ribs should've done the trick. Any lesser man would've gasped and ingested enough water to destroy his will to fight, but this man was nothing short of a warrior to his core.

Instead of fighting back or throwing wasted swatting blows with his hands, he drove his fists into the water and against the mucky bottom. He fully extended his arms and pushed his face and upper body from the stream. In one blinding motion, he spun away and reversed our positions.

I found myself on my knees in water just over my belt and the man's arms laced around my neck. I thrust backward in repeating powerful bucks, but I couldn't shuck him from my back. His relentless determination to lock the choke hold served only to strengthen my resolve. I bucked, twisted, and drove my chin into his forearm. Turning my head to the left, I hoped to press my chin into the bend of his elbow to break the hold before he could lock his right arm behind the crown of my skull. If he completed the hold, I'd be unconscious in seconds and fully at his mercy.

My shoulder and neck muscles ached and screamed for release, but I continued my quest for the soft flesh inside of his elbow. I threw my shoulders like a rodeo bull, hoping to disorient him and put him in front of me again, but no matter what I tried, he kept his left arm threaded tightly around my neck and his right arm pumping against my attempts to deny him the hold he clearly wanted.

Accepting that I would never get my chin in the crevice I so badly wanted, I reached over my head, grabbed two handfuls of hair, and threw my right shoulder toward the water. It worked, and man was soon upside down above my head and falling fast toward the surface of the now filthy water.

I had won. As soon as the splash came, I would crush his face with my heel and destroy not only his will to continue the fight, but also his ability.

I can't remember every mistake I made during the fight, but believing I'd won was my one unforgivable sin. I relaxed, let gravity do its cruel work, and waited for the splash. But instead of seeing and hearing the splash, I felt the man clench my shirt at my shoulders and tuck his knees beneath his body. His momentum, coupled with his grasp of my shirt, dragged me with him toward the waiting stream.

We landed on our sides, facing each other, and instead of chalking up the fight to the good guys, I watched in horrified slow motion as a strap of leather roared through the air from the end of the man's arm. The bulbous protrusion from the leather met my temple, and the warrior's dance ended beneath a veil of darkness.

Chapter 31
Alone With Myself

"Self-assessment" is what they called it at The Ranch. Clark's name for it was "waking up stupid." And I called it "un-ringing my bell." No matter how it's labeled, the first few seconds of consciousness after having been solidly in the spirit world are the epitome of terrifying confusion. Calming my breathing and willing my heart to stop pounding through my skull, I tried to piece together my situation.

I'm bound, hands, knees, and feet, gagged with a piece of cloth, and hooded. I'm moving in a vehicle. Whoever they are, they've done this before. Whoever the fighter was, he's big, strong, well trained, and experienced. Are my ribs broken? Maybe. The taste of blood on the rag in my mouth means I'm cut somewhere on my face, likely my nose. It's definitely broken. I'm alive, heart beating, lungs clear, head calm. Stay calm. Keep breathing. Listen, feel, count time. Pain? Not really. Just discomfort. No, it hurts . . . ribs and nose. Assets? I'm not dying . . . yet. I'm relatively unhurt. I still have my prosthetic. No headache, so probably no concussion. I'm not in shock. Those are all good things. Liabilities? Bound, blinded, lost time, unknown location, alone. SERE: Survival, Evasion, Resistance, Escape. I've survived so far, and they aren't trying to kill me yet. Evasion didn't work out. I can still resist. I will escape. Is my team alive? Are they wounded? Are they searching for me? Was the whole thing an elaborate ambush? Who would ambush us? Who were the men we killed at the church? Calm down. Breathe. Listen.

I pressed my feet against something hard and immovable and then raised my head to feel for confinement. The engine roar in my ears, the bouncing, and the wind blowing across my hands told me I was likely in the back of a truck.

Which direction are we going? How many captors are in the truck with me? Is anybody watching me?

I tested my theory of being alone by raising and lowering my head multiple times. No one spoke or kicked me or stepped on my skull, so I pulled my knees to my chest and forced my bound hands beneath my butt. The pain in my wrists and shoulders left me yearning to cry out, but I stifled the nearly overwhelming desire. With my hands behind my knees, there was only one remaining step to getting them in front of me. I had to force my hands and wrists beneath my feet one at a time. The maneuver was painful but necessary.

I slipped my wrists beneath my left heel and felt my bindings catch on the tread of my boot.

Pull the knees higher. Pull harder. Press the hands. You have to do it. Just do it.

I summoned the will from somewhere deep inside my soul and pulled with everything I had. My knees rose a fraction of an inch, and the bindings skipped across the boot treads. The pain was excruciating, and I let out a low, animalistic groan, but still, no one spoke or made any effort to stop me.

After catching my breath and preparing myself for the next wave of gut-wrenching pain, I shoved my wrists beneath my prosthetic and waited for the catch. It didn't come. The bindings slid across the sole as if someone had oiled the bottom of the boot, as well as the bindings.

Why had it been so easy? Is the prosthetic slightly shorter than my left leg? No . . . no, no, no! It's not oil. It's blood. My blood. How badly am I cut? Which hand? Am I seconds away from bleeding out from an open artery in my wrist? Calm down. Breathe. Survive. Evade. Resist. Escape.

One step closer to freedom with my hands in front of my body, my options expanded exponentially. I reached for my face and discovered a coarse bag over my head, tied loosely around my neck. I threaded a finger beneath the fabric and pulled the gag from my mouth. The rush of comparatively cool air that flooded my mouth and throat and lungs felt like an angel's kiss.

Don't stop. You don't have time to celebrate. Escape!

I pressed two fingertips against my nose, and bolts of lightning exploded behind my eyes.

Stay away from what used to be your nose. Get your hands free.

Suddenly, my foundation shuddered and bounced, sending my head bouncing like a rubber ball against the hard surface on which I lay. I silently prayed for that to never happen again, but the prayer of the assassin went unheard or unanswered as the vehicle continued to buck and bounce over the harsh surface of the road or field or whatever we were driving on.

I dug my thumbs beneath the binding at my neck and pulled, but nothing moved. I methodically slid my fingers around the perimeter of the bag at my neck and was quickly rewarded with the feeling of a simple knot. I worked the twisted string as the bouncing continued. It took several minutes, but the string finally parted, and I forced the bag upward across my battered face.

Blinding light poured in, and I blinked against the onslaught until I was capable of making out rough shapes and colors before me.

I was right. It was a truck bed. A rusty, filthy truck bed.

It's a small victory, but we still don't have time to celebrate. Escape.

I examined the bindings on my wrists. The mystery of the blood was solved in an instant. The spurs of the barbed wire wrapped twice around my wrists were buried in my flesh, but thankfully, the damage was little more than flesh wounds, and I hadn't opened any arteries yet.

I contorted my thumbs and index fingers to untwist the wire. With every motion, the barbs penetrated deeper into my flesh, but the pain didn't matter. I had the rest of my life to figure out how to escape, and the clock was ticking.

It may have taken only seconds, or perhaps hours, to twist my way out of the barbed wire handcuffs, but I'd done it, and I was one step closer to freedom.

I tried to ignore the pain and press on, but the blood concerned me. Even though the individual cuts were minor, there were more of them than I could count. Stopping the bleeding would soon become a priority.

I intentionally left the bag over my head to give the appearance that I was still well controlled—should anyone from the cab of the truck sneak a peek—so I lifted the front of the bag and examined the bindings at my knees and ankles. The two bindings were actually one piece of nylon rope that looked a lot like a ski rope. On the off chance that it had not been confiscated while I was unconscious, I reached for my pocketknife and found exactly what I expected: an empty pocket.

I refocused on the rope and examined the knots. They were simple but plentiful. Obviously, my abductor lived by the adage, "If you can't tie a knot, tie a lot."

One of the hallmarks of a poorly tied knot is often its difficulty in being untied. The overhand and accidental reef knots fell into this category, and I struggled with each bend of the rope until tiny shards of nylon were lodged deeply beneath my fingernails and blood from my fingertips joined the dripping liquid from my wrists. Frustrated, I growled as I picked and pulled at each infuriating knot. Finally, I remembered the words of the SERE instructor back at The Ranch: "Everything can be abraded with enough time and effort."

The rusty, crackling bed of the truck offered more than ample sharp edges, so I pressed my prosthetic against the bed and pumped my legs back and forth, feeling the rusted metal grabbing at the nylon with every pass. It was working, but not quickly, and I was expending energy I may have needed should I have gotten caught.

I paced my strokes, remembering Clark's admonition about my run time and cardiovascular fitness. As always, he'd been correct, and I was less than optimum. By the time the rope finally separated, I was winded, covered in blood, sweat, and mosquito bites. But I was free.

It took fifteen seconds—which felt like decades—to catch my breath before I mustered the courage to peer into the cab of the truck. The driver was hidden beneath a floppy bush hat soaked with years of sweat and filth. There was no rear-view mirror on the windshield, so I had no way of identifying my captor. Nothing good awaited me at our destination, and I gained no benefit by kicking my way through the back glass of the truck. So, my decision was made, and I crept over the wooden tailgate and hoped he would have a reason to slow down in the coming minutes.

Hanging outside the tailgate with my hip and the sides of my boots pressed into the jagged timber masquerading as a rear bumper, I watched the dirty, rock-dotted trail pass beneath me at thirty miles per hour. I would survive the fall and ultimate collision with the ground, but avoiding broken bones would be impossible. If I was unlucky enough to strike one of the rocks with my head, surviving would fall well into the unlikely category.

I waited as long as I could and prepared for the fall and roll. Just as I released the top edge of the tailgate with my fingertips, the truck bucked again, just as it had done previously, and I was catapulted from the tailgate, sending my body flying upward before crashing onto the craggy earth. I crossed my ankles and pulled my arms tightly against my chest, protecting my head and face with my battered hands.

The initial contact with the ground knocked the wind from my lungs again and sent me tumbling in every direction. Forcing myself to stay as compact as possible, I rolled to a stop and hopped into a crouch as I watched the truck slide to a stop.

The driver exploded from the cab, and I ran into the tree line as quickly as I could propel myself, but the torture my body had endured during the fight, confinement, and ultimate escape left me unstable and slow. The man would catch me at some point, but maybe he would be more winded than me when it happened.

Do not surrender! Run! Fight only if there is no other option!

The soles of my boots thudded into the ground like pounding hoofbeats, and I forced myself to continue, begging my legs to accelerate with every stride. My breath came fast and hard, and the pain in my legs, ribs, and head exploded with every step. I was running out of assets and stocking up on liabilities with every inch my attacker gained.

I'd prepared for and endured collisions at home plate a thousand times on the baseball field, so the thought of him tackling me didn't frighten me. That would merely bring the episode full circle and leave the two of us in another desperate ground fight. I lost the first one, but my life depended on me winning the next.

Despite my preparation, the collision never came. He never launched himself onto my back and forced me to the dirt. Instead, he fired two pistol shots into the ground at my galloping feet. He didn't have to miss, and I let my desire to live overcome my desperation to escape.

My feet thudded to a stop, and I hit my knees with my hands above my head. My pounding heart sounded like a relentless pile driver, and my breathing roared like a blacksmith's bellows forcing air into the forge's fire.

The hoofbeats behind me turned silent, and the man grabbed a handful of my hair, forcing my head through ninety degrees and turning my face skyward to meet his gaze. He roared in furious Spanish, "Who are you, and what do you want?"

Frozen by disbelief, pain, and self-loathing for having been caught a second time, I stared upward into eyes I'd known for three decades—into a face I'd seen every day in my own reflection. I sucked in enough air to force the words from my throat . . .

"I'm your brother."

Chapter 32
A Long Story

The man standing over me and holding my Glock in his hand with the muzzle pressed to my forehead wore the leathered skin of life in the tropical sun and the scars of a life spent in the company of dangerous men. His hard expression flashed to uncertainty and back again an instant before his actions reverted to his familiar state of violence.

He landed a boot against my neck, sending me crashing to the ground. Refusing to submit to his will, I twisted and pulled my knees back beneath my body in an effort to reclaim my previous position, but he threw a second crushing kick to my chest and pinned my right foot to the ground with the barrel of my Glock.

He leaned close, his sour breath assaulting my beaten and bloodied face. In growling Spanish, he said, "Why are you chasing me? If you refuse to answer, I will blow your foot to hell and ask again. Next, you will lose your knee, and I will continue until I get an answer I believe."

I moved my face within inches of his and said, "Do it!"

Without hesitation, he pulled the trigger and sent a single nine-millimeter round into the most solid section of my titanium foot, and I didn't flinch. His confidence melted into sheer disbelief, and his mouth fell open.

Moving with speed I didn't know I possessed, I seized his moment of weakness and snatched the pistol from his failing grip.
The impossibility of shooting a man in the foot and drawing no
reaction overwhelmed his sense of violent reality, and I continued
my motion forward, forcing him onto his back with the muzzle of
my reclaimed pistol thrust painfully into his crotch. Using the two
languages I knew he understood completely, violence and Spanish,
I said, "Now it's my turn to pull the trigger and your turn to try
not to flinch or bleed or die."

Just as I expected, he lunged forward to continue the fight, but I
caught him in the throat with a perfectly placed punch. The blow
sent him back to the ground, and I shoved the pistol beneath his
nose hard enough to split his upper lip under his filthy mustache.

I roared, "We can continue to fight if that's really what you
want, but I've lost my last battle with you. I will empty this pistol
into your skull if you do anything other than relax. ¿Comprende?"

When he spoke, his English was strong, but his tone was uncertain. "How did you do that?"

"How did I do what?"

He motioned toward my foot with his chin. "That thing with
your foot."

I took full advantage of the opportunity and tightened my jaw.
"I did it because there are parts of me that are not human, and
those parts of me will live on for eons after my flesh and blood
have turned to dust. Are you still interested in waging war against
a man like me?"

He may have ignored the question, or perhaps regarded it as
rhetorical, but either way, he changed the subject. "You claim to
be my brother, but I have no brother. I fell from the heavens and
tore open the earth. Hundreds of people saw it happen."

"Yeah, I saw it, too. I was just a child, and the Heaven you fell
from was the arms of our mother during the worst earthquake this

part of the world has ever seen. Everyone, especially our parents, believed you were dead. You didn't crash into the ground. The earth opened up and swallowed you in the aftermath of the earth-quakes. You've fallen victim to the lies you've been told, and especially the lies you've told yourself. You're nothing special, el Lagarto. Lizards are just slimy belly crawlers, and that's exactly what you are."

He ground his teeth together and spat in my face.

I repaid the blow with a butt-strike to his face with the Glock. Blood and spittle flew, and I moved closer. "I warned you once. The fighting is over. We're going to talk like men and not behave like animals. As I told you, I've lost my last battle with you. The next one will end with you being torn from limb to limb. Do not test me!"

He squinted and shook off the pain from my punch. "How did you find me?"

I pulled my pistol from his face and created distance between us so I could stop any attack he might attempt. "You found me, and if your men harmed mine in any way, you *will* pay for their sins in a hell I will create just for you."

He closed his eyes. "The threats aren't necessary. Your men aren't hurt. But mine are . . ."

I nodded slowly. "That's what happens when we're attacked. It never ends well for those who *think* they can defeat us."

"Who are you, and more than that, *what* are you?"

I took a long, considerate breath. "I told you already. I'm your brother. My name is Chase Fulton, and I'm an American."

He held up a finger and waved it between us. "We're the same. You're a mercenary like me."

"No, I'm no mercenary. I'm just a man who came a long way to find you."

He couldn't take his eyes off the burned hole in the top of my right boot. The wonder in his eyes reminded me of the look I must've worn the day Dr. Robert "Rocket" Richter told me my parents were spies. A curtain was drawn back, and I was allowed a look into a world I never knew existed. Now it was my turn to pull back the same curtain.

I grabbed the right leg of my pants and pulled it up, exposing the titanium rod protruding from my stump and connecting my prosthetic foot to the rest of my body.

He stared down at the device and shook his head. "How did it happen?"

"I killed a man on a ship in Western Africa. I lost it in the fight."

The shake of his head morphed into a nod. "See, you *are* a mercenary."

"Perhaps I am. But long before either of us was anything, we were brothers."

"Tell me about them."

"Tell you about who?"

He licked his lips. "Our parents."

I considered my answer and told him the truth. "They were missionaries."

"Were?"

I swallowed hard. "Yes, were. They died in Panama when I was still a boy."

"Both of them are dead?"

"Yes. They were killed by men like . . ."

He sighed. "Men like me?"

I considered the question for a long moment. "I don't know. The only things I know about you right now is that we share the same DNA and you've got twice as many feet as I do."

He didn't allow it to happen, but he couldn't stop it. The chuckle came and sounded exactly like mine. "What do you want to know?" he asked.

I stammered. "I don't know. I guess I want to know everything."

He stared into the few white bulbous clouds floating overhead. "Are we really brothers?"

"Yeah, I think we really are."

"Do we have more brothers?"

I fought back the sickening pain from so many years before. "No, we *had* a sister, but she was killed with our parents. All that remains of our family is you, me, and a cousin named Maebelle. She's a chef in Miami."

"Miami in Florida?"

It was my turn to laugh. "That's the only Miami I know."

His eyes turned back skyward. "Look up there. Do they ever call to you?"

I followed his line of sight. "If you mean the clouds, the answer is yes. They've always called to me, and I'd rather be up there than anywhere else."

As if I hadn't answered, he squinted against the sun. "You said we only have a cousin, but I have a daughter."

"A daughter? So, I have a niece?"

"Yes, una sobrina. Her name is Angelina, and she's six . . . or maybe seven."

I furrowed my brow. "You don't know how old your own daughter is?"

"I've only seen her twice that her mother knows, but I sometimes wait near her school to watch her come and go. She's beautiful and perfect."

"I'm sure she is. I have a wife, Penny, but no children. I got hurt on a mountain in Afghanistan, and I can't have children."

"That's sad. Children are the only meaningful thing we leave behind when we die."

I wasn't certain I agreed with his position, but that discussion could be added to the list of ten thousand other things I wanted to talk about with my only brother. Instead of continuing down that road, I said, "Listen . . . I need to talk to my team. Did you pick up my comms from the stream?"

He motioned toward his truck. "Yes. I have your weapons and your radio. I can't give you back the weapons, but I will let you tell your men you're alive." He climbed to his feet and offered a hand.

I hesitantly took it, and he pulled me from the ground. I followed him to the truck, still uncertain over his comment about the weapons.

As we approached the vehicle, he turned and held up a hand. "Wait here. I'll get your radio."

I stopped and studied his expression. "It's not exactly a radio. It's a satellite uplink."

His eyes widened into saucers. "Satellite?"

Before I could answer, he held up both hands and ordered, "Stay right there."

He backed away toward the truck while keeping me in sight. When he made it to the open driver's door, he reached inside, feeling for the commo gear. He came away from the door with my comms in one hand and my M4 rifle in the other. He tossed the transmitter about halfway to me, and I took a step forward. The crack and thunder of two rounds exiting the muzzle of the rifle burst through the air, and the satellite transmitter vanished into thousands of tiny shards of black plastic and green circuitry.

I leapt backward and pulled my Glock just as he shouldered the rifle with his finger covering the trigger. "Don't do it," I yelled. "I'm not here to hurt you."

"Put down the pistol. Don't make me kill you, Chase . . . if that's really your name."

I raised the pistol and focused on the center of his chest.

He yelled, "Put it down! Now!"

"I don't want to hurt you," I said as confidently as possible. "I just want some time with you. That's all."

He pressed the trigger, and the searing whistle of the round passing my head at well above the speed of sound sent tremors down my spine. His face contorted into the menacing face of a coldblooded killer. "I will not miss again, mercenary. You will put down the pistol . . . now."

His was the look of a man fully intent on taking my life. I'd seen the look before, and I'd ripped the life out of every skull who dared stare at me with such intent. One press of my trigger would drop him where he stood, but no matter how fervently my brain screamed for my index finger to squeeze, the screams were ignored in defiant immovability. I simply could not put a bullet in my own brother, regardless of his willingness to do so to me.

I don't know how long we remained in the frozen standoff. It felt like hours but was likely less than a second. I knelt and laid my Glock on the grass. I didn't look up, but the approaching shadow said he was moving toward me, perhaps to put a round through the top of my head or maybe to retrieve the Glock.

He pressed the round, hot muzzle of my M4 against the top of my head.

I trembled. "You don't have to kill me. I only came here to look into your eyes and tell you that you have a brother. Nothing more."

He spoke in soft, confident Spanish. "No one comes to Guatemala with a fire team simply to look into someone else's eyes. We may be brothers by blood, but my true brothers are the men who took out your team on the other side of the stream."

"I don't have any reason to lie to you. I wanted to see you and tell you about our family. I don't want anything from you."

His voice rose, and he pressed the muzzle tighter against my head. "You're a liar. At best, you're a mercenary sent to kill me. At worst, you're DEA sent to apprehend me. I can't allow either of these things to happen."

"Why would the DEA want to apprehend you?"

I was answered by the telltale sound of the barely perceptible tick of my M4's trigger made at the beginning of its travel.

Hesitation was a luxury I couldn't afford, so I lunged in desperation toward my Glock while throwing my left arm up to hopefully sweep the rifle away, but I was too slow. My instant of hesitation was punctuated by the soul-shredding explosion only inches above my head.

Chapter 33
Let's Play a Game

I collapsed to the ground, expecting the all-encompassing darkness to envelop me. I dreamed of a thousand years with Penny's face in my hands and sunlight dancing on the streaks of blonde in her hair. "I love you" danced from her lips, and I opened my eyes to welcome the light that lay just beyond the veil of darkness, separating the world of the living from the world of souls devoid of bodies and pain and sorrow.

Instead of the warmth of the loving, welcoming light, I saw my brother careening backward, his face and arms blackened from the explosion. My M4 lay twisted in demolished ruin at his feet, and he pawed feverishly at his eyes with both fists.

Logic abandoned me, but the caveman parts of my brain did not. The tiny amygdala sent a flash message to the hypothalamus, triggering my sympathetic nervous system and dispatching electrical lightning bolts through the autonomic nerves that commanded the glands to pour adrenaline into my bloodstream. All of this happened in an impossibly minuscule portion of time, and the arcs and sparks morphed into pulsing muscles and a thundering heartrate.

Springing from my kneeling position, I drove my left shoulder into his gut, lifting him from his feet and forcing him backward toward the truck. As if having been fired from a massive cannon, Diablo de Agua landed on my brother's shoulders like a primitive tree-dwelling beast. Hunter added his momentum to the melee from my left and sent the four of us crashing to the ground.

Refusing to cease his aggression, Diablo wrapped the Lizard into a headlock, the likes of which I'd never seen. Both of his arms, in conjunction with his legs, enveloped the man's head and neck while Hunter punished his ribs with crushing knee strikes. In seconds, Diablo's unorthodox lock rendered the man unconscious and seemingly lifeless.

I rolled onto my back and stared into the perfect blue sky dotted with billows of white. Through gasps of thirsty breath, I asked, "Where did you guys come from? Is everyone still alive?"

Diablo ignored the question and bound the man, hand and foot, giving him the look of a defeated rodeo calf. Hunter dusted off his pants and gave Lizard one final love tap with the heel of his boot. "Yeah, all of us good guys are still alive, but the bad guys aren't having a good day. They're standing in line in front of Saint Peter."

I caught my breath. "I'd be in that line with them if you guys hadn't shown up."

Hunter picked up what remained of my M4 rifle and tossed it toward me. "It wasn't us who saved your bacon. It was Singer. Mongo ordered him to kill that guy, but apparently, he 'missed.'"

"Singer doesn't miss," I said.

"Yeah, we all know that. Are you all right?"

"I've had better days, but I'm sure glad to see you."

Hunter wiped the sweat from his brow. "I've seen you fight a bunch of men, but I've never seen anybody get the jump on you the way he did."

I surveyed my brother's limp form. "He's faster than anybody I've ever seen."

Diablo looked up and rolled his eyes. "Really?"

"Okay, maybe not you, but I've never fought anybody who moved like that."

Hunter said, "That's why me and Diablo hit him together. It was obvious you were about to lose another round."

"How long will he be out?" I asked.

Diablo shook his head. "Not long. Maybe five minutes, maybe less."

"Where are Mongo and Singer?"

Hunter pointed toward the northwest. "Here they come."

When the team was reassembled, I asked, "How did you find me?"

"We didn't find you," Mongo said. "Skipper tracked your sat-com until your hermano over there blew it to bits."

I sat up. "Thank you, Skipper."

Tony tossed me his comms. "Here. Tell her yourself."

I stuck the earpiece in place and pressed the button. "What would I do without you?"

"Get dead . . . a lot. Are you okay?"

"Yeah, I'm okay, thanks to you and my *real* brothers."

"Is he dead?" she asked.

I gave him another look. "No, he's alive, but Diablo left him unconscious and tied up like a pretzel."

"Good. Don't let him free again."

"Speaking of not letting him free . . . He's worried we're from the DEA and here to arrest him. Can you find out if there's an international warrant in place?"

She hesitated. "We don't know his name yet."

"Run el Lagarto for now. I'll get his real name out of him when he wakes up from Diablo's goodnight kiss."

Although I couldn't hear the keystrokes, I could almost see her fingers flying across the keys.

Almost a minute later, she said, "Is it spelled L-a-g-a-r-t-o?"

"As far as I know, but he's coming around. Stand by."

I reached for Hunter's canteen, and he stuck it in my palm. I pulled off the lid and landed a foot on the man's chest. When the contents of the canteen hit him in the face, he squirmed and spat as if he were drowning.

I gave him an open-handed slap across his left cheek and grabbed his chin. "You screwed up, Lagarto. Your men are dead, and I'm not."

He squinted, forced open his eyes, and tugged at his bindings. "My men are dead?"

"That's right. And you're on the verge of joining them if you don't cooperate. Tell me your name."

He slowly eyed each of us. "So, I was right. You *are* mercenaries. DEA men wouldn't have survived."

I slapped him again, and he flinched. "Your name! Now!"

He blinked away the pain. "You know my name. I am el Lagarto."

I held out my hand, and Tony slapped a pistol into my palm. I clenched the weapon, racked the slide, and stuck the muzzle to the man's forehead. "Your name."

He squeezed his eyes closed as if willing the weapon to fire. "That is the only name I have."

I pulled my pistol from his face and stuck my boot beneath his chin. "You like games, do you? Okay, then, let's play a little game I like to call Too Far. It works like this. Since I've learned you're not afraid of dying, I'm going to push you deeper and deeper into your worst nightmare until I find out what you *are* afraid of."

Hunter took a knee beside el Lagarto and rubbed his hands together. "Boy oh boy, this is going to be fun to watch. Chase is the undisputed world champion of this game. You're in for a real treat."

I lowered my muzzle to his crotch. "We could start here, but last time, the guy bled out before I could win the game. Maybe we'll start a little lower since I owe you one through the foot. How does that sound?"

He squirmed and drew his bound feet as close to his body as possible.

I grinned. "Oh, you must be ticklish. I think we hit a nerve already. Since your feet seem to be important to you, we'll save those for round eleven."

I withdrew my multitool from my pocket and unfolded the cutting pliers. "Hold his wrist, Mongo. I'm starting with a thumb."

The giant took el Lagarto's wrist in his viselike grip and held his hand toward me.

I slid the jaws of the cutting pliers just beneath the second knuckle of his thumb and locked eyes with him. "Name?"

"You won't do it," he growled through clenched teeth.

Mongo laughed. "Not only will he do it, but he'll do it and play in your blood when he's finished. You boys come from a long line of ruthless, hardcore fighters. I know which one of you I've got my money on to come out on top, and it ain't you, lizard man."

I applied enough pressure to separate the flesh around the knuckle, and he roared like an animal. I continued squeezing and grinning.

"Listen close," I said. "This is one of the best parts. I love the sound the knuckle makes when it comes apart."

He roared in pain as I squeezed, but I stopped the pressure when blood began to pool on Mongo's forearm.

"You're making too much noise," I said. "We won't be able to hear the sound if you keep yelling like that. Are you ready to continue?"

Sweat poured from his face, and he flushed pale even beneath his sun-darkened skin. "I'm telling you, that is my only name. I have no other. There was no one to name me as a baby."

"Somebody fed you and changed your diaper. What did that somebody call you?"

"El Lagarto is all I have ever been."

I set my jaw and regripped the multitool. His thumb was coming off no matter how badly it sickened me. I swallowed hard and took a long breath. The instant I squeezed, Singer yelled out. "Chase! Wait!"

I looked up to see our sniper pulling his microphone to his lips. "Go ahead, Skipper."

I couldn't hear her voice through the sat-com, so I reached for my earpiece. It was dangling beneath my ear, so I thumbed it back into place just in time to hear Skipper say, "I've got Special Agent Ray White on the line. I'm patching him through."

The earpiece crackled, but finally, the voice boomed loud and clear. "Chase? This is Ray White in DC. What have you gotten yourself into now?"

I released the thumb. "I have el Lagarto in custody. I've not gotten his real name out of him yet, but I have a feeling he's just one digit away from spilling his guts."

"Take it easy, Chase. I've got the boys on it. Whoever this guy is, they tell me he may not have a name. Just hold tight."

Hunter gave our victim a shove. "You're one lucky SOB. You know that?"

A few seconds later, White said, "Do you really have this guy rolled up?"

"Yeah, we do. Why?"

"Uh, can you get him back to the States?"

"What's going on, Ray? What's this about?"

"It's a little hard to explain. Since Nine Eleven, we've changed the way we interact with other government agencies. I'm sure you know about that."

I said, "I don't need a history lesson, Ray. Just tell me what's going on."

"Who, uh, sent you down there to pick him up?"

"Nobody sent me. I'm—*we're*—here because we believe this guy is my brother. We're here on our own dime. Now spit it out, Ray. I'm a little busy cutting off some fingers."

He groaned. "I'd recommend stopping if it's el Lagarto's fingers you're lopping off. The Agency wants him back."

"Back? What do you mean, they want him back? Which agency?"

"*The* Agency, Chase."

"The CIA?"

White cleared his throat. "Look, I don't have time to get caught up in the middle of whatever this is, so I'm handing you off to a case officer from Langley. I've got enough to deal with trying to keep your little girlfriend in harness."

"She's not my girlfriend, Ray, and I can't recommend harnessing her. You won't like what she does with your wagon."

"Yeah, I'm learning that same lesson. Anyway, hang on. I'm putting you on with some Boy Scout who still thinks information only flows one direction."

"I'm not interested in what the Agency wants. I've got work to do."

A series of clicks sounded in my earpiece, and a distant voice asked, "Is this Supervisory Special Agent Fulton?"

I clenched my teeth. "No, this is Chase."

Chapter 34
Along Came a Spider

The previous few hours of my life felt like a warped, twisted psychological experiment designed by a demented sadist, and the Cain and Abel symbolism wasn't lost on me. I'd been attacked by my brother and survived. I had attacked him, and he survived. We shared a moment of confession and even talked about our shared love of the sky. In that moment, I may have been the most fulfilled of any moment I would ever experience on this Earth, but like so many beautiful things in life, the moment was fleeting and culminated in a crescendo of violence and the acceptance of the inevitability of death's brutal sword. The brothers of my choice snatched me from the jaws of certain death at the hand of a man far less of a brother than any of the men surrounding me.

The voice in my earpiece yanked me back to cruel reality. "Agent Fulton? Are you there?"

"It's Chase, and yes, I'm here. Who are you?"

"My name isn't important . . ."

Before he could continue, I said, "It is if continuing this conversation is important. You'll give me your name, and my analyst will verify who and what you are before this goes any further."

"That's not how this works."

"That's exactly how it works, and one of us will flinch in the next five seconds. Either you'll give in and tell me who and what you are, or you'll be all alone on this call, and you'll never hear my voice again. Five . . . four . . . three . . . two . . ."

"Okay, okay," he said with frustration lacing through every syllable. "My name is Seymour, Alex Seymour, and I'm an Agency case officer at Langley. My direct superior is—"

Skipper interrupted. "Okay, Case Officer Seymour. You check out. Tell us what you want."

Seymour stumbled. "Who was that?"

I said, "That was an analyst far superior to any you have in your basement, Seymour. Now, tell me what you want."

"It's not what I want, Agent . . . I mean, Chase. It's what the Agency wants. We want you to bring el Lagarto in out of the cold."

"Out of the cold? Are you saying he's an Agency asset?"

"I'm not at liberty to divulge the identity of Agency assets, but it's safe to say—"

"Look, Seymour. I'm in the middle of the Guatemalan rain forest with a guy who looks a lot like me and is tied up at my feet. We're both bloody, bruised, and beaten up. I'm looking around, and I don't see any of your guys with blood pouring from their broken noses, so I think it goes without saying that I'm the only one in any kind of position to negotiate. We play this my way, or you're free to come on down here yourself and see how you fare against the two dozen guys who tried to kill us in the past two days. So, what's it going to be?"

His sigh was either resolution or submission, and I could almost see him pulling at the knot of his power tie. Whatever he said next would disclose the verdict.

Partial submission turned out to be the next step. "Okay, Fulton. Here's what I *can* tell you. El Lagarto has, in the past, cooperated with certain undertakings related to U.S. National interests in the region—"

"Goodbye, Seymour."

"Wait! Just wait! I have to get authorization to divulge anything else."

"Two minutes," I said. "That's what you get. And when you come back, you'll be talking with our analyst, Elizabeth. If you pass her smell test, she'll reconnect you to me. I've got too much real work to do here to listen to elevator music while you keep me on hold. Two minutes, and not a second longer. Go!"

I silenced the comms and placed a heel on el Lagarto's kneecap. "Tell me everything you know about the American CIA."

He laughed. Tied up, beaten up, and surrounded by some of the deadliest men alive, he actually laughed. "A garden of snakes. That's what I know about your CIA. They promise me and people like me money and safety and security as if they've cornered the market on such things. 'Support this man. Kill that man. Prop up this candidate. Overthrow this one.' It's always the same."

"Wait a minute. Are you telling me you work for the CIA?"

"Everybody works for the CIA down here. Your government is the largest employer in Central America. How do you not know this?"

I took a knee beside him. "The CIA wants me to deliver you to them in the States. Why would they want me to do that?"

He stared down at his bindings. "Why does a spider spin a web?"

"To catch the fly."

He aimed his chin toward his wrists and ankles. "It looks like I am the fly."

I motioned toward his truck. "I think you were the spider while I was in the back of your truck. Where were you taking me?"

"I was taking you somewhere safe."

"Safe for you, or for me?"

He closed his eyes. "There is no place safe for you in this part of the world, my brother. Not as long as you're spinning webs for the CIA."

"I'm not working for the CIA," I demanded. "I was telling the truth when I told you I came here to find you, completely of my own accord."

"I know you believe that, but you are foolish and naïve."

Before I could react, Skipper's voice filled my ear. "He checks out, Chase. I think you should listen to him."

"Patch him back in."

The line clicked and popped until Skipper said, "Go ahead, Mr. Seymour. Chase is on the line."

Mr. Seymour, I thought. *That's interesting.*

"All right, Seymour. Let's hear it."

"The man you have in custody is a friend of the United States, and we owe him a great debt of both gratitude and financial reward. We want you to bring him home so we can make sure he receives everything he's earned."

"Stand by, Seymour."

I covered my mic. "Get a set of comms on him. I want him to hear this."

Hunter stuck an earpiece into el Lagarto's left ear and gave me a nod.

"Say that again, Seymour."

The case officer repeated his speech as if reading it from a cue card.

"What are you offering?" el Lagarto asked.

I said, "He can't hear you. You don't have a mic—only an earpiece. But I'll ask him for you."

"My brother wants to know what the CIA is offering."

Seymour said, "We're not offering. We're guaranteeing a significant financial reward and relocation anywhere in the world in return for his cooperation in planning operations in Central America."

"Wait a minute," I said. "You first told me that you owe this man a financial debt, as well as gratitude, for what he's already done. Now it sounds like you're negotiating a job. Those aren't the same things."

In typical bureaucratic fashion, Seymour said, "We do owe him a great deal, and he will be rewarded, but what we truly want is his cooperation and insider knowledge on future projects."

I looked down at the bound man at my feet. "What do you say? Do you want to go to the States?"

He spoke softly. "Are you certain he can't hear me?"

I covered my mic. "Yes, I'm certain."

"Look in my eyes and tell me you're not CIA."

I knelt again and locked eyes with him. "I am not now, nor have I ever been an officer of the Central Intelligence Agency."

He blinked in rapid succession. "And if I said I would walk away and never harm you, would you let me go?"

Without blinking, I said, "Why were you willing to kill me?"

"Because I wasn't convinced you were my brother. The story is almost impossible to believe."

"I understand, but do you believe me now?"

He nodded. "I do."

"Then, the answer is yes. If you want me to cut you loose so you can disappear back into your world, that's what I'll do to prove to you I'm not spinning a web for the CIA."

He bowed his head, obviously in deep thought—or perhaps nefarious plotting. When he raised his head and opened his eyes, he said, "If I agree to come with you, will I be a prisoner?"

I keyed my mic. "Open the line with Seymour."

Skipper said, "Okay, the line is open."

"Are you there, Seymour?"

"I'm here."

"If I bring my brother home, he will not be your prisoner nor mine. You will arrange for an immunity agreement with the Department of Justice for any crimes he may have allegedly committed in the past. These are not negotiating points. They are the conditions on which I will bring my brother back to the United States. He will not be incarcerated or otherwise held against his will by any agency of the United States for any prior acts, criminal or otherwise. Are you tracking?"

He said, "I don't have the authority to—"

I cut in. "Then the Agency made a terrible decision putting you on the phone with me. Goodbye, Seymour."

"Okay! Don't cut me off. I'll get it done. But it will take some time."

"It'll take some time for us to get back to the States, as well, but we won't put a foot on dry ground until we have everything in writing and approved by the Attorney General."

"Chase, you're being unreasonable."

I laughed. "When was the last time you fought twelve men with a pair of nuns watching?"

"What?"

"That was only part of what yesterday held for me. We won, by the way. Oh, and hang on just a second . . ." I turned to Mongo. "How many of his men did you put down back there?"

"Eight, and two got away."

I opened the mic again. "Add eight more men to that body count. Seymour, when was the last time you faced more than thirty men determined to kill you in two days?"

The line was silent, so I said. "I almost forgot. I've spent close to a hundred thousand bucks out of my pocket to find el Lagarto.

When did you last write a check that big out of *your* account to fund a mission?"

He still didn't answer, so I continued. "I see. Now, tell me again how I'm being unreasonable."

He finally spoke. "I'll have your paperwork within twenty-four hours."

"Good. Now we're getting somewhere. And about that financial reward you owe . . . Let's have a number."

"I'm not authorized—"

"Good," I said. "That sounds like a quarter of a million dollars to me. My analyst will have the offshore account created and opened by the time I say goodbye. You can deliver the payment there and send the paperwork to the analyst. When all of that is done and verified, I'll let you know if I can talk my brother into coming home with me."

Seymour said, "I don't think you understand how things work in Washington. I can't just snap my fingers and make all of this happen overnight."

"That's fine. While you're dragging your feet, think about bringing your team of operatives down here to the jungle. The bad guys are dangerous, but the mosquitoes are downright demons. Good luck, Seymour."

I plucked the earpiece from el Lagarto and shut down my comms. "Have you ever been to the States?"

He shook his head.

"Do you want to go?"

He looked over his shoulder at Mongo. "Did you really kill eight of my men?"

The big man shook his head. "No. We killed all ten of them, but I didn't want the CIA believing we'd paved the yellow brick road through the jungle for them."

El Lagarto wiggled his captive hands. "I have no reason to harm you anymore."

I nodded to Hunter, and he drew his knife. El Lagarto was free with two passes of Hunter's blade, but my partner clearly wasn't convinced I'd made the best decision.

He pressed the tip of the blade beneath the man's chin. "Immunity paperwork be damned. If you so much as hiccup toward any member of this team—this family—I'll carve your heart out and shove it down your throat. ¿Comprende, bandito?"

He raised his chin, exposing a trickle of blood on the glistening blade. "Banditos are from Mexico. Apparently, I'm from wherever Chase is from."

Hunter wiped his blade on el Lagarto's cheek. "Chase may not have the stomach to kill you, but my gut feels just fine about ending you where you stand, so just give me a reason."

El Lagarto held out a hand, and I pulled him to his feet.

He said, "Your men love you, and that says more about your character than any paper the CIA writes for me. Take me home with you, brother."

Chapter 35
Take the Long Way Home

Mongo spun in circles scanning the tree line. "Has anybody seen Diablo?"

My heart sank, and I joined Mongo in his visual search.

El Lagarto said, "You mean the little guy who choked me out, right?"

Mongo said, "Yeah, why?"

"He's not the devil. He's la Fiera, the wild beast."

I said, "No matter what you call him, I think it's safe to say he's gone." I brought my comms to life. "Disco, Chase, over."

Our chief pilot said, "Go for Disco."

"Get Skipper to pass you our location, and put the chopper on those coordinates."

"Do you want me or Leo on the controls?"

"You. Leave Leo there with the Caravan, but bring the keys with you."

Twenty minutes later, the *whop-whop* of the Huey resounded through the trees. Disco eased the machine onto the ground a hundred feet away, and we loaded up.

I slapped our pilot on the shoulder. "Disco, meet the Lizard."

Disco gave him a salute but received only a nod in return.

I asked, "Do you want to ride up front?"

El Lagarto motioned toward the cockpit. "Up there?"

"Yes, up there. It's fine if you want to."

"I don't know how to make it fly. This is my first time."

"Your first time in a Huey?"

"My first time in a helicopter."

"But I thought you said the clouds call to you."

"Oh, yes. All my life. But I've never touched one."

I gave our pilot another tap on the shoulder. "Trade places with me."

Without hesitation, Disco lowered the collective and brought the engine to flight idle.

I hopped from the chopper and grabbed my brother's shirt. "Come on. Get up here with me."

I opened the door and helped him inside. "Don't touch anything until I get in." I rounded the nose and climbed aboard. "Put your right hand on the stick and your feet on the pedals. You can follow me through the takeoff."

"You can fly this?"

I gave him a grin and took my little brother for his first helicopter ride. As we climbed out to the northeast, I said, "There's nothing to it. Just push forward ever so slightly to go forward, and make it go straight with your feet."

He jerked his hand from the cyclic and his feet from the pedals. "No! I can't."

"Sure you can. It's in your blood. Trust me."

He hesitantly took the cyclic in his hand and slid his feet back onto the pedals. I covered the controls and kept him from turning us inside out, but in minutes, he had the chopper obeying his every command.

"What if I want to go up or down?"

I pointed between our seats. Put your left hand on the handle on your side that looks just like mine. It's called the collective control. Pull to go up, and push to go down. It's really that simple, but do it gently."

He gripped the collective and made small changes in altitude. The grin never left his face, and the wonder never left his eyes. "This isn't so hard," he said.

"No, flying isn't hard, but landing and taking off requires a lot of practice."

"You will teach me?" he asked.

I couldn't believe the size of the lump in my throat.

We made our way back to the airfield, where I flew the approach and landed with my brother holding the controls with me and following my every movement.

I shut down the turbines, and we dismounted the chopper. Leo stood from beneath the Caravan, yawning and stretching from his demanding nap while guarding the airplane. He glared at my copilot with disdain in his eyes, but he didn't say a word.

El Lagarto pointed back and forth between the Caravan and the chopper. "These belong to the CIA?"

"No. I told you I don't work for the CIA. The chopper is his, and the airplane is mine."

He stared at the massive aircraft. "That's yours? And you can fly it, as well?"

I chuckled. "Yes to both questions. Believe it or not, it's a lot easier to fly than the helicopter. It has fewer moving parts. Go ahead. Climb up there and have a look."

He turned with uncertainty on his face and raised an eyebrow. "Really?"

"Yes. Go ahead."

He climbed the ladder and pulled open the door. Hunter shoved Tony toward the Caravan, sending him bounding up the rear ladder and into the cabin.

"What was that about?" I asked.

Hunter said, "There's a pile of guns and ammo in there, and you just turned him loose. I know he's your brother and all, but we can't forget that he's also the guy who stuck your gun to your head and would've killed you if Singer hadn't blown the rifle out of his hand."

I bowed my head. "Of course, you're right. It's just weird knowing I have a brother and actually having him with me."

Hunter threw an arm around my shoulders. "Just be careful."

"Thanks. I don't know what I'd do if I didn't have you watching my back."

"It ain't your back that needs watching. It's your noggin, College Boy."

"College Boy? Did Clark hand that one down to you?"

He tried to imitate our handler's crooked grin. "Somebody's got to keep you straight, and I guess that somebody is me now."

"You've got a long way to go to master that crooked smile. I've seen women all over the world faint when Clark does it. Somehow, it doesn't seem to work so well for you."

His look turned solemn. "What's the plan? Are we taking him back to Bonaventure or dropping him off at Langley?"

"We'll see," I said. "For now, we're just watching and waiting."

"I think you're doing the waiting, and the rest of the team and I are doing the watching."

"I hear you. And I appreciate you keeping me in check. I've never done anything like this before."

He threw a pulled punch to my gut. "Nobody's ever done anything like this before. Just keep your head on straight, and I'll make sure you keep it on your shoulders."

I took a seat on the portside pontoon of the Caravan and called Skipper. "I need to talk to Captain Sprayberry aboard the *Lori Danielle*. Can you make that happen?"

"Can I make it happen?" She huffed. "I can get you in touch with the man in the moon if that's what you want. Give me thirty seconds."

"Chase, how are you?"

"I'm good, Captain. How's the boat?"

"Shipshape. We're wrapping up the shakedown now. There were a few minor glitches, but all in all, she's ready for action."

"These glitches . . . Are the engineers addressing them?"

"They are. In fact, they've cleaned off the entire punch list except for one little vibration nobody can explain when we transition from foils back to displacement."

"That sounds pretty picky to me," I said. "Wouldn't every machine vibrate a little when it transitions from a flying machine to a boat?"

"It's not exactly a flying machine when we're up on the foils. It's still a boat, but I get your point. It's enough of an issue for me to want somebody to explain why it's doing it before I accept the ship."

"I like your style, Barry. If it ain't right, fix it."

"You can thank Captain Stinnett for that. He's chewed me out more times than I can remember for letting little things slip by."

"Thanks to Captain Stinnett, then, but that's not why I'm calling. How soon can you be in Puerto Barrios, Guatemala?"

I could hear him fumbling with charts. "Are you still using paper charts?"

He said, "I'm a little bit old-school. Charts work when batteries go dead. GPS systems don't. Let's see . . . We're off the Bahama bank now, so that looks like about a thousand miles. It'll be tempting to play hide-and-seek with the Cubans on the way by, but I think I can resist if you're in a hurry. We can make it in less than thirty-six hours if we stay off the foils, but if it's an emergency, we can cut that time in half."

I scanned my team and drew a timetable in my head. "Start this way on the thirty-six-hour plan, and leave the Cubans alone. If I need you sooner, I'll let you know."

"Aye-aye."

I said, "Skipper, let me know when it's just you and me on the line."

"Okay . . . It's just us now."

"Here's what's going to happen. Seymour is going to balk at at least one of the things we demanded. Those guys at Langley always have to have it their way, but we're going to make them understand that we're not Burger King. They can have it our way or no way at all. I'm putting my brother on the *Lori Danielle*. At sea, he'll be untouchable. When the Agency fulfills their commitment, we'll deliver him ashore."

She grunted. "I think you mean *if* they fulfill their commitment. There's a huge difference. What's the plan if they don't come through?"

"We'll burn that bridge when we come to it. For now, keep me posted on the ship's position, and we're going to clean up the mess we made down here before we pop smoke and bail out. Do you have anything for me?"

She clicked her tongue against her teeth. "Yeah, there's one thing. That thing in Virginia when you saved the little girl from the kidnappers has gotten some media attention."

"Please tell me they didn't release our names or pictures. That's the last thing we need."

"No, nothing like that, but Christopher Abbot, the CEO of Abbot Shipbuilding, is a wealthy, powerful man. Somehow, he found out who we are. Well, not exactly who *we* are, but who *you* are, and he wants a meeting."

"A meeting? With me? No, I'm not doing it. We saved that little girl because she's an innocent child, not because she's the granddaughter of a billionaire. I'm not interested."

She cleared her throat. "I don't think you understand. Abbot is a former classmate of the president. He and his wife have spent more nights in the Lincoln Bedroom than the Lincolns. If Christopher Abbot wants a meeting, Christopher Abbot gets a meeting."

"Skipper, I don't have time for this right now. Put them off until we complete this mission, and then we'll talk about it."

"I'll do my best, but even I have my limits."

I gathered the team and briefed the remainder of the mission. No one protested except Leo.

"I don't take checks," he said.

"I know you don't, Leo, but we're not finished with you yet. We have two more flights, and you can spend every renegade peso we give you on wild women and booze."

"That's my plan. I'll probably just waste the rest of it."

"All right. Let's get ourselves and our gear back to Puerto San Jose. I'll take Hunter, Tony, and el Lagarto with me in the Caravan. Mongo, Singer, and Disco will fly with Leo in the Huey."

We split up and headed for our trusty steeds.

El Lagarto stepped in front of me and checked over my shoulder. "You're afraid of me, brother."

"Why would you say that?"

"You ordered the man you call Hunter and his student to fly with us. He threatened me before, and I believe he's not the kind of man to make idle threats. You're bringing him with us to protect you from me, aren't you?"

I laid a hand on his shoulder. "Hunter and Tony are the two lightest members of the team. The Caravan is full of gear, so Mongo wouldn't fit. If I were afraid of you, you'd still be in chains. Just in case you have thoughts of doing anything to make me afraid of you,

you should know that your assessment of Hunter is right on the money. He doesn't bluff nor hesitate. Keep that in mind."

We shared a moment like two wild dogs staring into each other's souls, and I realized he was correct. Hunter was exactly the man I wanted covering my six when things fell apart. Maybe subconsciously, I was afraid of him, and maybe he was using me to escape the hell that had been his only home for nearly three decades.

He flinched first, and I gave him a wink, but I don't know why. "Get in the right seat. I'll be there in a minute, and you can get a little stick time on the ride south." I stepped away and caught Singer's elbow. "I need you."

He froze in his tracks. "I'm listening."

After checking over my shoulder, I said, "Tell me why I couldn't shoot him."

Singer stepped close. "You're the psychologist. Why do you think you couldn't do it?"

I poured the scenario through the sieve of nearly eight years of psychological education, and all that stayed on the screen was rocky uncertainty. "I don't know. Any other man on Earth would've eaten two nine-millimeter rounds in a standoff like that."

Singer lowered his chin. "Any other man? How about me? Would you have killed me in the same situation?"

"No, of course not you. You're my brother, and I love you."

He gave my arm a squeeze. "As humans, we all have a self-preservation instinct. Most of us would do almost anything to stay alive, but men like you and me put ourselves in harm's way every day and prove that we're willing to sacrifice ourselves to preserve the ones we love. He's your brother, regardless of what he's done or how evil he is under the skin that looks just like you. It's that simple, Chase. Even though you only met him hours ago, you love him more than you love yourself. You proved that when you laid down your pistol."

"Maybe you're right."

Singer squeezed again. "I watched it all through my scope. I know exactly what happened, and that man is alive only because you chose not to kill him."

"What do you mean? You could've killed him, but you didn't."

"You're right. I could've put that round in his ear just as easily as I put it in the ejection port of that rifle, but I watched you choose to let him live, so I couldn't override that choice. I fired to save your life. I hit the rifle to save his."

He threw an arm around me and hugged me like no one else could. "None of this is easy, and the hardest part isn't over. Stay strong. God won't let anything happen to us that He can't get us out of. We're on the winning team, Cowboy. Don't you forget that."

Chapter 36
Surprise . . . Surprise

"You were right. This is much easier than flying the helicopter. Are these aircraft really yours?"

I sat with my arms folded across my chest and watched my brother at the controls of the Caravan. "This one is mine, but the helicopter belongs to Leo, the other pilot."

"This means you're rich."

The shake of my head was involuntary but honest. "No, owning airplanes and having money in the bank doesn't make me rich." I shot a thumb toward the cabin of the plane. "Having a wife and men like those two and the ones on the chopper, that's what makes me rich."

He seemed to ignore the sentiment. "But you're also financially wealthy."

"I'm comfortable financially, and when the CIA deposits your reward into the account Skipper's setting up, you'll be on your way to being financially wealthy. I just hope someday you'll also be rich."

He glanced between our seats. "You trust them with your life, but you don't trust your own brother."

"They've earned my trust."

* * *

We easily beat the chopper back to Puerto San Jose, and we camped out in the general aviation terminal while waiting for the rest of our team to arrive. They showed up right on schedule, and I met Leo as he exited the Huey. He stuck his right hand in mine, and I stuck a stack of good ol' American sawbucks in his left.

"As always, it was a pleasure working with you. There's just one more little thing I need before you go."

Leo looked down and mentally counted the stack. "Whatever you want must be a big one. This is way more than we agreed on."

"It is," I said. "We're going to load everything we can fit onto your chopper, excluding the guns and ammo, of course, and you're going to deliver it to a pair of nuns living on top of a mountain."

He nodded and almost smiled. "You're a good man, Chase. The world could stand a few more just like you."

I motioned toward the Caravan. "It's already got another one who looks just like me."

Leo leaned in. "Don't let him fool you. He ain't you, and if you give him half a chance, he'll slit your throat and take everything you've got."

"He's my brother, Leo."

"Maybe by blood, but that's where the similarities end. Be careful. Maybe I'll see you again, and maybe we won't have to kill anybody next time."

We loaded provisions onto the helicopter until Leo could barely pull it off the ground, and he disappeared on the same *whop-whop* of the rotors on which he'd appeared.

* * *

We made our way to the resort, where the mission felt like it began a lifetime ago. Once again, Skipper scored us a luxurious suite where we could lick our wounds and wait for our ship to come in.

We showered, shaved, and doctored our wounds. Room service delivered a meal fit for a king, and we devoured it as if we hadn't eaten in days.

"Is this really how you live?" el Lagarto asked.

Hunter wiped his mouth. "No, we don't normally rough it like this. We're accustomed to much nicer places."

The team tried holding straight faces, but the laughter won out over our ability to mess with el Lagarto.

After a day and a half of catching up for twenty-six years of lost time, my sat-phone chimed. "Chase, it's Captain Sprayberry. We're two hours out of Puerto Barrio. Do you want us in the harbor?"

"How are the seas?" I asked.

"Dead calm with six knots out of the north. You couldn't ask for better weather at sea."

That brought a smile to my face. "Lay off about ten miles and shoot me your coordinates. We'll rendezvous there, and I'll brief you on the rest of the mission. Make room for two."

"Yes, sir. Oh, and we've got a couple surprises for you when you get on board."

"I don't like surprises," I said.

"Trust me. You'll like these."

I hung up. "It looks like it's time to go home, guys. El Lagarto and I will sail home aboard the *Lori Danielle*. Captain Sprayberry says the seas are dead calm, so we'll take the Caravan to rendezvous with him. Hunter and Tony can take the airplane home from there, and the rest of you can fly home with Disco in the Citation."

Almost everyone agreed to my plan, but Singer wanted to chat. "Let's walk outside for a minute."

I said, "Sure. What's on your mind?"

He slid the door closed behind us as we stepped onto the balcony. "Are you sure you shouldn't take at least one of us with you for security?"

"There's a security team on the ship. We'll be fine. You've seen him for the past two days. Do you really think he's a threat?"

"Did he apologize for pressing the muzzle of *your* rifle against your head?"

I closed my eyes and sighed. "Thank you for worrying, but you're worrying over nothing. We'll be fine."

"Okay, but don't let your guard down too much. If anything were to happen to you and I wasn't there to look after you, I'd never forgive myself."

The look in his eyes was sincere concern, and I wanted to do everything I could to put his mind at ease. "How about this? You can come with us on the ship. Would that make you feel better?"

His shoulders fell as if a mighty weight had been lifted. "Yeah, Chase. That would make me feel a lot better."

We blasted off into the afternoon sun and headed for the calm waters of the Caribbean Sea. Captain Sprayberry was right—the surface looked like an inland lake as we flew over the new *Lori Danielle*.

I scanned the decks and couldn't believe my eyes. "Hey, Hunter. Check it out. It looks like we scored a Little Bird."

Hunter pressed his face to the window and stared down at the solid black helicopter perched on the pad at the stern of the ship. "Christmas came early. I love it!"

El Lagarto said, "Is the ship yours, too?"

"Sort of. It technically belongs to a non-profit oceanographic research company, but you might say we're timeshare owners."

"I don't know what that means."

"That's the idea. Now, snug up that seatbelt, and let's see if I can remember how to land on the water."

I flew the approach from astern of the *Lori Danielle* and made the best water landing of my life. The officer of the deck deployed a tender and tied alongside our port pontoon.

"Our elevator has arrived," I said.

Singer was first into the rigid hull inflatable boat, and my brother and I followed close behind. Hunter gave us a sharp salute and climbed away into the northern sky.

The crane operator lifted us from the water and deposited the RHIB perfectly on its cradle.

When I stepped from the tender onto the deck, I couldn't believe my eyes. "What are you doing here?"

Wild auburn hair danced on what little wind blew across the deck, and Penny said, "Captain Sprayberry told me he needed somebody to drive this thing, so of course I volunteered."

She threw her arms around me, and we embraced as if we'd been apart far too long. Perhaps we had.

When we parted, I held out an open hand. "Penny, meet your brother-in-law, Lagarto."

She stared at the man who could've been my twin, and he stared back at her as if he'd never seen a beautiful woman before. He stuck out a hand, and she slapped it away.

"We don't shake hands in this family. We're huggers."

She threw her arms around him, and he closed his eyes in her embrace. As she tried to pull away, he held her an instant longer than he should have.

He threw up his hands. "I'm so sorry. It's just that I feel like I know you. Chase has told me so much about you that you already feel like family."

His little speech didn't erase the transgression, and the look on Singer's face confirmed my suspicion.

Captain Sprayberry came through a hatch onto the deck and

announced, "Welcome aboard. It looks like you've already seen surprise number one."

I shook his hand. "I have indeed, and I must admit that Penny is exactly the kind of surprise I love."

"I thought you'd approve. But surprise number two is no slouch." He turned and pointed toward the chopper on the pad overhead. "That's an MH-Six-M straight from Boeing. It's still in testing before they roll it out to the military, and I think we're the perfect test bed for it."

I stared up at the beautiful piece of hardware. "I couldn't agree more. Have you flown in it yet?"

Captain Sprayberry gave me a wry smile. "Not only have I flown *in* it, but I've also *flown* it."

"I didn't know you were a pilot."

"If it's got wings or rotors, I can make it dance."

Through my grin, I said, "I guess that's surprise number three."

"Speaking of surprises. It looks like you brought an extra body. We were only expecting two."

"I'm sorry about that. It was a last-minute change. I should've told you."

"No worries," he said. "We'll pour an extra cup of water in the soup and pull out another cot."

As we walked toward the hatch leading to the ship's interior, the executive officer, Greg "Long John" Silver, stepped through.

"I'm sorry to interrupt, but we have classified traffic for Mr. Fulton."

"What is it?" I asked.

Long John said, "It's a classified message from Langley, sir."

Captain Sprayberry said, "Go with the XO, Chase. I'll see that the quartermaster gets everyone settled in for the ride home."

I laid a hand on the captain's shoulder and whispered, "He's not a prisoner, but he may be unpredictable. Put a couple security officers on him for now."

He gave me a nod. "We're way ahead of you. The two sailors who picked you up in the RHIB are two of our best, and they're well armed. They won't let him out of their sight."

I turned to Singer. "Are you good with that?"

"If the captain says they're solid, I am."

"Good. In that case, come with me. If Langley presses my jackass button, I may need you to keep me calm."

Singer eyed Penny and el Lagarto. "Are you sure?"

"I'm sure. It'll be fine."

I gave Penny a kiss, and Singer and I followed Long John to the radio room. He scanned his thumbprint and entered his access code before pushing through the door. A young sailor stood from the console when we came in.

Long John said, "Thank you, Mr. Wells. We'll take it from here."

Without a word, Wells stepped between us and out the door. Long John slid two pairs of headphones across the console, and we donned them.

I pulled the mic to my lips. "Fulton here."

"Mr. Fulton, my name is Thomasson, and I'm Mr. Seymour's superior."

"Okay, Thomasson, what do you have for me?"

"I have some good news for el Lagarto. Everything you asked for has been provided, and your analyst has verification. May I assume you have the man in your custody?"

"He's not in custody, Thomasson. We cleared that up with Seymour. My brother is not now, nor will he ever be in custody for any acts he may have performed in the past. You are clear on that, right?"

"Of course. Forgive me. I used the wrong term. I meant, is he with you?"

"Yes, he's with me, and we'll be happy to drop him off anywhere on the East Coast as soon as I double-check everything with my analyst. Stand by."

I pulled my sat-phone from my pocket and dialed Skipper.

She didn't wait for me to ask and answered the phone saying, "I have everything, including the deposit into the Cayman account. Everything is in order."

"Thank you, Skipper. That's all I needed. We're safely aboard the ship and headed home."

"Before you go, how did you like your surprises?"

"I love them both. But I'll always prefer one of them over any other surprise."

"Yeah, I know how much you love helicopters. Bye, Chase."

I pulled the mic back to my lips. "Okay, Mr. Thomasson. It looks like everything's in order. Where should we plan to make landfall?"

"We think the naval base is the best place."

"I'm afraid you'll have to be a little more specific. The East Coast is littered with naval bases."

He paused and said, "Guantanamo."

Singer laid a hand on my arm and mouthed, "Don't get excited."

I took a long breath. "Look, Thomasson, we've made this crystal clear from the jump. My brother isn't a prisoner, and I'm not surrendering him to any detention center at Guantanamo or anywhere else."

"No, you misunderstand. He's not going to be held at Gitmo. He's free to come and go as he pleases, but we can discuss matters and plan certain scenarios down there that wouldn't exactly fall on the legal side of the fence if it were done at Langley. I'm sure you understand what I mean."

"Okay, Thomasson. If you screw me or my brother on this, you can kiss your bureaucratic pension good bye. I have some extremely powerful friends, and one of them just happens to live at an address you'd recognize on Pennsylvania Avenue."

"The threats aren't necessary. The Agency takes our responsibility very seriously in matters such as these."

I hissed, "In my experience, Thomasson, the CIA has never taken responsibility for anything, be it serious or otherwise. And I'm not making threats. I'm simply explaining what will happen to your career if you've been less than honest about anything. I'll consider delivering my brother to Cuba, and if I convince myself you're telling the truth, I'll be in touch."

Thomasson began a standard-issue government speech, but I pulled off my headset and laid it on the console. "How far is it to Gitmo?"

"About a thousand miles," Long John said.

I turned to Singer, and he gave me a confident nod, so I said, "Take us to Cuba, Mr. Silver."

We followed the XO back through the secure hatch of the radio room and came face-to-face with the ship's yeoman purser.

"Oh, hey!" she said in her perpetually cheerful tone.

"Hello, Ronda. How are things in the bank vault?"

"So far, it's all black ink," she said. "But this is a ship, so we'll probably be in the red before long."

"I think it's safe for you to throw your red pens overboard."

The XO said, "Ronda, would you mind showing Chase and Singer down to their cabins?"

"Sure, no problem. Follow me, gentlemen."

Long John headed for the bridge, and we fell in trail of the ship's CFO. She said, "I met your wife, and she is delightful. If you ask me, you outkicked your coverage with that one."

"I couldn't agree more, but let's not tell her that. I've still got her convinced she's lucky to have me."

We descended two decks, and Ronda said, "We're almost there. Your berths are just around this corner and down the corridor."

"Thank you. I think we can find them from here. I don't want to keep you from important work."

Almost before I finished my sentence, Ronda threw both hands over her mouth and muffled a scream. I sidestepped her, and terror pierced my chest. Singer obviously saw the carnage the same instant I did, and we burst into a sprint down the narrow corridor. The limp bodies of the two security officers lay on the steel deck in expanding puddles of blood. Both of their holsters were empty.

Singer and I drew our sidearms in unison and kicked the two cabin doors behind the bodies.

Singer yelled, "Clear!"

My heart sank, and I yelled back, "Clear! Find them!"

I shot a look back down the corridor where Ronda stood, still in shock and disbelief.

I yelled again, "Notify the captain! The prisoner is gone, and he's got Penny!"

As if yanked from her trance, she pulled the small radio from her belt and spoke into the mic, but I didn't wait to hear the captain's reply. Singer and I bolted through the aft hatch onto the deck. We scanned the space until we saw el Lagarto behind the wheel of the RHIB, suspended by the winch cable with the remote control for the crane in his hand. Penny lay across the seat, and the instant I saw her lifeless form, I charged across the deck with my pistol raised and Singer keeping pace beside me.

The Lizard saw us coming and yanked Penny to his chest as a human shield. She slowly lifted her head, revealing a bloody wound at her left temple. He stuck the remote into his left hand holding her against his body and raised one of the guard's pistols to her head.

288 · CAP DANIELS

"Drop it now or die!" I yelled. My warning only served to send him shrinking farther behind my wife's body as the crane lifted the RHIB ever closer to the rail.

The ship's public address system burst to life, and Captain Sprayberry's voice echoed, but I ignored him. Nothing he could announce would change the coming seconds of my life.

With less than half of his face exposed over Penny's shoulder, el Lagarto yelled, "Stop! If you take another step, I'll kill her!"

I followed his command, but not because of his warning. With a target no larger than the palm of my hand, I took one long, calming breath and steadied my grip.

The sound of a single pistol shot echoed from only inches away. The steel cable supporting the RHIB exploded into splayed strands of metal wire, and the tender fell to the deck. Before the boat came to rest, I pressed the trigger of my Glock twice. What I could see of el Lagarto's head turned instantly to a cloud of pink mist, and Penny slumped onto the portside tube.

In the aftermath of the horrific scene on the stern deck of the *Lori Danielle*, I ran to my wife and yanked what I believed was my handkerchief from my pocket and pressed it against the wound at her temple.

A pair of medics materialized and gently laid Penny on a gurney as she reached up for me.

I took her hand in mine. "You're going to be okay."

One of the medics lifted the handkerchief from her face and placed it in my hand. "You hang on to that, sir, and we'll get her down to the medical bay."

I stepped aside as they wheeled her away and stared down at the bloody rag in my hand. Stretching it to its limits, I could barely make out the simple pattern on the cloth that had once been a piece of a faithful nun's worn cotton dress.

I stared down into the RHIB, where the body of the man who'd been my brother, but only biologically, lay splayed across the console. I ripped the pistol from his dead hand and emptied it into his corpse, sending lead, blood, and flesh pouring onto the deck.

Singer stepped against me and pulled the pistol from my hand. "Go with Penny. I've got this."

I turned to see the medics clearing the hatch I'd run through only seconds before. The purser, Ronda, stood beside the opening with an arm outstretched, and I crossed the cold steel deck and took her hand.

She said, "Come with me. I'll take you down to medical."

The world around me seemed empty as I sank into depths I'd never before known. The world seemed so far away through a continuously narrowing tunnel of fading light. I staggered, and Ronda said, "Stay with me, Chase. She's going to be okay. Just stay with me."

When I could finally focus again, I found myself sitting in a reclining chair with an IV in each arm and a cacophony of sounds echoing in my head.

A voice I recognized but couldn't place said, "Chase, how do you feel?"

I groaned. "Is Penny alive?"

Dr. Shadrack's voice finally registered when he said, "Nobody dies in my sick bay. You know that. She's going to be fine. It was just a nasty blow to the head."

Relieved, I blinked and tried to crawl from deep within my sunken soul.

"Don't try to get up," the doctor said. "I'll take you to her."

The reclining chair that held me turned out to be a wheelchair of sorts, and he rolled me to Penny's side. She reached for my hand, and I gave it to her.

"I'm so sorry," I said.

She squeezed my hand. "No, Chase. Don't be sorry. You saved my life."

"No . . . I think you saved mine."

Penny whispered, "Look over there."

I followed her gaze to the two security officers resting peacefully in a pair of hospital beds. "They're alive?"

"Yes, they're alive. As weird as it sounds, the doctor said they're lucky they were just stab wounds, not gunshots."

"Gunshots make a lot of noise."

Epilogue

Every man needs a place to go where everything makes sense—where he can be alone with his demons or surrounded by his angels. The gazebo at Bonaventure was that place for me. It would be impossible to count the number of hours I spent in that worn Adirondack chair overlooking the aged cannon guarding the western bank of the North River in Saint Marys, Georgia.

On that particular autumn afternoon, it was just me and the demons until my guardian angel laid his hand on my shoulder.

"Mind if I join you, College Boy?" Clark Johnson didn't wait for me to answer. He set a fresh glass of old whiskey beside my hand and settled into the chair next to me. "How you doing?"

I moved my head in tiny shifts left and right. "I'm done."

He stared out over the river and lifted his glass to his lips. "Yeah, I know that feeling, but it'll pass. It always does."

"Not this time. I made every mistake possible. I almost got the woman I love killed. I shot my own brother twenty times. I misread everything, and I got it all wrong. All of it."

He studied the cubes of ice floating in his whiskey. "Yep, me too."

I turned to face him. "What are you talking about?"

He let his breath come long and deep and then held a folded sheet of paper toward me. I took it from his fingers and unfolded it. As I read the words, a sickening emptiness poured over me again.

Chase,

I'm sorry. I had to do it. They said they'd kill me if I didn't convince you to find your brother for them. It turns out they didn't have to kill me. I did it for them.

Phil McCall

I held the paper above my lighter and watched it melt into an orange flame and black smoke.

"How did we miss it?"

Clark sighed. "I don't know. He was good enough to fool you, me, and my dad."

"It got past Skipper."

"Yes, it did. There will always be somebody better than us . . . Always."

"They were going to kill my brother, weren't they?"

He took another drink. "Probably. He knew too much. They couldn't let him live, and they couldn't risk having what he knew get out. It would've done too much damage."

I swirled my ice cubes and watched them drift slowly to a stop. "It never ends, does it?"

"Not for people like you and me and your brother. They won this time. They silenced him forever, and they used us to do it. That's why you're not done. You're not the kind of man who rides the bench."

I placed my tumbler on the wooden decking beside my foot and pulled a package from beneath my chair. I laid it on the arm of Clark's seat and reclaimed my whiskey.

"What's this?" he asked.

"Go ahead. Open it up."

He untwisted the red string from the button and unfolded the flap. He peered into the pouch and then dumped it onto his lap.

One by one, he lifted the roughly bound notebooks and thumbed through the pages of the seven books that made up el Lagarto's diaries.

"How did you . . ."

"That's not important. What matters is that I have them. I have them right where I want them."

* * *

With Penny on my arm and Singer refusing to leave my side, I took the meeting with Christopher Abbot. I believe I got to see him as few people have.

One of the country's wealthiest men sat in the library at Bonaventure with his hands folded in front of him, and he let tears of gratitude roll down his weathered face. "Chase, my family will never be able to repay you for what you did to protect my grand-daughter, but I want you to know that I own the largest ship-building company in North America. I insist that you let me build you the best ship your mind can dream up."

"Mr. Abbot, I have everything I need and want right here at Bonaventure. I would've saved your granddaughter even if you were destitute and couldn't pay a dime. I don't want a reward of any kind from you, but if you insist, I do have a project in mind that needs and deserves *our* support."

"Name it."

I tapped the arm of my chair. "My friend, Singer, leads the choir at the First Missionary Baptist Church."

Abbot leaned forward. "I'll build you the finest church that's ever been built."

Singer and I smiled in unison, and I said, "That's exactly what we wanted to hear, Mr. Abbot. If you'll write the check, Singer and his merry band of missionaries will make sure a certain pair of nuns way up on a mountain in Guatemala get the church and school they need. The sisters will never let Central America forget your granddaughter's name."

About the Author

Cap Daniels

Cap Daniels is a former sailing charter captain, scuba and sailing instructor, pilot, Air Force combat veteran, and civil servant of the U.S. Department of Defense. Raised far from the ocean in rural East Tennessee, his early infatuation with salt water was sparked by the fascinating, and sometimes true, sea stories told by his father, a retired Navy Chief Petty Officer. Those stories of adventure on the high seas sent Cap in search of adventure of his own, which eventually landed him on Florida's Gulf Coast where he spends as much time as possible on, in, and under the waters of the Emerald Coast.

With a headful of larger-than-life characters and their thrilling exploits, Cap pours his love of adventure and passion for the ocean onto the pages of the Chase Fulton Novels and the Avenging Angel — Seven Deadly Sins series.

Visit www.CapDaniels.com to join the mailing list to receive newsletter and release updates.

Connect with Cap Daniels:

Facebook: www.Facebook.com/WriterCapDaniels
Instagram: https://www.instagram.com/authorcapdaniels/
BookBub: https://www.bookbub.com/profile/cap-daniels

Also by Cap Daniels

9 781951 021344